FAMILY
MATTERS

Other Five Star titles
by Justine Wittich:

The Shocking Miss Shaw
Chloe and the Spy

FAMILY MATTERS

JUSTINE WITTICH

Five Star • Waterville, Maine

First Edition
First Printing: August 2004

Set in 11 pt. Plantin.

Printed in the United States on permanent paper.

ISBN 1-59414-234-3 (hc : alk. paper)

For Sherry Hartzler, Donna MacMeans and Barb Whittington, who critiqued and hauled me back when I went astray while writing *Family Matters*.

And, as always, for Pete, who never knows what I'll write next.

ONE

A chill of foreboding stopped Jenny Tyler halfway up the sidewalk to the tidy bungalow. "Mr. Dolan must have gone away and forgotten to have his mail stopped," she told herself sturdily before climbing the wooden steps to the tiny porch.

The lace curtains at the window beside the door were shredded. Mail overflowed the wrought-iron mailbox; circulars dangled from the hooks beneath it.

Just as she reached the top tread, the lace parted. She stepped sideways so quickly her foot slipped on a newspaper.

The cat's face pressed against the glass. Frantic blue eyes stared from a chocolate-furred face, and an almost human cry poured from the wide-open mouth.

Her stomach clenched, then relaxed so suddenly she wanted to wrap her arms around herself to hold it together. Something was terribly wrong. Lips scarcely moving, she murmured, "Not today, God. Please." She rubbed a suddenly sweaty palm on the thigh of her linen slacks, mortified to discover that her hand shook.

Maybe he'd fallen. Accidents happened all the time, didn't they?

Over the past month, each time she passed this way the wiry little man had been puttering in his yard, shaking his head over the rabbit population's assault on his tulip bed, searching for signs of grubs amongst the emerging blades of grass and murmuring affectionately to his still bare-caned rosebushes, a habit which had endeared him to Jenny.

Since her daily walks were her only breaks from her easel, she'd looked forward to their brief chats. The elderly man's friendliness made her feel a part of the pleasant community—as much a part as she would allow herself to be. The members of the art league were the only people she'd met, and she hadn't encouraged friendships outside of the monthly meetings.

The cat screamed again. Refusing to give in to apprehension, Jenny pressed the doorbell. When there was no answer, she pressed again, this time leaning forward to listen. Choc's agitated Siamese voice chattered from behind the door. In reply, she called, "Mr. Dolan? Are you there? It's Jenny Tyler. I'm here about the Summer Arts Festival."

She raised her hand, knocked on the door—and nearly fell inside as it swung open beneath her touch.

The chocolate point butted her ankles, a fierce purr shaking his body. Jenny knelt and stroked the cat's sleek back, horrified to feel his ribs beneath her fingers. "Where's Mr. Dolan, Choc?"

At the sound of her voice, Choc turned to run toward the rear of the house, looking back over his shoulder as if urging Jenny to follow. Worried little sounds punctuated his movements.

Jenny sniffed. The sweet, sickening odor pervading the stuffy house was unfamiliar, but she had an excellent imagination. Her stomach contracted into a queasy knot. "Why me, Lord?" she said, her voice sounding thin even to her own ears. After another moment's hesitation, she yielded to the demands of the determined cat.

"All right. Food comes first." She had a strong suspicion she needn't hurry to look for Mr. Dolan, so she scooped up the cat and headed for the kitchen.

Her apprehension grew when she saw the innards of the

couch and two upholstered chairs strewn across the ripped carpeting of the small living room. Books, their covers torn off, mingled with crumpled papers scattered over the worn carpet. An old-fashioned whatnot hung crookedly over the couch, inexpensive figurines of animals clustered at the low ends of the off-kilter shelves.

Averting her eyes, Jenny passed through the room. If she pretended nothing was out of place, she could feed the cat, leave, and return to the sanctuary of her studio, erasing whatever she'd seen here from her memory. She would make an anonymous phone call to the police, then forget the whole matter.

Sugar and cereal crunched beneath the soles of her leather sandals when she reached the kitchen. Spilled flour swirled across the green marble pattern of the countertop. The faucet over the double sink dripped steadily, its patter the only sound in the room. Every instinct told her to run, not get involved.

The stench was stronger in here. Her insides roiled again. She choked down the bile rising in her throat.

Clinging to the pattern of denial that had kept her sane for six years, she pushed aside a burst package of paper napkins on the counter, revealing canned cat food in a neat stack. "Here we go, Choc," she said in a voice she didn't recognize.

The cat wove around her ankles, purring. She popped the lid and emptied the can into the ceramic bowl on the mat beside the door. The water dish beside it was dry. "You poor baby. How long have you been without water?" As she twisted the handle of the faucet she realized where the animal had been drinking. Cat hairs and paw prints marred the interior of the sink.

Jenny watched him devour the contents of his dish,

reminded of the house-proud little widower whose daily life had revolved around his garden and his pet, with television and newspapers filling his evenings.

But the sickish smell reminded her of . . . "Oh, God." Mr. Dolan hadn't gone anywhere. "Why me? Why can't I just leave and pretend I was never here?" she demanded. Jenny took a deep breath without thinking. Her stomach heaved. "You can't spend the rest of your life hiding from trouble," she told herself.

She straightened, swallowed another wave of nausea, then set out in search of Mr. Dolan.

He lay on the floor of his ransacked bedroom. The pleasant little gentleman hadn't died peacefully. His arm was twisted at an unnatural angle; dried blood splattered his upper body and pooled around his head. Mattress filling had settled obscenely around his balding pate, giving the impression of a fuzzy halo. Jenny's mind tilted off balance.

Dropping the long manila envelope half-full of arts festival donations, she fled. Horrible gagging sounds filled her ears as she staggered on trembling legs to the japonica bush beside the front steps. There, after a painful interlude, the sounds ceased.

An hour later, Jenny leaned against the headrest in the squad car, squeezed her eyes shut, then forced them wide open. She wished she could cry, but she had long ago given up on the myth concerning the healing power of tears. The scene imprinted on her brain made her nauseous all over again, but her stomach had nothing left to give.

"Excuse me, Ms. Tyler." The young officer who approached sounded uncomfortable about interrupting her misery.

"Yes?" She forced the acknowledgment through her dry throat.

"The coroner's given the okay to take away the body. When we're done searchin' and printin', we gotta seal up the house." He smiled weakly. "Ah . . . would you be willing to take the cat home with you until we find out if there's family who wants him? He's in there screamin' somethin' awful. Won't let no one catch him." He sucked the scratch on the side of his hand.

Jenny remembered the confusion in Choc's eyes and nodded. She and the cat were friends. Then she remembered the sickening stench that filled the house. "I . . . I don't think I can go back in there."

"We've had the windows open, ma'am. It's lots better now." He looked over his shoulder at the sound of the door opening. The paramedics were coming out.

"I'll help you, ma'am. Looks like a nice little cat. He's just awful scared."

Jenny turned her head away from the sight of the plastic bag on the gurney. Her stomach contracted, and she willed herself not to be sick again. She had to get home, away from this. But inside the house was a little cat who needed comforting.

In the end, capturing the animal was easy. When Jenny entered, a cream-colored streak erupted from beneath the remains of the living room sofa and threw itself at her ankles. She scooped the animal into her arms, where he burrowed his head beneath the lapel of her blazer. She concentrated on the cat's terror, blocking out the memory of her discovery.

"There's a bunch of cat food and a bag of litter in the pantry. I'll bring 'em for you." Her escort's footsteps faded, only to be replaced by a heavier tread. Jenny looked up apprehensively as a tall, thin man with a paunch entered the room. His sagging features reminded her of an aging hunting dog.

"I'm Chief Pierce, Ms. Tyler. I know all this has been a pretty bad shock. I'd appreciate it if you came down to the station to give us a formal statement tomorrow." He clutched the arts festival envelope beneath his arm. "Let me give you a lift home."

The chief's rumbling voice, combined with the warm, lithe body plastered against her, nearly broke Jenny's rigid control. She swallowed hard, fighting the hysteria that had been building since the moment she'd seen the tattered curtains. Soon after her marriage, nearly seven years earlier, she'd learned to disguise her true state of mind, and she reminded herself that the first officers to arrive at the scene had been as affected by the contents of the bedroom as she. One of the patrolmen had bent double behind the same bush which had received her lunch.

She managed a wan smile and a feeble attempt at humor. "I think I would have preferred to meet you in a speed trap."

Chief Pierce's gaze never left her while he called to the young officer to bring the cat supplies to his car. He led her out the door. Jenny kept her features composed beneath his assessing gaze. Although she had lived in Donhaven since the end of January, she'd done her best to help the gossip grapevine overlook her, keeping to herself and staying as close as possible to her rented house a mile beyond the city limits.

She settled into the front seat of the cruiser, then waited until he'd backed the car into the street to ask, "How did Mr. Dolan die?"

"Looks like someone slit his throat," Pierce said bluntly.

Jenny shuddered. "Why?"

His eyes on the road, the chief replied, "That's what we're paid to find out."

"How long has he been dead?"

"Doc Morrow'll know better after the autopsy. He guessed maybe a week."

"Will . . . will my name have to be released to the press?" A local reporter had circulated through the crowd of neighbors who'd gathered, and Jenny wanted nothing to do with the press.

Pierce drove on in silence. As they nosed onto Jenny's driveway, he eyed her curiously, switched off the ignition and said, "Damn reporters will bug me until somethin' happens somewhere else. Then they'll move on. Unless, a' course, we turn up a suspect right away. I'll do my best to keep you anonymous, but I can't make any promises."

Still clutching the cat, Jenny felt her eyes fill with tears. "My husband was murdered late last year. The publicity was . . . difficult for me. One reason I came here is to live quietly." She saw no reason to tell him she was hiding until she verified that certain promises were being kept.

When Pierce's eyes narrowed, she realized her error. She shouldn't have mentioned how Trent died, but today's discovery had jolted her—her mind didn't seem to be working clearly. Surely no one could connect her mother's maiden name to Trent, or to the Travino family.

"I'll call you a 'concerned neighbor' when I talk to him. I should be able to keep the official log under lock and key," the chief said soothingly. He opened the cruiser door and scanned the front of her redwood and stone house. "Let me carry in this other stuff for you."

Swearing viciously, Gabe Daniels watched the paramedics drive away. He was too late. Again. Apparently, this time Winston DeWitt's escape was permanent.

Crime tape surrounded the ordinary yard and house. Earlier, a deputy had assisted a slight, blonde woman from the police car at the curb. "Sonovabitch!" He pounded the steering wheel of his rented Jeep Cherokee, venting his frustration.

Four years ago, he had traced DeWitt to a remote Iowa farm, only to discover that his bird had flown three hours earlier. A neighbor had seen DeWitt at his mailbox at mid-morning that day, the last reported sighting of the larcenous CPA until three days ago, when a longtime Magnacorp employee had spotted him at a reservation desk at Port Columbus and heard him give his name as Carl Dolan and his residence as Donhaven, this remote, godforsaken town in southeastern Ohio.

He watched the skinny blonde broad enter the house, then exit minutes later clutching something to her chest. The cop with her treated her as if she owned the town. Sunlight glinted off his badge. Gold. Probably the chief. Whoever the skirt was, she was getting an official ride home. He checked his watch. Three-thirty. He'd give the chief an hour to get rid of his passenger. Then he'd present his credentials at headquarters.

That should give him plenty of time to find what passed for a motel in this backwater and phone in his report. Gabe ran his hand over the healthy growth of whiskers on his cheeks and scowled at his wrinkled silk trousers. His suit jacket looked no better. The way things were going, by the time he checked into the motel and called Sterling he probably wouldn't have time to shave and change clothes. He shrugged. His appearance didn't bother him nearly so much as the thought of his boss's reaction. "Sterling's going to shit a brick," he predicted.

Jenny emptied cat food into a china bowl while Choc paced the white tile floor. The little cat had clung to her

14

throughout the short ride, then dogged her heels since they'd entered her house, viewing with disinterest the plastic dishpan of litter she'd positioned in the corner of the pantry. Food was obviously foremost in his thoughts.

She set his meal on the floor and filled a matching bowl with water. The violets painted on the thin china shimmered beneath the liquid as she set it down. Jenny chuckled softly. "Quite a fancy table setting for a cat, but after what you've been through, you deserve it." While he ate, she stroked his sleek back, surprised to discover she received as much comfort as she gave. Caring for the animal's needs made the horror of the day recede. "You're safe with me, Choc. If no one claims you, I'll adopt you myself."

The cat purred appreciatively, a soothing sound that made Jenny realize she wanted nothing more than to curl into a fetal position and escape in sleep. Although it was only mid-afternoon, she scrambled an egg and forced herself to eat it and a slice of toast before heading upstairs to bed. Sleep would mask the fears lurking at the edges of her mind—at least until morning.

Although she slept as soon as her head hit the pillow, her mind wouldn't rest. Disturbing dreams jostled each other like birds at a feeder, returning in disconnected segments. Six hours later, Jenny awoke. She crawled out of bed, accepting the fact that dreamless sleep would be a long time returning—perhaps not until she felt safe, and anonymous, once more.

The cat lay curled in a knot at the corner of her bed. Before pulling a short terry robe over her sleep shirt, she smoothed his silky fur. "At least you can sleep soundly," she told him. When he made no response, Jenny went downstairs and poured herself some wine.

Goblet in hand, she wandered the room that spanned the

back of the house, flicking switches until light erased every shadow. She paused at the windows overlooking the ravine below, visualizing exotic dangers in the dark and shadows, dangers she would willingly exchange for those that haunted her. Anything would be preferable to the memories awakened this afternoon.

Stars twinkled, oblivious to her distress; a sliver of moon rode the sky. She wished she could erase the vision of poor Mr. Dolan. Why had he been killed? What had the murderer been looking for? She was so immersed in thought that at first she missed the polite tapping at her front door. When the sound penetrated her consciousness, her wrist jerked, and the wine in the blue goblet she'd just raised to her lips sloshed down her chin.

Setting down the glass, Jenny pulled out a tissue and patted her skin. She looked at her watch. "It's nearly midnight! I didn't think anyone in this town stayed up this late," she murmured shakily as she crossed to the front door. For a moment, panic filled her, and she nearly stopped at the closet to retrieve the tote holding her Lady Smith. Common sense told her no one who was really a threat bothered to knock. Flipping the outside light switch, she squinted through the peephole.

Chief Pierce stood on her front step. She released a breath she'd been unaware she was holding.

Unhooking the chain and freeing the dead bolt, Jenny swung the door wide open. "What happened?"

"Didn't mean to scare you, Ms. Tyler. It's just that somethin's turned up in the Dolan case, and this fella insisted on talking to you tonight. Since your lights were on . . ."

Jenny stiffened when her gaze lit on Chief Pierce's companion. Outwardly, he was everything she despised. The man looked as if he hadn't shaved in two days. Black, curling hair that appeared to have been finger-combed fell over his forehead, brushing equally dark eyebrows. Dark, deep-set eyes stared at her unblinkingly, making her throw up mind barriers. Why did she get the feeling he could read her thoughts?

Other women would surely find his harshly carved features compelling; Jenny found them overwhelmingly masculine, and she'd had enough of masculinity to last her a lifetime. Expensive tailoring couldn't conceal his powerful shoulders and chest, but the suit was a wrinkled mess, and his tie hung free of his unbuttoned shirt collar, which revealed black, curling hair.

His unwavering gaze remained fixed on her face throughout her inspection.

She forced herself to meet his intent stare for a heartbeat, then turned away. The sooner she spoke with him and the chief, the sooner she could rid herself of them. Dropping her hands to her sides in a gesture of surrender, Jenny motioned them inside. "I hope this won't take long. It's very late."

As they entered, Pierce apologized once again before explaining, "I had the dispatcher fax all the prints we found in Dolan's house to the National Crime Information Center in Washington as soon as we got back to the station."

Pierce continued talking while she closed the door and led the way to the back of the house. "Seems our corpse's name wasn't Dolan after all, but by the time we heard from them, we already had a pretty good idea about that. Gabe here had come in and identified the body."

Pointing to the lurid dust jacket of the police procedural on the coffee table, Jenny countered, "In books it takes forever to get identification from NCIC." She was sure a psychologist would impute some dark emotional flaw to her fascination with detective stories, particularly in view of her past.

"Yeah. Well, this was a fluke. You better take over, Gabe." He gestured toward his companion. "This is Gabe Daniels, Ms. Tyler. He troubleshoots for Sterling Thomas . . . you know, the rich guy who's on television all the time tellin' the president what he ought to do."

Jenny didn't offer to shake hands. "What has this to do with me?" she demanded, her heart beating high in her throat.

Gabe resented the way she had pretended not to see him when she greeted the chief—as if he were dirt on her door-step. He resented even more the way her blue-green gaze had ignored him ever since. Women usually reacted to him positively, but this one pretended he didn't exist, and he hadn't done anything to annoy her. Yet. The rebellious side of him decided that if the opportunity presented itself he might do just that, simply to even the score. He recognized the type. She was a tight-assed, scrawny blonde who spoke the same way as those snotty upper-class babes who attended his grandfather's parties.

Reluctantly shelving his prejudices, Gabe reverted to training. "Nothing at all, Ms. Tyler. May we sit down?" At her nod, he sank into the plump pillows of the overstuffed couch. He knew better than anyone that he wore the same silk shirt he'd put on at five that morning; his beard had been rasping against the collar since lunch. He was also aware he looked like a thug, but that didn't explain the frost in the lady's eyes. What she thought of him didn't matter, he reminded himself.

"Sterling's been looking for your Mr. Dolan for years. His contact at NCIC scans all new prints and matches so he can let us know immediately if Dolan's prints turned up, dead or alive."

Frost edged her response. "How very convenient for Mr. Thomas to have such a connection."

Gabe himself was cynical about Sterling's high-level network, but Jenny's tone made the contact sound like a member of al-Qaeda. He said harshly, "Dolan wasn't really Dolan. He was Winston DeWitt, who worked as comptroller at Sterling Starjet, a division of Magnacorp. Five years ago the bastard embezzled three million dollars. He disappeared, turned up a year later, then got away from us again. Since you knew him, I thought you might be able to help, Ms. Tyler. Or is it Mrs.?" He stared at her hands.

The slender fingers of her right hand fumbled with her naked third finger, as if seeking succor from a band which was no longer there.

Jenny sat up straight and crossed her hands in her lap, looking directly at him for the first time since he'd arrived. "Ms. Tyler, if you please. My husband is gone and forgotten." She stopped, her eyes widening as if horrified by the impression her words might make, then continued. "As I told Chief Pierce earlier today, I didn't know Mr. Dolan . . . DeWitt, well. I walk nearly every day, even in cold weather. He spent a great deal of time in his yard, and we visited over the fence."

She crossed her ankles precisely, as if she wore Ferragamos instead of scuffed terry-cloth slippers. The movement drew Gabe's attention to the length of bare leg revealed by her knee-length robe. In spite of the fact that she looked at him as if he were a garden slug, he couldn't help noticing that Ms. Tyler's pins were first-class. "Excuse me, ma'am. You knew him well enough to go into his house . . . and you've brought his cat home."

"Yes, but . . ."

"I've talked with his neighbors. They all say he kept to

himself. None of them knew much about him, and no one had seen him this week. The Kiroski kid fed the cat while he was away for a few days last month, but the boy doesn't know zilch. Do you know where Dolan went on that trip, Ms. Tyler?"

"He never said. I didn't even know he'd left town . . . he once told me he found everything he needed right here."

"Well, somebody put seventy-two thousand miles on his Taurus in three years. And he's the original owner. I ran a check."

"I wouldn't know. I've only lived here since January. He seemed like such a nice man . . . a gentle man." She tugged the belt of her robe tight, as if she wished it were Gabe's necktie. "I simply discovered the body . . ." Her voice broke.

Gabe looked to Pierce for help. The police chief avoided eye contact. Gabe sighed. "I'd appreciate it if you'd think back over every conversation you had with him. He may have said something revealing . . . something you don't realize might be helpful."

"Such as, 'By the way, I have three million dollars in an old pickle crock in the basement'? Or do you suspect I took the money when I found the body?"

"I didn't mean that, dammit." Gabe was tired and weary of bickering. Jenny Tyler, with her pure contralto and precise diction, her elegant profile and her little neck fragile beneath the tidy line of her blunt-cut blonde hair, made him want to emphasize his own roughness. He stood, well aware that his size was intimidating. "My job is to track down loose ends, and three million dollars definitely falls in that category. DeWitt screwed my boss, and Sterling's a man who doesn't like to get screwed unless he can enjoy it."

Jenny stood also. She tilted her head back until she

looked into his eyes. Her fingers worried her ring finger, but her gaze was steady. "Poor Sterling Thomas. My heart bleeds for him."

She picked up the blue goblet from the table and drank from it defiantly before bargaining. "I'll help you by telling you what little, what very little, I recall about Dolan . . . DeWitt . . . whatever you call him. In return I want your promise that Mr. Thomas's influence erases my name from any publicly accessible report concerning the murder."

A little warning bell rang in Gabe's brain. "You got yourself a deal. Tomorrow?"

"That will do nicely. I have drawings that must be on their way to my publisher by noon. Will one o'clock be convenient?"

TWO

Early the next morning, Jenny returned the orange juice to the refrigerator and reached up cautiously to scratch the cat's neck. "You feel safe up here, don't you, sweetheart." The cat shrank toward the back of the appliance, and she withdrew her hand. He'd followed her downstairs, eaten his breakfast, then taken himself to the highest point in the room.

"Believe me, Choc, I understand." No one knew better than she the obsessive need for safety. She pressed down the toaster lever and waited for her wheat bread to brown. The impending interview with Gabe Daniels filled her with dread. Last night his presence had made her feel . . . annoyed? Antagonistic? Alive? As quickly as the third choice popped into her mind, Jenny told herself not to be ridiculous. She simply didn't want to spend any more time with him than necessary.

Why was he so insistent on questioning her? She couldn't know anything of importance. His challenging dark gaze made her want to withdraw even further into herself, and she refused to allow him to intimidate her. She'd tell him what little she knew and send him on his way, then resume her quiet, and safe, existence.

When the toast popped up, she spread it with marmalade and cut it into tidy halves with rather more force than necessary. She could handle Gabe Daniels. After all, she'd survived six years of hell, hadn't she? Ignoring the doubts nibbling at her insides, she carried her breakfast upstairs to her studio.

★ ★ ★ ★ ★

At that same moment, Gabe leaned against his rented car, staring delightedly at DeWitt's tidy, deserted bungalow. The house had a faintly neglected air, as if the decay of the body within had permeated the wood and nails that made up the building. The front door hung crookedly on its hinges. Last night's break-in meant the murderer hadn't found what he wanted. The clue he needed might even be amongst the mountain of paper the police had gathered before they sealed the house.

"There couldn't have been much left," he mused, enjoying Chief Pierce's annoyance. "Whoever took him out did a thorough sweep, then your crew carried away everything but the furniture and the kitchen sink. Last night's bunch must have thought they were in Mother Hubbard's cupboard." He rubbed his hands together delightedly. "I'd say they were from a different company than the one who did the hit, wouldn't you? I wonder what he's been up to recently?"

Gabe stopped to consider the possibilities and found himself back at the only logical choice. For the fourth time since he'd arrived, he asked, "Are you sure you don't have drug activity here, or in the county? This reads to me like the bastard was playing two suppliers against each other."

Pierce shook his head, his drooping features placid. "Stick around here a while, and you'll discover towns like this keep crime averages as low as they are. I'm not sayin' we don't have drugs available, but nothin' points to Dolan. He paid his bills, didn't give wild parties, didn't spit on the sidewalk or molest children. His neighbors all say how nice he was, but they don't know anything about him. He was just 'nice.' "

"Hell!" Gabe pulled at the knot on his silk tie and unbuttoned the second button of his shirt. He ran his other hand through his hair. "That's what everyone at Sterling

Starjet said about him, before an audit showed three million dollars missing. Along with Winston DeWitt." He made a mental note to have his sources find out which Mafia family claimed distribution rights to this parcel of the Midwest.

Pierce's lids narrowed. "Are you certain this is your man? He sure didn't live like he had that kind of money."

"If I had any doubt, I wouldn't have identified the body. According to people who knew him back then, the sonovabitch didn't know how to have a good time. I figure he got his biggest jollies from outwitting Sterling," Gabe growled. "Even though he was boring as dirt, he's been up to something in this backwater. Someone that bent wouldn't retire. He found another way to turn a dishonest dollar, and along the way he annoyed someone enough for them to off him."

Seemingly unoffended by the description of his town, Pierce replied, "Can't help you, son. What little action we have is pretty tame. The biggest excitement here is the last day of school, when the seniors roar around in pickup trucks and toilet paper everything that'll stand still." His thin lips split in a proud grin. "I work to keep it that way."

Gabe gave the peace officer a dark look. "Well, hold on to your hat, friend, because the well-known article just hit the fan. You got yourself a big-time crime that just hasn't been identified yet. DeWitt was so crooked he probably won't lie straight in his coffin." He hooked his finger in the perfectly tailored collar of his silk suit jacket, threw it over his shoulder and pushed himself away from the car. "Let's go back to the station. I want to get a start on the paper you collected from his house before I talk to the merry widow."

Due to lack of space in the station, the green garbage bags of evidence had been dumped in one of the two empty cells. Gabe settled on the cot, dragged one between his knees, and pulled out a piece of torn paper. Large red print lauded the charms of a local pizza restaurant. "Damn. Did this guy save everything?"

"That's only what was on the floor and in the trash baskets. There's another sack full of real garbage locked in the police garage. The boys there are already complainin' about the smell," Pierce answered from his desk, which sat opposite the cell. His voice indicated enjoyment of Gabe's discomfort. "Nice of you to do our work for us."

"Yeah, sure." Gabe looked at the crumpled grocery list he had unfolded. "What the hell is Tidy Cat?"

"The stuff you put in litter boxes."

"Probably lots of it bagged in the garage," Gabe said, wrinkling his nose at the prospect of searching that mess, then continued to dig. The new prints in the house after last night's break-in indicated two intruders. He pulled out an envelope featuring Ed McMahon's face in the upper right-hand corner. "Your number was up, all right, DeWitt. But your luck was out." He discarded the envelope and called to the chief, "You should have fingerprinted all this stuff, you know."

Grim humor laced Pierce's reply. "It would probably only take a month or two."

Gabe continued to mumble and comment as he searched. "You got a report on those other prints yet?"

"I thought you'd never ask. They belonged to a pair of small-time drug pushers from the Bronx." Pierce paused, then continued, "They turned up dead three days ago, stuffed in a Dumpster behind a public library in Queens."

"Damn and hell!" Gabe erupted from the cell, a scrap of paper still clutched in his hand. "When did you hear? Why didn't you call me?"

"About six this morning. I didn't call you then because I didn't want to disturb the night clerk at the Traveler's Rest. I might have interrupted somethin'. Her boyfriend spends the night to keep her from being bored."

Spring sunlight blazed through a spotless window behind Gabe's shoulders. A trickle of perspiration made its way down his back. Although he'd shaved and dressed only three hours earlier, he knew he looked as though he'd been doing manual labor for hours. He didn't need a mirror to know his cheeks already sported a heavy beard pattern or that his shirt was nearly out of his trousers. The trousers themselves were wrinkled and twisted sideways. He jerked them back in place.

"Great. Just great," he muttered. "Didn't I tell you? When there's nothing you can put your finger on, look for the pros behind the mess. What do you bet someone else hits town before nightfall to make sure the Tyler woman didn't carry off something incriminating? How do you intend to protect her?" Gabe had no idea why he asked. Just because Jenny Tyler was attractive, blonde and alone, her safety was no concern of his.

Pierce tilted his chair farther back and scratched his shoulder. "Can't see why she'd be in trouble. All she did was discover the body. I figure we'll take things as they come. Besides, you're here to help out."

"Don't look at me to do your work. I'm only staying long enough to make sure I haven't missed anything. Then I'll be off to follow the money trail. I don't give a damn who offed DeWitt. Good riddance. I sure didn't sign on to babysit some skinny broad who's riddled with hang-ups." He gazed blindly at the scrap he held while his mind pictured Sterling's response to the latest news. The old man was going to get crazy, a state he expressed with chilling silence. Gabe squirmed inwardly.

Pierce's grin widened. "Shucks. After the way you two hit it off last night you should be real eager to play Sir Galahad."

"Yeah, right." Gabe turned abruptly toward the empty cell. Jenny Tyler's instant aversion still pricked his ego, but when he recalled how her cool, upper-class inflections affected him, he had to admit he felt pretty much the same way about her. "I'm cutting short this paper chase. I just ran out of patience."

As he sank to the thin mattress his gaze focused on the scrap of paper. A lone capital S showed at the ragged edge of 100 percent linen. He set the scrap carefully on the empty bunk and began to search the bag for the remainder.

Ten minutes later he gave up, gathered the discards from beside the cot and crammed them into an empty bag, which he carried to the desk where Pierce was filling out a report. He set his burden on the floor. "I think this is pure garbage, but you're welcome to take your turn." He held out the scrap he'd set aside. "Can I borrow this? I'll keep it in an evidence bag."

"By law, that's ours." Pierce's shaggy eyebrows raised, then lowered. "You'll have to sign for it, son." He rummaged through the drawer on his left.

Gabe acknowledged the bending of the rules with a nod. "I've seen similar print before, only I can't remember where. Maybe if I stare at the damn thing long enough it'll come to me. I'll bet a twenty that scrap didn't arrive with one of the credit card offers our friend was saving."

Pierce found what he wanted and adjusted his bifocals before peering at the paper. "Looks like a form of some kind."

"Yeah, but for what?" Recognition teased at Gabe's memory. He accepted the bag, inserted the scrap and signed the paper Pierce pushed toward him. "By the time I identify it, the damn thing probably won't matter. Until then I'll keep jabbing at my memory. I'll let you know if I get a brainstorm."

"Going to the Widow Tyler's?" Pierce queried.

"After I report to Sterling and grab a sandwich." Gabe rebuttoned his shirt and tucked in his shirttail, draping his tie around his neck before grabbing his jacket from the hook next to the door.

The chief's eyes twinkled with sly humor. "Maybe you ought to shave before you go out there."

Gabe cursed as he shrugged into the coat. "Waste of time. Why disappoint the nice lady? She already thinks I'm a gangster."

"Before the Justice Department called back about you, I kind of thought you were. You have friends in high places."

Gabe's scowl was automatic. "I don't know any of those people anymore. Sterling just pulls strings and sends me off." Although influence eased his path, Gabe preferred to operate on his own, using the skills honed during ten years as a Drug Enforcement Agency investigator. Even there, Sterling's long reach occasionally intruded.

"The guy I talked to said different."

"He performs when Sterling yanks his chain. Just like all of us," Gabe threw his coat over his shoulder and walked out.

He arrived on Jenny's doorstep full of resentment. Sterling's latest instructions were ridiculous. The man knew nothing about what happened out in the field, yet he dictated every move Gabe made, from the way he dressed to the way he performed his job. Every so often the idea of striking out on his own had great appeal, in spite of . . .

The door before him swung open. "You're very prompt, Mr. Daniels," Jenny said.

"Yes, ma'am." Before his conversation with Sterling, he'd promised himself not to use profanity and rudeness to annoy her. Now all bets were off. With luck, she'd cooperate and they could treat each other with civility. Even armed with that resolve, he would probably screw up. The way she looked down her straight little nose at him made him want to inquire if she smelled something bad, and then name the substance. At the same time, he wished her cotton twill skirt were shorter. Only a hint of the slender, subtly curved calf he'd seen last night showed. First-class, all the way.

She led him to the room at the back of the house. Today, natural light flowed through the windows overlooking the ravine and flooded every corner. "Would you care for some coffee?"

"No. No, thanks . . . I've already had too much today." In daylight, the room disconcerted him. Off-white walls showcased paintings of all sizes, paintings done in bright, primary colors, paintings alive with light and movement. Hers? The furnishings were casual, the upholstery mauve, natural and pale green linen. If a decor represented the inhabitant's personality, Jenny Tyler's interior was as classy and repressed as she appeared to be. But the passion and assertiveness of the paintings didn't match.

"Water or lemonade, then?"

At the negative shake of his head, she sank to a striped chair opposite the couch. He felt her intent gaze on him as he removed a miniature tape recorder from his briefcase and inserted a fresh tape. Looking up, he saw her focus on the laptop computer and fax machine nestled inside his case.

"From the looks of that setup, I assume Mr. Thomas hasn't yet seen fit to assign you an office," she observed dryly.

Gabe almost smiled. He snapped the back of the recorder in place and put it on the glass-topped coffee table. "Actually, I have an office, but I don't spend much time in it."

She fidgeted with her empty ring finger, the gesture he'd noticed the night before, then said lightly, "I suppose now you'll warn me that what I say can be held against me."

As much as it went against the grain, Gabe apologized. "I'm sorry about last night, Ms. Tyler. My mother tried to teach me better manners."

"If I recall correctly, I wasn't particularly cooperative. Perhaps we can start over. I really want to assist you if I can. It's just that I doubt I know anything helpful."

Her blue-green gaze tangled with his. The agreeable answer had caught him off balance, and he nearly smiled a second time. Then he saw her expression change and thought better of it. Sterling's bombshell had pissed him off, and he wasn't prepared to relinquish his anger just yet. Besides, a little fear might make her more forthcoming. Gabe lowered his eyebrows and scowled.

Not the least bit intimidated, she asked, "Do you really think you can solve this murder by yourself?"

Gabe's good intentions vanished. "Who said I gave a damn about solving the murder? All I want to do is find out where DeWitt hid the cash."

"You mean you're going to all this trouble simply to recover money your employer lost three years ago? He must be extremely patient if he's given you all this time to look for it."

Her sarcasm hit a nerve. "Listen, lady. I'm damn good.

If I weren't, Sterling wouldn't keep me around." He glowered at her, employing an expression which usually ended all opposition.

Unfazed, Jenny continued, "Has Mr. Sterling gone hungry because of the loss of this money?"

"No, dammit! Sterling may have more money than most rich bastards, but he's entitled to what's his. He wants it back." Gabe ran his fingers through his already rumpled hair. He loosened his necktie and unbuttoned his collar. "All right. What's your connection with Sterling? Half an hour ago, I was ordered to stick around until I was sure none of the bad guys thought you were connected with DeWitt."

"Such generosity makes my cup overflow. To think I've only watched him on television."

Her inflection left him no doubts about how distasteful she found the situation. "I'm quite sure the danger is all in his mind. My primary concern is keeping my name out of the press. If you and Chief Pierce take care of that, I'm more than capable of protecting myself."

Gabe reassessed Jenny. Perhaps she wasn't the serene, pliant little blonde she appeared to be. In addition to great legs, the lady had moxie, but could she back it up? "Not if we don't identify whoever DeWitt crossed, real quick. His house was searched again last night. Looks to me like another major player is pissed off. What if one of them suspects you carried away something besides the cat?"

He wasn't prepared for the way her skin paled. "If that's the case, you're in double trouble. The bad guys nipping at your butt and a camcorder in your face. News shows love people like you, people who look as if they never came within miles of anything dirty, but who find themselves in a pile of shit."

"Is that last supposed to be a compliment? You make my heart flutter, Mr. Daniels."

There was fear in her eyes. Why? "Look. I didn't come here to argue. How about a truce?" Damn! He'd neglected to instruct Sterling's experts to develop a profile on her. Last night something she said had set off his alarm system, but then last night his mind had been nearly fried with exhaustion.

"No one wants peace more than I. Where do you want me to start?" she said brightly.

Gabe scowled at her. What was percolating in the brain beneath that tidy haircut? His fingers moved involuntarily to touch her, and he put the brakes on them. Still, he wondered if that hair was as soft as it looked. Perhaps there were worse jobs than keeping a close eye on the little widow. "With the first time you met DeWitt."

Half an hour later, thirty minutes filled with information as trivial as Dolan's partiality for meatloaf and mashed potatoes, Jenny said suddenly, "Now that you've taken me back step by step, I remember something odd. We were talking about my paintings and my work as a children's book illustrator, and he commented that he'd switched careers overnight once . . . about five years earlier. Then he changed the subject." She crossed her legs, and Gabe realized his attention was focused on the soft, stone-colored twill inching up her calf. The progress of that piece of fabric was excruciatingly slow.

"He claimed he was retired, and mentioned that although he lived on the income from some very clever investments, he kept a financial cushion in a safe place. Since his finances were none of my business, I didn't pry."

Gabe swallowed a snort. Why couldn't she be one of those nosy broads with insatiable curiosity? "Naturally. And you never saw anyone else at his house? A strange car

32

parked in the drive, or at the curb?" he persisted.

"Never. In fact, I didn't even know he owned a car." Jenny tucked her legs beneath her on the seat. "We only chatted about day-to-day things."

Gabe employed every ounce of his considerable skill in taking her back through each of her encounters with Dolan/DeWitt. She was protesting this when he sensed movement in the doorway. Her attention swung away from him, and he swallowed a curse. "Be very quiet," she cautioned. "Don't look around."

He tensed, straining to see from the corner of his eye what held her attention. Then her voice, crooning and warm, flowed over his nerve endings. Gabe would have sworn his temperature rose.

"Hi, Choc. Want to investigate? It's all right, baby. No one here will hurt you . . . you can sit in that big patch of sunlight over there, right on the rug. The whole place is yours."

Her soft cajolery stopped, and he watched the cat cross the open space, body close to the floor, ears twitching like antennae. "Is this the first time he's come in here?"

"He slept at the foot of my bed last night. This morning he was on top of the refrigerator, tucked back beneath the cupboard above it. This is the first time I've seen him explore." Jenny's voice was low, as if she were still speaking to the cat. Gabe's question answered, she returned her attention to the animal. "Pretty Choc. Doesn't that sun feel good?"

Gabe kept his own voice soft. "What's that around his neck?"

"A flea collar, I think. An extremely elegant one. He hasn't let me close enough to inspect. Oh, good. He's washing." Relief filled her voice. "That's a good sign."

"You seem to know a lot about cats."

"I had one before I married. My husband made me give her away. He claimed to be allergic to them." Her voice was devoid of emotion.

The set of her chin and the emptiness in her eyes made Gabe sit up and take notice. Each time she referred to her husband and her marriage, he got the feeling she looked on that time as something that had happened to someone else. Maybe even on a different planet. Although it was none of his business, he surprised himself by asking, "Why did you marry him?"

Her careful word choice revealed more than her voice, which was expressionless. "Believe it or not, I was deeply in love, or so I thought at the time. I already had a successful career as an illustrator, and my paintings were beginning to sell, so I didn't even have the excuse that I was looking for a meal ticket."

"So what happened?"

Her gaze on the cat, Jenny spoke softly, but steel threaded her voice. "People and things are frequently not what they seem, Mr. Daniels. Haven't you ever noticed?" She straightened her shoulders and regarded him coolly. "My marital history has nothing to do with recovering Mr. Thomas's millions. What else do you want to know?"

"Why are you hiding?" he asked softly.

Jenny swung her feet to the floor and met his gaze defiantly. "Why should you think I'm hiding?"

"Get real, lady. You want your name kept out of the papers, and you back off when I ask the simplest question about your past." Gabe wanted her to hate him; maybe then he could ignore the way his hands itched to rumple her cornsilk hair.

"I still have no assurance you will be able to accomplish that," she countered, ignoring the second part of his statement. "Only your promise."

"You bought a bundle of moonshine. Do you think for a minute any idiot couldn't discover who found the body? Who was in the house? Who had befriended the old bastard? In a town this size, that might take someone half-sharp all of five minutes." He nearly told her about the two dead murderers, then decided to save the information for another time.

"You're deliberately trying to frighten me," she accused.

"Finally figured that out, did you? You're not the first person I've ever met who I've had to convince I mean what I say. You have my protection, but I need some answers. The evidence so far points to DeWitt getting cute with some real bad people. Not just crooks, Ms. Tyler . . . organizations that don't stop at anything. Not even . . ."

The shrill ring of the telephone interrupted Gabe's words. The cat sprang up and disappeared, the scrabble of his claws on the waxed treads to the second floor the only sound until the phone rang a second time. Jenny reached for the portable on the table beside her chair. "Hello . . . Yes, he's right here." She passed him the phone.

"Daniels," he answered. Pierce's laconic voice reminded him that he should have given the chief his cell phone number. As the rest of his message sank in, Gabe realized it wouldn't have made any difference. "How long ago? . . . Anybody we know inside? . . . Yeah, I'll be right there."

Jenny had risen, her luminous blue-green eyes wide with apprehension. Her hands were clenched together, the fingers tightly entwined. "What happened?"

Gabe wondered why she reacted to every crisis as if this one might be the big one, the final act that would destroy her. He stood slowly. "DeWitt's house just exploded. It's my guess whoever gave it the toss last night set timed explosives."

"But why destroy the house? What if someone had been inside?" Jenny's face turned white and her features crumpled.

Gabe had to stop himself from reaching for her. If she fainted, she would just have to pick herself up off the floor.

In a remote wooded area ten miles from Donhaven, Donnie Snow surveyed his marijuana plot with satisfaction. Planted in a clearing deep in a remote area of the state park, the carefully transplanted seedlings were thriving. The profits from this patch would be a nice addition to his income from distributing cocaine to selected pushers. He circled the area, checking his trip wires and traps. Anyone foolish enough to investigate his enterprise would be in for a shock.

"Too bad about Dolan," he mused. "I wonder who'll take over the old man's place in the pipeline."

Donnie checked his watch for the fifth time in as many minutes. The order to get the cat's flea collar from the Tyler broad's place had come by phone that morning, and he'd sent his brothers to watch for her to leave so they could retrieve the collar while he checked the hidden plot. Perhaps he should have gone with Tommie and Bobbie, but he'd needed the solitude to recover from the destruction caused by the explosives his new boss had sent him. He'd left as soon as Dolan's house blew.

Now he had another worry. He didn't want to tell his employers his bad feeling about the black-haired dude hanging around Dolan's house and kissing up to the cops. Somehow he didn't think they'd be impressed with his explanation that the guy just didn't smell right.

Pierce he could handle, but this stranger was an unknown factor. If the lady at the top expected him to tangle with pros, she'd have to pay extra. He'd taken on enough risk by switching employers. Then he smiled. Having a foot in two camps might pay off. Besides, the five grand they'd promised to pay for the flea collar would make a nice nest egg.

THREE

Gabe headed for the door, but Jenny beat him to it. "Where the hell do you think you're going?" he demanded. As she reached for the knob, he seized her wrist.

Although the top of her head barely reached his shoulder, Jenny stared down her nose at the fingers pinioning her wrist. She forced herself to ignore the tingle his touch sent up her arm, concentrating instead on the little victory when he released her. It had taken her years to develop such control.

"I'm going with you," she said. "I don't understand any of this, and I don't care who he used to be, but Mr. Dolan was my friend. He loved that house and his rose garden." She tilted her head back to meet his scowl with one of her own. "If you refuse to take me, I can quite easily drive there on my own."

He swore beneath his breath before grinding out, "You would, wouldn't you. All right, come on." He took her hand and tugged her behind him to his rented Jeep.

Sighing with relief, Jenny climbed into the passenger side. She wasn't sure why she felt compelled to see the destruction, but she didn't want to be left alone with her imagination. Gabe started the engine before his door slammed. "You're a pain in the ass, you know that?"

"I appreciate your sharing that touching observation with me," she responded calmly, then grabbed for the dashboard as the Jeep backed wildly into the road, fishtailing as it roared down the highway. "You overcorrected," she couldn't help pointing out.

"Any more help with the driving, and you can walk." He favored her with a black look. "In case you didn't notice, Dolan's murder wasn't tidy like the ones in books, Ms. Tyler. The only similarity was that the two men who probably murdered him left fingerprints. A couple of nights ago the owners of the prints were found in New York. Both of them were shot execution-style. This whole damn thing becomes screwier and more dangerous every minute."

He turned left on Pearl Street and nosed the Jeep to the curb behind a police car, ignoring the patrolman who motioned them away. "If you're hoarding any information that will help, now's the time to spill it."

Her heart beat thickly in her throat. New York? Her in-laws had promised her . . . "But I don't know anything!" Jenny couldn't keep the panic out of her voice. Suddenly she wondered if showing up at the scene of the explosion was wise.

Gabe jerked the keys from the ignition and turned to arrow a harsh look at her. "I sure hate to think you're keeping anything back. Sterling doesn't want anyone hurt, but he might change his mind if he thought you were keeping secrets."

She swallowed the lump of fear in her throat. "Mr. Daniels, I assure you I've told you everything I recall about Mr. Dolan. Besides, I never asked for Mr. Thomas's protection." A flashback of the little man as she'd last seen him made her stomach clench. Bile rose in her throat. Panicky tears blurred her vision. Surely his murder had no connection to . . .

Gabe opened his door. "Then you'll be okay, Ms. Tyler."

As if his Rambo-type presence would be any protection if the Travinos had decided she was a risk. She scrambled out of the Jeep and joined him at the hood.

The street ahead was chaos. Donhaven's small fire department and even smaller police force were having difficulty restraining the spectators. Hoses aimed at the smoldering ruins did little but contain the flames. Jenny recalled the detailed discussions she'd heard about bombs. The one used here must have been one of the incendiary types—the kind employed when the intent was total destruction.

Flashing the contents of a small leather folder at the nearest policeman, Gabe seized her elbow and dragged her toward the tangle of canvas hoses snaking through an opening in the tidy hedge. The movement pulled his suit jacket open, and Jenny recognized the checkered handle of a Beretta Cougar holstered beneath his armpit. Looking up, she saw him eyeing her as if daring her to comment. Then he jerked his coat back in place and guided her to a corner of the yard, away from the organized confusion surrounding the house. "Stay here until I come back. I need to find Pierce."

Seeing the gun had stiffened Jenny's resolve. "Has it ever occurred to you that your presence might be what is attracting these unusual events?" She allowed herself a small smile of satisfaction at the surprise that flickered across his features. "After you return, I intend to ask some questions of my own."

As he strode toward the chief of police, Gabe shook his head in disbelief. What the hell had brought all that on? The stony determination in her eyes had startled him; it was a complete one-eighty from her distress minutes earlier. He stopped at Pierce's side.

"I see you brought Ms. Tyler with you. Was that real smart?" the chief inquired. His eyes were red-rimmed; flecks of soot dusted his balding head.

Gabe shrugged. "She claimed she'd come on her own if I didn't bring her. Seemed smarter to keep her where I could keep an eye on her in case . . ." Before he could continue, what remained of the house's walls caved inward. Sparks flew in every direction. He slapped at a red-hot cinder which landed on the left sleeve of his Italian-tailored suit. "Damn!" He doubted Sterling would honor a claim on his expense account. Shrugging resignedly, he switched his attention to the sight before them. "Pretty sophisticated explosives for a local to come up with."

"Kind of wondered about that myself," Pierce replied. "Fire inspector'll pin the thing down, but he don't generally hurry unless there's loss of life."

"You sure no one was in there?"

"Yep. We did a sweep after the break-in last night, and I left a couple of the boys in front and in back. I don't have that many personnel, but I had a feelin'. The thing just blew. Out of the blue, you might say." Pierce chuckled at his own feeble pun.

Gabe grinned. "Must have been a hell of a search your boys did."

"They're usually pretty good. Since they didn't spot anythin', I figure whoever planted the bomb knew what he was doin'. The stuff must have been under the floorboards." He scratched the bridge of his nose. "Afraid you were right, son. Now the big boys will be in town breathin' down my neck. I sure hate that. Bad enough I got you pokin' your nose in."

"What about our friend over there?" Gabe gestured toward Jenny, who gazed stonily at the fire. He wondered what she was thinking beneath the tight purity of her features. Her calm made the skin at the back of his neck tighten, a warning which had saved his hide more than once. He peered at her more closely. Her eyes were half-closed, like a gambler computing the odds before betting. He recognized the look; he'd worn it many times himself.

Pierce broke into his brooding. "Seems like the lady just showed up at the wrong place at the wrong time. Ran her name yesterday, as a matter of course. No record, and nothin' outstandin' against her. Pure as the driven show."

"We'll see. Sterling's creepy little nerds are doing a full workup. By the time they finish, I'll know what color polish she puts on her toenails." Gabe had a sudden burning need to know the details of the lady's life. If she were spotless, he would baby-sit as he'd been told. Otherwise, he'd leave town with a clear conscience.

"Kind of scary to know someone can turn your pockets inside out like that," Pierce said as he mopped at his bald head. "She seems like a nice lady. Keeps to herself."

Everyone had secrets, Gabe thought. His curiosity had to do with her late husband. He'd seen the bleakness in her eyes the night before, when she'd dismissed the man as if he were an unfortunate purchase from a boutique. The suspicion that Jenny Tyler was either hiding something or hiding from someone grew with every passing minute.

"Yeah, well, if she's an ax murderer, I'll get back to you on it," he said, inspecting the burn in his coat sleeve ruefully. Silk was so damn flammable. He cursed Sterling for mandating such impractical dress, particularly since denim was more his style. "I'm going to take the lady back to her house, unless you're planning a weenie roast over those coals. Then I want to dig through those bags of paper some more."

"I'm goin' straight to the office. Why don't you bring her in to make her statement before you take her home? Save us all some time." As if sensing his impatience with the idea of a delay, Pierce peered at him from beneath his shaggy brows. "You might need a favor from me later."

As he turned to follow, Gabe reflected that the old rascal was nearly as bad as Sterling Thomas.

Two hours later, Jenny stepped from Gabe's Jeep and made her way along the flagstone path to her front door. She felt drained, her thoughts so chaotic she didn't even protest when he killed the engine and followed her. Digging her key from her pocket with one hand, she opened the storm door with the other and jabbed at the lock. As the key brushed the opening, the door swung open. Before she could move, hard hands grasped her waist and swung her backward. "Stay put." Gabe's harsh order rumbled in her ear. A part of her registered the gun which had appeared in his hand.

He went in low, scanning the small foyer with one glance before moving into the hall. Jenny followed, stopping at the closet to retrieve her canvas tote. She shadowed him while he did a quick survey of the dining room and kitchen on their right, then headed for the spacious great room. Late afternoon sun streamed through the wall of windows, revealing chairs tipped at drunken angles against fallen wicker tables and tilted lamps. Broken glass and shards of her precious Indian pottery littered the gleaming floor. She cried out softly.

Gabe whirled, anger contorting his face. "Dammit, I told you to stay put," he snarled.

The pistol in his hand would have frightened Jenny if she hadn't been able to match his firepower. She leveled her Lady Smith at his Beretta. "This is my house. What makes you think you're any more capable of looking for an intruder than I am?"

"Christ! Put that thing away before you hurt yourself,"

he ordered. "Where'd you get that cannon?"

She looked fondly at the weapon in her hand. "It was the only honest gift my husband ever gave me." Fleetingly, she recalled the early days of her marriage, when learning to handle the pistol had been a lark, when Trent had treated her with teasing tenderness. Shaking her head to banish the memory, she turned and headed down the hall. "We're wasting time. Someone may be upstairs."

The ruffled valance above the curtains in her bedroom hung at an odd angle. In her studio, her drafting board lay on its side. Everywhere, chairs and small tables were either overturned or pushed out of place.

When they found no one, Jenny remembered. She rushed into the hall, calling, "Choc! Where are you, sweetheart?"

"Who cares about the damn cat! I want to know what you're hiding here," Gabe demanded as he stepped from the guest bedroom.

Jenny recalled Choc's wildly beating heart the day before; she understood all too well the animal's terror. Gabe's anger meant nothing when measured against that. "Choc's master was murdered and he was left with the body for nearly a week, hungry and terrified. Now he's been frightened again. I must find him."

Her whole body shook with the force of her anger. "Why don't you just go play with your toys? Report to the billionaire who holds your leash. Maybe he'll throw you a piece of fresh meat."

Turning on her heel, Jenny fled down the stairs to begin a more systematic search. As she hurried through the house, opening and closing cupboard doors and peering beneath furniture, she caught a glimpse of Gabe in the hall, talking on his cell phone. "Choc," she called softly, fighting to keep the panic out of her voice, "I know you're frightened, baby. Please come to me. I'll keep you safe, I promise."

After a quick survey of the kitchen, Jenny headed for the basement. With no regard for the possibility that someone could be down there lying in wait, she seized the doorknob and widened the opening, pressing the light switch with her other hand. She didn't want to startle the animal into retreating into a hiding place so obscure she would miss him, so she paused at the top of the stairs and called, "Choc? Are you down here, baby?" As she descended the stairs, she called again. Looking down, she saw blood on the gray tile floor leading to the laundry room.

Pushing back terror that threatened to engulf her, Jenny called once more: "Choc?" She held her pistol steady with both hands and edged cautiously toward the louvered door. A nudge of her hip swung it inward, and she turned on the overhead light.

An empty plastic basket had been knocked from the counter where she folded laundry. She stepped around it and instinctively looked upward. Round, terrified blue eyes peered from between the joists overhead. The cat perched on top of the wall separating the laundry from the storage room. His fur was fluffed and his tail twitched angrily. A wide pattern of red droplets splashed across the walls, most of it on the wall and counter beneath him.

"Choc!" Jenny fought to keep panic out of her voice while she locked the safety and set her gun on the dryer. "Oh, baby, I'm so glad to find you. You're hurt, poor darling." Pulling a stool to the edge of the shelf, she used it to climb onto the Formica surface. Crouching below him, she crooned, "Will you come to me, Choc? Let me see where you're hurt."

Footsteps on the stairs warned her of Gabe's approach.

In the same soft chant, hoping she spoke loud enough for her voice to reach him, she said, "He won't hurt you, Choc. I promise. You can trust me."

She rose to her knees and extended her arms until her hands were six inches from the cat. Without moving, she concentrated on holding his blue gaze with her own. Within seconds, a tentative paw reached toward her, and she stretched farther. Moments later, he climbed cautiously into her cupped hands. "Good kitty. Good Choc," she murmured as she brought him to her chest. Rapid heartbeats racked the cat's body.

Gabe's strong hands spanned her waist. "Hold on to him. I'll lift you down." His voice was quiet and gentle.

When her feet touched the floor, Jenny pulled away from his touch. She didn't need anyone to prop her up or take care of her. "His back left paw is bleeding. I have to call a vet."

"Yeah, and his sissy collar's gone." Gabe eyed Choc disgustedly. "Sonovabitch! That's what they came for. The freaking collar."

Jenny clutched the cat closer. "I'm sorry to hear you missed such an important clue, but my concern right now is for Choc. If you'll just step aside, I'll attend to him."

Gabe crowded her against the edge of the table. If he leaned toward her . . .

He did. His big body surrounded her as Gabe reached behind her back. She realized with dismay that what she felt wasn't fear; the heat curling through her body was something much more dangerous. Attraction. His warm breath brushed her ear as he said, "Here. Wrap him in this towel before he makes a run for it." She shivered, scarcely making sense of his next words. "His claws will lock in the nap and he'll be trapped, at least until we get him to a vet. I'll go upstairs and check the phone book." He wrapped her fingers around the towel and left the room.

Dizzied by the quick practicality of his suggestion, Jenny realized she'd been holding her breath. She exhaled, the sound sounding loud in the enclosed space. She heard Gabe's voice from upstairs and quickly confined the cat before joining him.

"His claw's been ripped out," Dr. Alicia Hall said disgustedly. "The only consolation is that somewhere there's a thief with a deep scratch. A really deep scratch. If God was watching, an infected scratch." She smoothed her hands over Choc's quivering sides and rubbed his forehead. "I'll have to anesthetize him so I can remove the nail bed and stitch it. He needs to stay overnight. You can pick him up in the morning."

Jenny reached to scratch the struggling cat's ears. "He's been through so much. The poor thing will think he's been abandoned again." The curiosity in the gray-haired woman's eyes made her sigh. She explained how she came to have the cat, adding, "Mr. Dolan was very attached to him."

The veterinarian nodded sympathetically while ruffling the dark cream-colored fur along the cat's flank. He was calm beneath her capable hands. "Believe me, the anesthetic will leave him so woozy he won't be aware of anything till morning. You can come for him anytime after eight-thirty."

Gabe's voice was surprisingly soft as he moved closer to the table. "The little guy really must be hurting. He's tougher than I would have expected for such a fancy cat." He smoothed Choc's back, awkwardly at first, then more confidently when the cat responded with a rumbling purr. His lean fingers nearly spanned the little animal; his arm brushed hers. Inexplicably, Jenny once again felt surrounded. She realized she was breathing shallowly, her gaze locked on the seductively repetitive strokes.

"How old is he?" Gabe asked.

As if in a trance, Jenny responded, "Ah, he's not quite two." She caught herself and said firmly, "At least that's what Mr. Dolan said." She felt Gabe's body tense. His fingers separated the fur on Choc's flank.

"What the hell is that, Doc?" He held open a furrow of fur.

Dr. Hall leaned closer and peered at the cat's skin. "The owner must have registered him." She moved Gabe's fingers aside and searched the cat's hide expertly. Dark lines flashed by like a deck of cards being shuffled.

"Registered?" Jenny asked.

"A national agency assigns pets a number. Then they're notified if the animal wanders off and is picked up by an animal control agency. He must have had an out-of-touch vet. Now they're implanting microchips. Much quicker and less trouble." The vet's attention focused sharply on the cat. "Funny place for it, though." She brushed the fur the wrong way once more, her other hand capably anchoring Choc. "Too many numbers, too."

Gabe reached into his inner pocket for an envelope and pen, causing his suit coat to fall open. The veterinarian looked from his holstered pistol to his face and demanded. "Are you with the police? Otherwise I have to ask you to hand over your weapon. I'll return it when you leave the premises."

"Hold your fire, Doc." He reached into another pocket and pulled out the flat leather case he'd shown the policeman earlier. Flipping it open to reveal the badge and photograph inside, he held it out at an angle. "This cat and those numbers are important evidence. Read them off to me."

Before he could return the case to his pocket, Jenny seized it. She could scarcely believe her eyes. *Dear heaven, what have I gotten myself into?* The badge was from the DEA. He claimed to be working for Sterling Thomas. For whom did Gabe really work?

She waited until Dr. Hall finished reciting numbers, then said coldly, "I'm afraid I must ask you to clarify some of the things you've told me, Mr. Daniels."

"Later, dammit," he replied. His lips curved in a triumphant smile as he reached out to pat Choc, whose eyes were dull with pain and exhaustion. "We'll pick him up in the morning, Doc. He's going to take a little trip. Where can I get one of those carrying cases?"

"Just one minute!" Jenny shouted. Both Gabe and the veterinarian stared at her. "The police put this cat in my care, and since I'm not going anywhere, neither is he." Anger felt wonderful. The last time she'd lost her temper was before Trent's death; since then she'd existed behind the shield of self-imposed detachment. Still, she shouldn't be surprised by her outburst. Gabe Daniels and his high-handed tactics made her crazy.

"Yeah, well, we'll talk about that later, too." He tugged at his necktie until the knot slipped completely. Turning to Dr. Hall, Gabe asked, "He'll be all right to travel, won't he?"

Dr. Hall surveyed him cynically. "Would it make any difference if I said no? The cat will be miserable and confused tomorrow . . . physically able to travel, but not happy about it. Actually, the confinement will be ideal until he heals. I'll see what I can do about locating a cat caddy, since you'd probably throw this poor animal into a grocery sack if I don't come up with one." She gathered up Choc and carried him to the door. "And now, I'm afraid you'll have to excuse me. I have a job to do."

Gabe turned a surprised expression toward Jenny. "Crusty broad, isn't she?"

She slapped away the hand he folded around her elbow. "She is not a broad, and neither am I. We're women who are sick and tired of having you steamroll over us." She stalked down the hall and out the front door of the clinic. "You're like a freight train at full speed. I have no intention of traveling anywhere, and Choc will be in no condition for a journey, even if I were so foolish as to give him over to your care." When he reached for the handle, she pushed his arm out of her way and opened the door herself. "Just take me home."

Gabe did as she asked, driving in silence all the way to her house. Killing the engine, he jerked his keys free and stepped out, then opened the rear door and reached inside to pull out a leather suit bag before looking at her challengingly. "As much as it will pain you to hear, you don't have much say about anything anymore. That tattoo is the key to a Swiss bank account, and I intend to guard that cat like the crown jewels until I deliver him to Sterling. Since I'm also under orders to keep you safe, you and Choc are a package."

He straightened and slung the bag over his other arm. Slamming the car door, he continued, "The cat's going to be in la-la-land all night, but there's no way in hell I'm going to leave you here on your own. I'm staying with you."

FOUR

"Absolutely not," Jenny declared. His right eyebrow arched and his gaze settled on her mouth. She resisted a need to lick her lips.

"What's your problem? Are you afraid you'll be overcome with lust?"

She stiffened. For a millisecond, she pictured herself in his arms, pressed against the wide chest that had brushed against hers earlier. Her cheeks warmed, and she reined in her imagination. "Not even in a four-star dream, Mr. Daniels."

A flash of humor showed in his dark eyes. "I doubt your imagination could script one of my four-stars, Ms. Tyler."

Then irritation replaced his humor. "Sterling's an old-fashioned sonovabitch. Chivalrous. He feels bad about you discovering DeWitt's body. And he's concerned for your safety. In his convoluted way of thinking, he feels he owes you something. Don't ask me to explain why."

Once more in control of her thoughts, Jenny lifted her chin and narrowed her eyes. "I don't need his help. Or yours. I don't even know who you are! Or who you really work for! You say you work for Sterling, but that badge you flashed said something else. Is it phony?" She waited for a response.

When he didn't answer, she continued, her voice rising with each word, "See? You can't tell me the truth! You have the number that was tattooed on the cat. Whoever had DeWitt killed must want it, too, and they'll figure you have the number and are going after the money. If you go away, they'll follow you. I can take care of myself." Before he could move to stop her, she marched to her front door, unlocked it and let herself in.

Her hands were shaking. She had shouted again. What was it about the man that made her lose control? And she'd lied to him. Deep down, she was terrified. A paranoid corner of her brain fostered the thought that perhaps Mr. Dolan's . . . no, DeWitt's . . . murder had nothing to do with Sterling Thomas's money. It was revenge concocted by Trent's family. They had changed their minds. Jenny leaned against the wall and shuddered. How could she have been so stupid as to believe she was free?

When her front door opened she swung around, nerves jumping. Gabe strode over the threshold and dropped his garment bag at her feet. "Don't ever walk away from me like that again, dammit."

"I told you to leave," she said, fighting to regain her composure. He looked overwhelmingly male and more than a little menacing. Even as she tried to convince herself those qualities made him an animal, a part of her responded in a way she'd hoped never again to experience.

Ignoring her, he walked past to the sunny room overlooking the ravine and looked around. "My team did a good job. Printed everything and then cleaned up." He propped his hands on his hips. His coat hung open, revealing the tail of his shirt hanging free of his waistband. And the shoulder holster.

Jenny realized belatedly that the room had been put back to rights. With a pang, she noticed the gaps where her treasured pottery had been displayed. Feeling perverse, she said, "I didn't give permission for this. I could have done it myself."

"You couldn't have printed the damn place if you took the rest of the year. My team is good." His smile reminded her of a satisfied shark. He walked over to the linen-covered couch, pushed aside four throw pillows covered with flower prints, and pressed down on the cushions. "A little soft, but that's probably for the best. Make it harder for me to sleep soundly."

"I feel sure you'd prefer a bed of nails. However, since you won't be sleeping on my couch, no comparison is necessary." Jenny felt better. She had her composure back.

He continued as if she hadn't spoken. "I know you'd prefer I use that nice guest room upstairs, but I want to be down here." His sudden smile told her he knew she thought no such thing. "Should be tough for someone to break in through the back, but this gives me good coverage of the front." His frown deepened. "By the way, your front door lock sucks."

Her control snapped. "That does it." She whirled and pointed to the door in question. "Out. Now. By the count of ten, or I'll call the police and have you arrested for unlawful entry. One . . . two . . ."

"Stop being so tight-assed and look at this realistically. Pierce doesn't have the manpower to protect you, and after the break-in today, you're a walking target. He's pretty shrewd, but he's not a magician." His scowl told her he wasn't any happier about the situation than she was.

"Three . . . four . . ."

"Enough already. What are you going to do when you get to ten, shoot me?" Impossibly, his black brows lowered even more.

"I can't. You took my gun after I found Choc." Jenny scanned the room for something blunt and preferably heavy. Seeing nothing adequate, she demanded, "Give it back."

He turned his back to her, walked to the broad window and looked out at the gathering dusk. "I don't trust females with guns. Women tend to fly off the handle."

Frustrated by his calm and his asinine chauvinism, Jenny accepted the futility of her ultimatum. She could never move him. "All right, Mr. Daniels. You may spend the night. And you may accompany me to pick up Choc, but then I expect you to leave . . . without either of us." Not one muscle of his broad-shouldered body moved. "However, this is my house, and I will tolerate neither your foul language nor your contemptuous references to women. One lapse and I will make you wish you had chosen to spend the night in a nest of vipers."

He whirled and glared at her. "You're some kind of prude, right? Who the h—"

Jenny interrupted him. "Stop right there. During my marriage, I heard every one of those words in every conceivable combination." She drew a deep breath to steady her voice, which had betrayed her by wobbling. "When I was finally free, I vowed never to live like that again."

The quizzical lift of his eyebrows warned her he was about to ask questions she had no intention of answering. Without a word, she whirled and headed upstairs. She could use her cell phone in her studio.

With narrowed eyes, Gabe watched her walk away from him. He told himself his curiosity was simply that of a trained investigator. The woman was a royal pain in the ass, just as he'd told her, but he'd nearly passed out that afternoon when she'd appeared, competently brandishing a gun. The Lady Smith was made for hands bigger than hers—strong, capable hands, not the slender fingers she'd wrapped around the custom grip. What kind of a man would gift her with a killing machine?

Her snotty finishing school accent still drove him nuts, but her voice wasn't abrasive. It was soft and pure, almost like music. And she wasn't really skinny; she was Grade A Choice, even though there wasn't much of her. The view of her backside as she walked away, must have raised his blood pressure fifteen points.

Gabe snorted at the absurdity of his thoughts. He'd have to get a grip on his hormones, or the Widow Tyler would need protection from her protector.

Jenny stared through her studio window at the mist rising in the ravine below. During her months here she'd found peace, and her work had never gone better. Her agent had passed on glowing comments from both writers and editors about her illustrations; and her paintings, the works she'd yet to show anyone, filled her with satisfaction. Looking at them objectively, she saw more freedom, more strength and brightness, in each one.

The silence at the other end of the telephone line ate at her nerves. She'd dialed Trent's uncle's number five minutes earlier, and one of his underlings had taken her name, promising to fetch him. Perhaps this was simply another, more subtle, way of informing her of a change in her status . . .

"Jenny, my beautiful one. I was in a meeting, and Charles dithered about interrupting. How goes it for you?"

The mellifluous voice flowed around her like warm honey. She fought the familiar spell it cast. "I could be better, Uncle G. I called to ask what you knew about the situation here in Donhaven."

"Jenny, love, I haven't the faintest idea what you're talking about."

"A man named Winston DeWitt, or Dolan, as he called

himself. Someone slit his throat, and I found the body. Then someone blew up his house. There's a suspicion he was connected to drug dealing."

Silence reigned at the other end of the telephone. Cold sweat began to form on her nape, and she shifted her feet as she swiped at it with her free hand.

"Not one of ours, Jenny. That's not our territory. I know of no . . . conflict with any other corporation."

"Then this has nothing to do with me? You haven't changed your mind?"

"Jenny, Jenny," he soothed. "I keep my promises. I promised we'd cut you completely free, and I made this clear to everyone. No one would dare go against my wishes."

Jenny chewed her lower lip. He sounded hurt. Was the pain genuine? Even if she'd been able to see his eyes, she wouldn't have been completely sure. His years as a Mafia don had given him total control of every nuance of his expression and his voice. He broke into her thoughts. "What kind of wolves are on the scene?"

Ah, well. I was the one who started this. "There's an investigator named Gabe Daniels, who works for Sterling Thomas, the industrialist. Apparently Mr. Dolan, who was really named DeWitt, embezzled a great deal of money from Thomas, and Daniels is quite serious about recovering the money. Then this afternoon Daniels flashed a DEA badge. Can he work for both?"

Full-bodied laughter rang in her ear. "Daniels? Heaven help us." Uncle G. chuckled. Jenny heard him sharing the news with someone in the room. More laughter sounded behind him.

"What is so funny?" she demanded.

"Little one, you must be very careful. Although Daniels

works for Thomas, he reverts to the government when it suits him, and they're glad to accept whatever he offers. He's ruthless and he's dangerous. When he makes up his mind, nothing gets in his way. Even Thomas becomes impatient with his single-mindedness at times. You haven't told him about your past, have you?"

Was that apprehension in his voice? Even if he meant what he said about her status, he didn't completely trust her. "Of course not. There's no other way he can find out, is there?"

"He probably has access to pipelines we can't seal, so you must reconcile yourself. Little one, you must watch your step. Promise me you will call if things become difficult?"

"I . . . I promise, Uncle G. But I won't involve you unless I've no other choice. You've been much too good to me already." She hoped he couldn't sense her fear.

"You're a good girl, Jenny. Trent should have done better by you. The boy was a disappointment to me."

Trent couldn't have disappointed his uncle more than he'd disappointed her, Jenny thought bitterly. "I understand, Uncle. If you hear anything, will you call me? Use my cell phone number."

"Of course. Remember, Jenny, be very careful."

A mechanical sound followed the disconnect. Either the call had been recorded or someone had tapped into the line. Uncle G. was paranoid about security, so it was probably the former. If the listener was the FBI, she could add them to the list of people who thought Jenny Tyler knew something she didn't. She knew one thing. This time she'd fight for herself. No one would ever again take control of her life.

Only after she'd replaced the receiver did she realize she hadn't asked about Tania. Perhaps she'd been wise not to.

Their friendship hadn't been obvious; both she and Trent's cousin had guarded their privacy. How she longed to hear Tania's voice.

Gabe had been inspecting the locks on the downstairs windows when he heard the shower running. Maybe the water would mellow her temper. He could put off telling her that security-wise, the place was like Swiss cheese; she'd only poker up again.

Not that he didn't enjoy penetrating her serene facade. Without it, she came alive. The first time, her eyes had flashed clear blue-green anger and her cheeks had flushed a warm rose, highlighting cheekbones as elegant as a piece of Ladros porcelain. The second time, he'd felt the same rush of attraction. Gabe had no intention of indulging himself a third time—he might give in to temptation and touch the merchandise. Then Sterling would bitch like a Mother Superior. Business was business. Always.

Disgusted with the direction his thoughts had strayed twice in the last half-hour, he focused on the job at hand.

Stripping off his tie, he slung it and his jacket over the back of the couch. He unbuttoned the top buttons of his shirt and rolled up his sleeves. After careful consideration, he selected a drop-leaf table near the inside wall as the place to set up shop. A little hacking was a satisfying way to end a day, and he was eager to see if his hunch would bear up under investigation.

An hour later, he gazed with satisfaction at the scrap of paper from Dolan's house. The envelope he'd used to record the number tattooed on the cat lay next to it.

Dialing the number he knew best on his cell phone, he tipped his chair onto its back legs and waited for Sterling to answer the secure line. With any luck, the old bastard was eating dinner. The idea made Gabe smile with satisfaction. When Sterling answered, he said without preamble, "The greedy sonovabitch didn't have sense enough to retire. My guess is he's been distributing drugs for one of the mobs, and there may be a rival involved. His Swiss bank account holds more than double what he stole from you . . . I just got out of their files, that's why . . . How? You don't want to know. I just faxed you a report." Gabe ran his fingers through his hair and waited.

After a moment he said, "Slater and his boys are watching tonight . . . As soon as the damn cat's able to travel . . . She'll come around. Trust me."

Without compunction, Jenny paused in the doorway to listen to Gabe's conversation. At his last words she gasped, crossed the room, and snatched the phone, all the while keeping her defiant gaze fixed on Gabe's frowning face. "Mr. Thomas? This is Jennifer Tyler. I'd like to inform you that I have no intention of 'coming around.' The cat has been placed in my care, and he, and I, are staying here. Your bloodhound is a paranoid, profane animal. I feel sure you mean well, but the sooner you remove him from my presence, the happier I will be. Good-bye."

Gabe took the phone from her fingers gingerly, as if afraid the instrument had become red-hot. He raised it to his ear, and Jenny had the satisfaction of seeing him wince. "Yes, Sterling, she is . . . No more than usual." He massaged his nape with one big, long-fingered hand. "But dammit . . ." He shot her a glance and said, "Don't worry, I'll apologize . . . Things have been moving pretty fast here. I hadn't gotten around to that . . . I'll try, sir . . . Right, I'll keep you up-to-date."

Was she imagining it or did he avoid meeting her gaze

while he folded the phone and set it on the table next to his other toys. "Was I clear enough for your employer?" she challenged. The sight of the black, curling, chest hair escaping his unbuttoned shirt distracted her, and she looked at his face, which was a mistake. He was grinning, showing white, even teeth. She groaned inwardly. On top of everything else, the miserable wretch had the audacity to possess a deep dimple in his left cheek.

"He gave me orders. The first was to apologize for swearing in your presence. Consider it done." His grin disappeared and he lowered the front legs of his chair. "The second was to let you in on exactly where we stand. Sterling said you sounded more intelligent than he'd expected," he added disgustedly. "Probably because of the way you talk." The doorbell rang.

"That must be the pizza I ordered. I don't know about you, but I'm starving." He stood and reached into his back pocket for his wallet. "Truce? At least while we eat?"

Caught off guard by his sincerity, Jenny nearly groaned. A pizza delivery less than a year earlier had changed her life forever. Perhaps it was a sign of recovery that she found herself even able to contemplate remaining in the same room with one. "I'll make salads." The unpleasant reminder of her past was timely. In his present mode, Gabe was entirely too likeable.

She hurried to the kitchen. Pulling down a glass bowl, she filled it with torn romaine and spinach leaves, and was slicing thin rings of sweet red onions across the top when Gabe came in and set the pizza box on the round, glass-topped table. Without comment, he set places with the plates and flatware she provided. She handed him the vinegar and oil cruets, steeling herself against the fragrance wafting up from the table. "Would you like a beer? I have Beck's," she offered, satisfaction filling her when his eyebrows rose halfway up his forehead.

"I'm surprised a proper lady like you would have such a thing in her house."

Jenny took that for a yes, and was surprised when he came to stand behind her at the refrigerator door. "Much as I'm tempted, I have to stay awake tonight. That Pepsi will do." His voice rumbled close to her ear, and the tiny nerves across the top of her shoulder jumped in response.

"Whatever you want," she said, determined to ignore the sensations. Reaching for a cola for herself, she popped the top and poured it over ice cubes in her tumbler. She eyed him skeptically. "Aren't you imagining danger behind every bush?"

Not bothering with ice and a glass, Gabe took his drink to the table, where he stood waiting for her to join him. She shook her head and motioned for him to sit, ignoring his questioning look. "That number on the cat's back is for DeWitt's Swiss bank account. When I recognized it, the fragment of a deposit slip I'd dug out of the debris triggered the name of the bank. I hacked into their records while you were upstairs." He separated a slice of pizza from the box and bit into it.

She just couldn't do it. Jenny opened the freezer and pulled out a frozen chicken/pasta dinner and programmed the microwave while absorbing the realization that he must be more than a casual hacker to bypass the intricate codes she was sure protected a Swiss bank. Finally she commented, "You appear to be proficient in a number of fields, perhaps even law. Wasn't that illegal?" She busied herself dressing her salad.

"Yeah, it might have been," he said carelessly. His grin flashed once more. "Anyway, DeWitt has over twice what he stole from Sterling in his account. Since the only reason he'd bury himself in hick heaven would be to make a profit, I'm assuming he was a middleman in someone's drug operation."

Jenny dribbled herbed vinegar over her salad and returned the cruets to the counter. His voice came from behind her. "All right, since you're not saying, I'll ask. Is there something wrong with the pizza?"

"I don't know. I haven't tasted it," she replied coolly, turning to remove her dinner from the microwave.

Leaning back in his chair, he glared at her from narrowed eyes. "You really have that cold bitch routine down pat."

Jenny slid the plastic container onto a plate, carried it to the table and sat. Still not answering, she touched her finger to the surface to make sure the food was warm. The creamy sauce clung to her finger and she brought it to her mouth. Gabe's sudden stillness drew her gaze, and she shivered. His dark eyes watched her finger with such intensity that warmth spread low in her belly. She swallowed the smooth mixture, which felt as if it had swelled to the size of an apricot, then said, "You've made a wild assumption about Mr. Dolan, and now you're making one about me."

"Not in Dolan's case. Drugs are the only source for that kind of money. The small-timers who took him out were probably killed soon after they reported in. Only the big outfits reach this far that efficiently." He reached for another slice of pizza. "As far as you're concerned, maybe I did. Make an assumption, I mean."

"Did it ever occur to you that I simply don't like pizza?" Jenny was tired of the discussion. Uncle G.'s organization was immense, with fingers all over the country and beyond. Oh, God, what if he'd lied to her? The cold finger of fear inching up her spine dispelled the heat she'd felt seconds earlier. She didn't realize her expression had changed until she looked up to see concern on Gabe's face.

"I shouldn't have reminded you about the murderers. I'm so used to talking shop I forgot."

"No . . . I'm not shocked. I was . . . simply thinking of how sad it is to see that kind of thing happen in this part of the country. Most of us only think of gangs and the syndicates in connection with large cities." She knew she was babbling nonsense, but she couldn't stop. It was either that or tell him how intimately she was acquainted with the inner workings of organized crime. Hadn't she been married to a "company" lawyer?

His expression was scornful. "Yeah, well those good old days were a lot of years ago. Sterling's got a wild hair that they'll try to get the cat, and he doesn't want them to have either the number or the animal. He thinks you're in danger, too, because you found the body and you were friends with the old guy, and you sure as . . . heck aren't safe here, even with a bodyguard, so he wants you both in one of his compounds until everything blows over. Just in case someone assumes you know more than you do."

Jenny gave up all pretense of eating. "I suppose he intends to restrict my contact with the outside world." At the thought, her stomach felt as if it had been squeezed by a large, cold hand. She would die before she went back to that kind of existence. Swallowing her panic, she protested, "I can't leave my studio. I've several contracts to fulfill, with others pending."

His eyes were unreadable. "Sterling will make sure you have everything you need. He'll even set you up a place to work. Lord knows he has plenty of room." He picked up his fork and began to eat salad as if everything were settled.

"You're being remarkably obtuse. Surely I needn't explain the necessity of my own studio, my own space, to . . ."

"Get yourself knocked off?" he said. He reached for another slice of pizza.

Jenny's temper erupted, bypassing the dread taking over her nervous system. She felt murderous. "Don't be ridiculous." Her fingers clenched the handle of her fork tightly, and she realized he was staring at her hand.

"It's not necessary to kill the messenger," he explained in a patient voice she hadn't heard him use thus far. "This is what Sterling wants, and what he wants, he gets. You can take that to the bank." His mouth twisted wryly. "I'm living proof."

"What do you mean by that?"

His features flattened and his eyes went blank. "Just what I said. When he's in the driver's seat, no one else gets a map."

"Then I'll be an unpleasant surprise for him," she said firmly. She stood. "I don't believe we have anything more to say to each other this evening. I put a pillow and some bedding next to the fresh towels in the bathroom off the hall, Mr. Daniels. I wish you a pleasant night."

Dressed in black jeans and turtleneck, Gabe propped the pillow on the arm of the sofa and rested his head against it, contemplating the night. Faint starlight glowed over the wooded ravine. A creature of the city, he had difficulty visualizing any predator other than the two-legged variety prowling that shadowed unknown. Still, his antennae for danger told him an attempt of some kind would be made before morning.

Picking up his handheld communicator, he listened to the code-filled conversations of the three-member team stationed strategically around the perimeter of Jenny's lot.

Soft light from a squat wrought-iron lamp on the chest next to the front door glowed, lighting the foyer dimly. He and Ms. Tyler had had quite a disagreement about that, but he'd finally given in. Since he had every intention of taking her with him when he left the next day, he figured the small concession might soften her up. He glanced at his watch. Three-forty-five. It shouldn't be too much longer now. In fact . . .

The roar of an engine in the driveway shattered the silence.

FIVE

For seconds that seemed like hours, Jenny lay rigid beneath the comforter, praying she had dreamt the gunshots and the sound of shattering glass. She waited for the circulation to return to her legs, which seemed to have the strength of overcooked noodles. An engine revved; gears ground painfully. The sound of the speeding car disappeared in the night.

Silence. What if Gabe was wounded, bleeding to death? The thought made her heart race faster. If he'd been killed trying to protect her . . . She drew several deep, cleansing breaths, then edged off the bed. When her feet touched the floor she slid to a crouch and crept to the door of her room. The doorknob wouldn't turn.

Oh, God. I locked myself in. The words sobbing inside her head accompanied her frantic fumbling with the button. When the door opened, she held her breath and listened, then crept along the hall runner toward the top of the stairs. She knelt there, her ears straining in the silence. Nothing. Her heart beating inside her ears, she whispered softly, "Gabe?"

Silence answered her. Waxed tread by waxed tread, she slipped down the stairs. The sound of her own breathing joined the beat of her heart in her ears. Her hands trembled. Once again she ventured softly, "Gabe?"

Starlight filtered through the unshuttered windows flanking the front door, which stood several inches ajar. The lamp in the foyer was dark. The entryway felt cold and empty. Fear more intense than any she had ever felt, even in those awful last years with Trent, swept through her. Reacting to a sudden, atavistic need for light, Jenny sprinted toward the switch. As her fingers reached the wall, the door swung wide and strong fingers gripped her wrist. The blood rushed from her head and she opened her mouth to scream. A hand clamped over her lips before a sound could escape, and she was dragged to one side of the door.

"Don't make a sound. I'm waiting to be sure they all left." Gabe's harsh whisper was so close his lips grazed her skin. His whisker-stubbled cheek brushed hers when she nodded jerkily, and his hand fell from her mouth. The other held her motionless. Relief and tingling awareness spread through her veins in equal amounts. He was safe. She nearly sagged against his warmth.

They stood like that for what seemed like eternity, Gabe's body tense, his breathing steady and calm, Jenny holding herself stiffly, denying a need for his closeness. Then she felt the tension in his arm ease. She pulled away and whispered furiously, "I was terrified. I thought you were lying down here dead."

"No chance. The second shot was mine." He spoke in normal tones. "I'm afraid you need a new storm insert."

His nonchalance infuriated Jenny so much she swore. "I don't give a damn about the door. Who were they? Where did they come from?"

"How the hell should I know? They were clumsy. They were also suckered, because I parked the Jeep in the garage and they thought I was gone." He paced nervously. "I heard them pull in and opened the door and stood to one side so I could see who it was. Since they thought you were here alone, the idiots parked in the driveway and toddled up the walk like Avon ladies. They weren't expecting the door to be open, and one of them looked as if he were reaching for a gun when one of my crew shot at him. That's when your door took the hit. They turned and ran. Pardon me if I didn't ask for their business cards."

He withdrew his pistol from the shoulder holster strapped over his turtleneck. "I'd better get another clip in case they come back with reinforcements."

Jenny had no intention of leaving their defense to Gabe. What did she really know about him? "Give me my gun," she demanded. Even in the dim light, she could see him stiffen.

"I'm serious. I want my pistol now."

He shrugged resignedly and strode down the hall to his briefcase, which stood next to the couch. The gun he carried made him look like a character in an old George Raft movie. She was suddenly aware she was clad in only a thin, sleeveless nightshirt. The tails ended just above her knees. The shiver that shook her had nothing to do with cold, nor with the fear she'd felt earlier, but with awareness. She forced herself to focus on what had happened.

"Aren't you going to call the police?"

His concentration on the task of replacing the clip was complete. "Why wake them up?" he asked absently, unzipping the outside pocket of the leather case.

"They should know about those men. They were men, weren't they?"

He slipped his hand inside and brought out her Smith & Wesson. "They were three males, probably the two who left their prints all over here this afternoon and a friend they scared up to help. I don't think they wanted directions to the interstate. I'll tell Pierce in the morning."

"But what did they want?"

"My best guess is you or the cat. The flea collar was a

wash-out, so one of you is the key." Impatience laced his voice.

He handed her the pistol. "Oh, hell. You might as well know. The reason I'm not calling Pierce right now is that he doesn't know I have a team here . . . or that your place was broken into yesterday." He pulled a flat object from his pocket and spoke into it. "Did you get a plate number? . . . You turkeys are slipping . . . I'm sure you winged one. A bullet wound should make a trace easier. He'll probably need treatment. Put someone on it." He jammed the communicator back into his jeans pocket.

In spite of the comfort of having her gun back, icy fingers of fear clawed at Jenny's stomach. "I don't understand any of this."

Gabe stood by the window, peering out above the shutters. "We don't know enough for anyone to understand. My take is that DeWitt tried to deal with another company to encroach on his boss's territory. He probably figured he'd worn out his welcome with the first one after he'd skimmed his share off the top of the profits. One of the organizations took him out. Maybe someone figured they'd appropriate his nest egg." He chuckled mirthlessly. "They'd be even more aggressive if they knew the stash included the three million he'd skimmed from Sterling."

"You're telling me you think I was just in the wrong place at the wrong time." Jenny pushed back a lock of hair which had tumbled across her cheek and absently hooked it behind her ear. With all her heart, she hoped that was true. The alternative was unspeakable. "I feel like a character in a play who is being dealt a page at a time. I prefer not to wait around for someone to tell me what to do next." She had another escape route, with proof of a totally different identity. She would go into hiding where none of these people, including Gabe, could find her.

He changed position and scanned the opposite side of the front yard and the wooded area beyond. "I take it you don't cotton to the idea that that's what I'm here for."

Jenny threw out the other possibility she'd considered. "What if your presence only attracts more trouble?"

He checked the dead bolt one more time and tucked his Beretta back into the holster. "Then whoever's after you doesn't know any better than to take me on. We're taking off tomorrow. It'll be a long day, so get some rest."

Her control shattered. "You haven't listened to a word I've said!" Without thinking, she advanced on him with her gun in her hand. "Stop giving me orders. I'm not going anywhere with you. Leave, and take the trouble with you."

"Jesus, woman! Don't wave that thing at me!" He reached forward and snatched the weapon from her, pulling her off balance. Unable to recover, she stumbled against his hard chest. He cursed roughly, holding her upright with one arm while he tucked her pistol in the waistband of his jeans behind his back.

Jenny felt his uneven heartbeat against her cheek. Her suddenly muzzy brain registered his uncompromisingly male scent. Without thinking, she inhaled deeply, hungry for the essence of him, just as his other arm came around her.

"Ms. Tyler, I don't know what the hell to do with you," he murmured, nudging her chin up with the back of his hand.

She saw the quick glitter of his dark eyes before he lowered his mouth to hers. Jenny instinctively braced herself for an assault. Instead his mouth was gentle, coaxing and molding until their lips fit to his satisfaction. When his tongue teased at her lower lip she opened to him and melded herself against his body.

How could she feel lost and cherished at the same time? She met the caress of his tongue with her own, kneading his back with her hands and even reveling in the bite of the holster's harness against her breast. How could a kiss from a comparative stranger make her feel as if she'd come home?

Sanity struck Gabe even as he filled his hands with the softness of her subtly rounded bottom. The effort it took to move them to the sides of her hips and set her back from him doubled the pain of denial stabbing his groin. His mouth felt bereft. "Jesus, woman, why did you attack me like that?"

His intentionally crude words had the desired effect. Jenny's slender body stiffened. In spite of the half-light, he would have sworn he saw a blaze of blue-green fire in her eyes before she stepped away. Fading starlight revealed her slender legs below her sleep shirt. In another minute he'd have pushed that soft cotton up to her slender waist and . . .

"You attacked me, you . . . you animal!" she spat.

Her voice shook. Was she furious that he'd touched her or disappointed that he'd stopped? Gabe was too shaken to make an attempt to sort it out.

"I want you gone tomorrow, as early as possible," she said coldly. With that she approached him once more, this time circling behind him.

Gabe felt a tug as Jenny jerked her pistol from his waistband. He stood helpless as she stomped up the stairs, wincing as her door slammed and the lock clicked into place. What could have possessed him? He replayed the last five minutes in his head; the memory of her flowery scent—and her taste—clouded his mind.

He'd lost control. Gabe sighed. He couldn't have picked a worse time to jump in over his head with the woman. Tomorrow he planned to kidnap her.

Far on the other side of Donhaven, Bobbie Snow frantically attempted to free himself from Donnie's iron grip. He howled when his brother pulled him closer to the light and dabbed at the bloody furrow along his left hip with an alcohol-soaked rag. "Hold still, dammit! It's just a graze, you big baby."

Bobbie screamed and jerked again, and Donnie shouted, "Tommie, hold on to his legs tighter."

"I can't, Donnie. My arm hurts. I think I ought to see a doctor," his other brother whined.

Disgusted with both of them, Donnie finished cleaning the bullet wound and glared at Tommie. "It's just a damn cat scratch. I've got a friggin' dog bite on my leg, and you don't hear me whining. We don't dare go near no doctor."

"It ain't just a scratch, Donnie. My arm's swellin'. I think I got that cat fever," Tommie moaned. He pulled back the gauze taped above his wrist and held out his arm, which was half again its normal size. "Look!"

Ignoring his brothers' complaints, Donnie rubbed antibiotic cream into Bobbie's wound and reached for a large gauze pad. "I got the claw out. You'll be fine." He stripped a piece of tape free of the spool and plastered it over the gauze.

"I need a doc for my hip, too," Bobbie said sullenly. He winced as a second strip of tape was slapped into place. "I need a tetanus shot."

"You're an idiot. This here's a bullet wound. Don't look like anythin' else. Emergency rooms got to report 'em. And you don't need no tetanus shot. Not unless that bullet's been in horseshit," he explained for the third time. "If you two would a' done a better job of scoutin', you'd a' knowed that mean dude was shackin' up with the Tyler woman."

Bobbie stood, groaning as he eased his leg into a fresh pair of jeans. "Can't be two places at once, Donnie. You made us go with you to break into that vet's."

Donnie shuddered as he recalled his fright the night before. He'd crawled through a high window at the back of the concrete block building, and the mixed breed had taken a chunk out of his calf before Tommie could pull him back up. And all because the flea collar had turned out to be just that. No indelible ink inscriptions and nothing concealed in the plastic.

The only reason they'd gone to the vet's after the first fiasco at the artist lady's house was that Bobbie recalled seeing the black-haired dude's Jeep in her parking lot. Even the remote possibility that the cat might be there made the place worth checking out. Their new boss hadn't been too pleased about the flea collar proving a dead end. She'd demanded the cat in no uncertain terms, and Bobbie intended to keep her happy.

Ever since the old man had been killed, they'd encountered nothing but failure.

Donnie wondered if his brothers needed to know about their new employer. This pipeline might prove to be even more lucrative than the old one through Dolan. He decided to keep the information to himself. Neither of them could keep his tongue in his head, and their recent blunders were a mark against them. He sighed and looked at the VCR to check the time.

The furnishings of the shabby house they'd inherited from their parents might not look like much, but Donnie had his own measurements of luxury—a refrigerator large enough to hold at least two cases of beer, a large-screen television, and a VCR.

Unless they could get solid with the new company,

they'd be unable to buy additional luxuries in the future. He shuddered, feeling as if someone had just walked over the family plot at the old county cemetery. "I got to go call the Dragon Lady."

Momentarily distracted from his throbbing arm, Tommie pushed his shock of dark hair out of his close-set brown eyes and said, "Is she really a Dragon Lady, Donnie? Like the one in those old comic books we stole?"

Amazed that his slow-witted brother could make the connection, Donnie patted his shoulder and said, "Not really. She's just mean and smart-mouthed. I gotta tell her we ain't gonna be errand boys no more." He swaggered toward the bedroom in an attempt to impress his brothers with his bravado. His insides were quaking; he hoped he didn't pee his pants.

Shortly after sunrise, Jenny Tyler grimaced at herself in the bathroom mirror. Three hours of restless tossing and turning had left her exhausted. The hot shower hadn't erased the dark shadows beneath her eyes. Was she so starved for affection that Gabe Daniels could kiss her senseless in less than one minute flat? She applied cover-up briskly, then bent over and brushed her damp hair before blow drying it, each brush stroke an attempt to rid herself of the embarrassing memory.

Exiting her bathroom, she opened the closet door and pulled out a pair of tailored khaki-colored slacks and a soft blue linen shirt. She would appear cool and detached if it killed her.

Earlier, the sound of the shower in the downstairs bathroom had verified her suspicion that Gabe didn't leave as she'd ordered last night. Not that she'd really expected him to, but the man would go this morning if she had to order him out at gunpoint. Once he was gone, her life would get back to normal. As normal as it could be while she searched out a new hiding place.

Jenny looked around wistfully. In the short time she'd been here, she'd become attached to the rented house. A home. Someday she'd have her own place. A place to come back to, no matter where she went. At the thought, she took a deep breath before heading downstairs to banish the man who had fractured her peace.

The smells of coffee and bacon frying greeted her at the top of the steps. Gabe Daniels had made himself at home in her kitchen with the audacity of a pickpocket. She ran down the stairs and burst into the kitchen. "What do you think you're doing? I told you to get out," she said in a hard voice.

"Making breakfast. You didn't follow up to make sure I left," he answered. "Besides, the vet's office opens in an hour."

Jenny stalked to the refrigerator and threw open the door. "I'll pick up Choc at my own convenience." She drew out a carton of grapefruit juice and poured a glassful. "You're not needed anymore." She drank, relishing the tart sting of the juice as it flowed down her throat. "Actually, you were never needed."

"Yeah. Next time you put out a welcome mat for some slug who slithers up the front walk you can deal with him yourself." He dug into the bread box and pulled out the package of wheat bread. "I couldn't find anything but this low-fat health stuff. No wonder you're so skinny." Shaking his head, he removed two slices and dropped them into the toaster.

Jenny felt her temperature rise. "I didn't ask for your help. Nor have I requested your opinion of my diet." She walked closer and said loudly, "Read my lips. I didn't invite you here. I want you to leave. Now. Be gone!"

As if he hadn't heard a word she said, Gabe turned to the stove. The omelet he folded onto a plate was golden brown at the edges. "Here. Sit down and eat." The toaster shot the bread upward, and he buttered the slices and put them on the plate next to the bacon. "Just tell me when you're ready. I'll be in the other room." He disappeared through the kitchen door.

If the food hadn't smelled so good, and if she hadn't been so hungry, Jenny would have hurled her plate at his broad, silk-covered shoulders. She doubted he would have noticed. His shirt was already pulled out on one side, and he had ignored her when she yelled. The idiot must have played football without a helmet.

Aware she'd need all the strength she could muster to contend with such an immovable object, she ate. At least Gabe Daniels did one thing she approved of. He cooked like an angel.

An hour later, Gabe eyed the molded plastic cat caddy skeptically. "That thing looks more like a space module than a travel cage. Is he going to fight being shut up?"

Dr. Hall held Choc cuddled in her arms. "Believe me, this cat's not going to notice anything much for five or six hours. After that he'll be too uncomfortable to make trouble. Too much stress tends to make Siamese retreat into themselves. Being caged should make him feel safe." She stroked the cat, then inspected the bandage on his left hind paw. "I'll give you a few tranquilizers for him in case he tears at the stitches the first few days. After that, it doesn't matter if he removes them himself. And don't keep him confined any longer than necessary."

"I'll shut him in my bedroom when I get him home," Jenny said, shooting Gabe a venomous look as she stepped in front of him. "With his food and litter and a Mozart CD to soothe him," she added defiantly. She opened the door to the caddy. "Put him in now, and I'll write you a check."

"Mr. Daniels has already taken care of the bill," Dr. Hall said, easing the cat through the opening.

Before Jenny could argue, Gabe said, "Sterling wanted to handle the expenses. He feels . . . responsible for Dolan." He watched the veterinarian close the screened door and reached for the handle.

"By the way, we had a break-in here last night," Dr. Hall said. "I leave my shepherd mix, Ironsides, in the building to guard the clinic while I'm gone. He apparently took a bite out of whoever tried to get in a window at the back. The police found a scrap of denim on the floor. They assumed someone was after drugs." She slanted Gabe a questioning look.

"Keep them pretty well locked up, don't you?"

"Always. My drug safe's like a miniature Fort Knox, and I make sure everyone knows it," she replied flatly.

Gabe shrugged. "Must have been some outsider who didn't know any better." He met her sharp gaze with one just as sharp.

"That's what I figured," she replied.

Jenny pushed Gabe's hand away from the caddy and wrapped her fingers around the handle. "Come on. I want to get Choc home."

"Thanks a lot, Doc," Gabe said before he followed her out the door. "Sorry I didn't think to warn you."

"No need to. Ironsides knows how to do his job."

As he followed Jenny to the Jeep, Gabe wondered if he shouldn't have bought Ironsides. He might need him for protection during the next few hours. He watched the graceful sway of Jenny's slender hips as she crossed the tidy parking lot, and he amended his time frame to the next few weeks. Why hadn't he noticed the sweet curve of her butt before last night? His hands curved instinctively at the memory of the softness her khaki slacks covered, and he forced his thoughts in another direction.

Minutes later they took the county road leading into town, the cat's caddy secured in the backseat by a seat belt. Aware of Jenny's suspicious gaze, Gabe kept his features expressionless and drove as carefully as if he were chauffeuring his maiden aunt to church. He also kept an eye on the road behind them.

Just outside the city limits, he abruptly increased his speed and turned left across the highway. At least the team he was playing against was predictable.

"You idiot! Where are you going?" Jenny cried. She grabbed his arm and attempted to turn the wheel back to the right.

He switched to four-wheel drive as the Jeep swooped through the shallow ditch and forged an opening through a natural fence of brambles and wild grape. Shaking off Jenny's hand, he shot a hard gaze in her direction and headed across a freshly plowed field. "Hold tight, Ms. Tyler. It's going to be a rough ride." In the rearview mirror, he saw the Honda that had followed them from the vet's office flounder in the first ten feet of turned earth and come to a halt, its wheels spinning.

"Stop! I want to go home. You can't do this."

The panic in her voice pierced his conscience, but he had no choice. "Lady, I am doing it." Gabe reached the other side of the field and turned onto the farm road his team had scouted out. The path was no more than a tractor trail through the weeds, an easy task for the Jeep.

Just when Gabe thought they were away free, a rifle bullet struck the rear right window and exited through the opposite side. Using his right hand, Gabe gripped Jenny's neck and pushed her head forward between her knees. He gunned the engine into the gentle curve around a stand of walnut and oak trees, taking them out of sight and out of range of the next shots. A hundred yards ahead stood a low, fabricated building of rusting metal built to store field equipment.

As they neared the shed, he released Jenny, before the brush of her soft hair against his fingers tempted him to linger. He had no business crossing that line again. Her silence was more disturbing than if she had continued to shout or had dissolved into hysterics. All color had drained from her face and her eyes were closed. The soft mouth that had responded to his so unexpectedly the night before drooped with resignation. But her hands were fisted on her lap. She looked like someone accustomed to being dealt unpleasant surprises; he suspected she had never learned to accept them without a fierce internal battle.

Gabe wanted nothing more than to gather her into his arms and comfort her. He grimaced. His wants had seldom been high on Sterling's priority list. Sterling wanted her, and he, Gabe, was going to take her to him. He knew one thing for sure. If the old man didn't play straight with Jenny Tyler, Sterling's lead dog would turn on him.

SIX

When they rolled to a stop, Gabe reached over and released her seat belt. "You okay?" he demanded.

Jenny despaired of ever being okay again. "I'm not bleeding anywhere, if that's what you mean."

A plaintive wail erupted from the backseat. "Guess the cat's all right, too," Gabe said briskly.

Two men Jenny had never seen before ran from the storage building toward the Jeep. They wore sharply tailored suits and white shirts, looking as if they'd come from their law offices, but they carried guns and were scanning the track behind the Jeep. One called, "We heard shots. How close are they?"

Gabe opened his door and jumped to the ground. "They're stuck not far from the road, but reinforcements will probably show up anytime. Let's get moving." Before Jenny could react, he leaned in and scooped up her tote bag. He removed her gun, handed the bag back to her, then headed for the metal shed. She pounded the seat in frustration, watching helplessly as the passenger door swung open and a lean, red-haired man with pointed features that reminded her of a fox offered his arm with all the courtesy of a prom date. "I'm Jim Slater, ma'am. Let me help you to the van."

Van? She accepted his help numbly. Nothing made sense anymore. Gabe had just taken her gun. Again. Control of her life had just been wrested from her. Again. Gabe Daniels and his egomaniac employer now had her trapped, body and soul. Jenny set her jaw. Keeping her would be tougher than they could imagine.

The shorter, stockier man had freed the cat caddy from the backseat, and was already leading the way to the storage shed. "Did you get everything?" Gabe called as he stepped from behind a gray Suburban. Jenny turned her head to look at him and her heart jolted at the sight of the automatic rifle he swung casually from one hand.

"All under control, Gabe. Ford will go back to Ms. Tyler's house until Maddy and Rick show up to take over." Jim Slater released Jenny's arm and slid open the side door. "Put the cat in first, Ford. Ms. Tyler can sit next to him."

Jenny watched the second man settle the cat as tenderly as if it were a baby. He turned and extended his hand. "Here, ma'am. Just step inside. There's a thermos of coffee and a cooler with soft drinks just behind the seat if you get thirsty."

Jenny climbed in and settled herself, disguising her rebellion by murmuring soothing words to Choc. Jim Slater swung in behind the wheel and started the engine.

Gabe climbed into the passenger seat, calling over his shoulder to Ford, "Don't take any chances. Lead them toward Port Columbus and then lose them. When you return the Jeep, be sure to tell them Sterling will pay for repairs."

"Teach your mother to suck eggs, Gabe," he answered cheekily. "See you later."

"Let's roll," Gabe grated, pulling the door shut. He leaned around the edge of his seat and eyed Jenny. Something that could have been compassion flashed in his dark eyes. "Ms. Tyler, you could have been killed back there. Maybe now you understand why I had to get you out of Donhaven. I promise, Sterling will make sure you're comfortable. Ford packed clothes for you at your place. They're in the back. Once we get you tucked away, all you have to do is ask for anything else you need. Anything at all."

In spite of his soothing voice and reassuring words, anger she'd suppressed for six years rose to the surface. A stranger had pawed through her belongings? She turned to look in the back, and saw her garment bag and largest suitcase occupying the seat. The dishpan of kitty litter and a bag of cat food were tucked next to the cooler. Her rage blazed, then retreated into a white heat, heat she planned to nurture. Forcing a cloying smile, she said, "How very considerate of you, Mr. Daniels. I do hope Mr. Ford packed my favorite bras and bikinis."

Gabe Daniels's wince was immensely gratifying.

Three and a half hours later the Suburban rolled through a gate to a perimeter landing strip at the Pittsburgh airport. Gabe was relieved to see Maddy and Rick in the black BMW parked beside Sterling's Grumman Gulfstream.

He turned to the backseat and broke the silence that had reigned since Jenny's snotty crack about her lingerie. "We'll take off as soon as we're cleared."

He'd stolen glances at her throughout the trip. When her eyes weren't closed, her gaze had been focused out the smoked glass window. The only movement she'd made had been to work her fingers through the grate at the front of the caddy and scratch the cat's head. Her silence made him jumpy as hell. Why hadn't she ranted and raved, protesting her abduction? The woman didn't even pout. She had simply retreated within herself . . . like a Siamese cat. Gabe would almost have preferred the tantrum.

"What destination are you filing on your flight plan?" she inquired.

Damn, that snooty accent had never been more pronounced. She sounded as if she didn't give a damn, when he knew better. Gabe definitely would have preferred screaming and crying. "I won't know myself until I radio ahead. Sterling moves around a lot."

Jenny's eyes burned with anger as she replied, "Bully for Sterling. Let me go on record, Mr. Daniels. I despise him for what you and he are doing to me, and I intend to make sure you both regret it."

Jim Slater made an unintelligible sound. Gabe pretended not to have heard either her defiance or Jim's reaction. Instead he sighed and opened his door. "Get Ms. Tyler and the cat settled onboard, Jim." He crossed the tarmac and climbed the steps Rick hastily rolled into place. The plane's door swung open as if by magic, and when the uniformed flight steward greeted him with a smile, he growled, "Shit, Will, it's nice to see a friendly face."

"Shit, it's nice to see you having a tough time of it, Gabe," the attendant replied, his eyes twinkling with wicked enjoyment. "Could this be payback for the easy ones?"

"I'll get my payback when Sterling tangles with Ms. Tyler. My money's on the lady. She's spitting fire." He looked around the cabin, which reminded him of a designer showroom in some damn store. "Count your blessings. She'll probably treat you like a prince, just to be contrary. When Slater brings her in, get her settled while I run the checklist and square us with the tower." He pulled off his suit coat and slung it over his shoulder, then stripped off his necktie and headed for the cockpit.

After he determined his destination, he had to decide how to explain the screwed-up mess to Sterling.

Half an hour later, at Will's gentle suggestion, Jenny made sure the cat caddy was secure and fastened her seat belt. She massaged her aching neck, then leaned back and rubbed her temples. Her stomach rumbled. The steward had promised her a meal as soon as they were airborne. Food couldn't erase the tension in her body, but it might help her rest. Where was Gabe? Surely he wouldn't put her on a plane and send her off to deal with Sterling Thomas by herself, although ridding herself of Gabe Daniels would be a blessing. She let her head fall back onto the pale blue glove leather upholstery and closed her eyes, accepting her fate. The arrogant bastard had indeed kidnaped her.

The Gulfstream vibrated as the engines gathered power. A soft chime sounded twice, and moments later she felt as if a giant hand had hefted them skyward. Jenny's ears popped, and she opened her mouth wide, working her jaws.

"My apologies, Ms. Tyler. I should have offered you this sooner."

Jenny opened her eyes to see the steward's hand in front of her face holding a cut glass bowl filled with a variety of chewing gums. She selected one blindly. What was his name? Oh, yes. "Thank you, Will. Flying makes my ears go crazy."

"Mine, too. I'll have some grilled sole and asparagus ready for you shortly. What would you like to drink? The wine selection is excellent."

Eyeing his youthful countenance, she said, "I suspect you're too young to serve it legally. Iced tea will be fine." She realized her mistake as soon as she'd spoken, but the slow blush that started at his chin and traveled up his cheeks was the giveaway. "I'm sorry. That was unforgivably rude."

He gave her a boyish smile. "I've been getting carded for eight years. Gabe tells me I should enjoy it while I have it."

"Speaking of Gabe, where is he? Don't tell me he and his friends simply threw me into your lap and left." Why did the idea of being abandoned by him hurt? Especially since moments ago the idea of losing him had pleased her.

Will laughed and gestured toward the cockpit door. "He's playing pilot. When he takes over the controls, I get demoted." With that, he turned and headed for the galley.

The plane leveled off and Jenny released her seat belt. She stood carefully, her body aching as if she had been sitting for a month. She wanted to walk in the sunshine. She wanted to throw open that door, jerk Gabe Daniels out of the pilot's seat and beat him to a pulp. Will wouldn't be able to come to his rescue; he'd be too busy trying to keep the plane in the air.

That little fantasy faded as she inspected her surroundings more closely. Sterling certainly didn't stint himself. There were even daffodils arranged in a crystal vase cleverly attached to the low table between two luxuriously upholstered lounge chairs. She headed for the bathroom Will had pointed out earlier.

For a moment, Jenny thought she had stepped into the Arabian Nights. In her wildest dreams, she had never imagined a facility like this in an airplane. Through the etched glass shower door, she glimpsed the same pale, dusty blue that graced the other fixtures. An intricately carved silver frame outlined the mirror above the sink. A cupboard with pierced silver doors held thick, dusty blue towels, along with luxurious soaps and any conceivable toiletry she might need. Closer inspection of the black-and-white print above the commode made her gasp. It wasn't a print. A Picasso? In the bathroom of an airplane?

She attended to her needs and returned to her seat. If there was any humor at all in her situation, it was the discovery of how the other half lived. Uncle G.'s taste had been somewhat garish. When any other members of the family indulged themselves, it had been done without taste, something Jenny certainly couldn't accuse Sterling Thomas of lacking.

"Gabe's going to join you for dinner. Sounds like you two have had a busy day," Will commented from his post beside the cozy leather-upholstered booth at the rear of the main cabin.

Jenny watched as he set two places with exquisite Irish linen place mats and heavy silver flatware. "That knife looks wonderfully sharp. You might want to rethink leaving me alone with him," she said.

Will's boyish face was stern when he looked over his shoulder at her. "From what I gather, you're in trouble, Ms. Tyler. If I were ever in danger, Gabe's the guy I'd want at my back. I know he can be rough. But there are reasons. Mr. Thomas demands more of him than he does the rest of us, and Gabe never fails to deliver." He positioned a lush double iris in a crystal bud vase and moved the wild greens salads directly above the forks before standing straight. "Give him a break, ma'am. He hasn't had many. If you'll excuse me, I'll be back with your dinner in a few minutes."

Jenny rubbed her hands on the thighs of her khaki slacks, then stopped when she realized she was only wrinkling them more. What did he mean about Gabe? The man was a human steamroller. Admittedly, he'd kept her alive thus far, but could she truly trust him? Or even Sterling Thomas, for that matter. Once before she'd allowed herself to trust. She'd bought a fairy tale, then lived to regret it. And she couldn't help wondering if Uncle G. had lied to her. He could have been toying with her the way Trent had. Everything that had happened during the past two days had the stamp of Uncle G.'s organization all over it.

Will brought two silver dome-covered plates. Setting one

86

at each place, he disappeared. On his return from the galley, he carried a tray with two Waterford tumblers of iced tea. "I'll go relieve Gabe," he said as he set them above the knives.

Jenny sighed and slipped into the cushioned booth. Using the silver tongs, she dropped a sugar cube into her glass. Stirring the tea would give her something to do. Maybe Gabe and Sterling meant well, but they had no idea of the price she'd paid for her freedom.

"Don't worry about breaking the crystal, Sterling probably has only another ten gross of the damn things." Gabe slipped into the seat opposite her, lifted the silver covers from the plates and set them aside. His tie and jacket were gone, and the sleeves of his wrinkled shirt were rolled up, revealing muscular forearms liberally sprinkled with dark hair. "Now you know why I made you eat a big breakfast. I didn't want you fainting on me before I had a chance to feed you again." He drank thirstily.

The fragrances rising from her plate were irresistible. Jenny didn't notice them until she'd forcibly wrenched her gaze away from Gabe's hands and the contractions of his throat as he swallowed. What on earth was wrong with her? She picked up her salad fork and, refusing to soften simply because he had expressed concern for her welfare, said dryly, "I'd think it would have been much easier to kidnap an unconscious person."

"Not really. The last time I tried that, she was a dead-weight. I kept knocking her head into door frames." He broke off a piece of dinner roll and buttered it, then put it in his mouth.

Jenny nearly choked on her first bite of salad. He'd actually made a joke! She kept her gaze on her plate, but peered through her lashes at him. A half-smile tugged at the corner of his mouth as he separated a bite of sole with his fork. She eyed the stubble covering his cheeks and chin. "Your beard must have been what made her faint."

The half-smile grew to three-quarters as he lifted his fork. "My one o'clock shadow is very popular with a certain type of woman," he said. His mobile lips closed around the wedge of fish. His gaze held hers steadily.

Somewhere in the vicinity of Jenny's stomach, nerves clenched. Oh, God! Is this some kind of roundabout foreplay? We haven't even progressed to using each other's first names yet. In desperation, she speared a tiny parsleyed potato and popped it into her mouth. She needed food; she was having delusions.

"Sorry about the food. Will isn't the usual chef on this plane, so the meal is pretty basic. I called at the last minute, and he didn't have much time."

Jenny looked at the perfectly grilled fish, the crimped lemon wedges, the tiny new potatoes sprinkled with parsley so fresh and green it nearly crunched, and the lightly steamed asparagus on her plate. "I suppose this will do," she said deprecatingly. She squeezed a lemon wedge over her sole. "Where are we headed?"

"Palm Springs. Sterling thought an obvious destination would be best. He owns a compound not far from Bob Hope's. We won't land until late, so you might want to take advantage of the bedroom."

Gabe continued to eat, and Jenny realized he was hungry and tired. She swallowed before commenting, "You must be as exhausted as I. How are you going to handle the controls all that time?"

He patted his mouth with the monogrammed napkin and grinned at her. "Who do you think's flying the damn plane right now?"

Jenny found herself grinning back. "Will, the man of all

trades. My brain's at half-power."

"You need sleep."

"I'd rather nap in that lounge chair. You can use the bedroom." As soon as the words left her mouth, Jenny saw the twinkle appear in his eyes. Odd. She'd thought they were black, but they weren't. They were blue. Midnight blue, as deep as the night sky. She felt color rise in her cheeks.

"We could always share the bed," he said. Then his grin faded and his expression tightened. "Sorry, that wouldn't work. I'm not sure I could leave you alone."

Jenny's throat closed. She hadn't imagined that the attraction was mutual. The kiss last night had been a joint effort, and she hated herself for remembering how her body had yearned for more. Her fingers shook as she reached for her dinner fork. "That wouldn't be a good idea. I . . . tend to strike out when someone wakes me suddenly," she choked out, purposely pretending to have misunderstood him.

A low yowl from across the cabin broke the rising tension. Jenny stood, picking up her plate. "He's hungry, poor thing. A little of this sole will suit his stomach better than cat food." She edged away from the table, self-consciously aware of his gaze focused on her. The lazy teasing had taken them to the brink of the impossible. Gabe Daniels couldn't have any way of knowing she had sworn off the outcome of seduction.

Gabe told himself he should be relieved. Jenny Tyler might be a little on the skinny side, but the way she moved did something to his libido, and the lost look in her blue-green eyes reached out to him. Besides, he remembered all too well the way her body had yielded beneath his fingers the night before. No.

After he stopped expressing amusement at Gabe's fall from grace, Sterling would proceed to have his head on a plate for messing around with a woman he was protecting. And this woman needed protection as much as any he'd ever met. He wondered if she had any idea what sort of danger she'd stumbled into, simply by being in the wrong place at the wrong time. The ten-million-dollar question was, why did he doubt the "wrong place, wrong time" scenario? The specialist's delay in forwarding her background report frustrated him. Sterling's man usually compiled one in a matter of hours.

Gabe watched Jenny feed the cat. She'd taken him from his cage, and the little animal, still wobbly, was propped on her lap nibbling bits of sole from the tips of her slender fingers. She hadn't eaten very much. Was it because he made her nervous? If he had a conscience, he'd feel guilty about hitting on her during dinner. Or could she be feeling the same awareness that was beginning to consume him? He threw his napkin on the table and stood. "I'm going to relieve Will. Don't bother with this mess. He'll straighten things up."

The fax bell rang. Moving to the cherry cabinet beside the cockpit door, Gabe swung open a carved panel and snatched the sheet curling from the machine. He scanned the information. "Shit."

She was beside him in a flash, the cat clutched in her arms. "What happened?"

Turning to hide the message from her, Gabe muttered, "Nothing you need to know right now."

Jenny stepped close, so close the toes of her loafers touched his. "Let me be the judge of that." She thrust the cat at him, releasing it so quickly he had no choice but to catch the animal. The paper fell, and she scooped up the fax before it hit the floor. Ten seconds later, she said, "I don't understand. Who were these people?"

"Brothers. Three small-time players who were in over their heads," Gabe replied. Choc's silky fur felt soothing. The look in the lady's eyes was not. "The cat left his claw in one of them yesterday when they broke into your house to steal his collar. I wounded another last night when they tried to get at you, and Ironsides bit the third one when they broke into the vet's."

"None of those injuries could be fatal, could they?"

He rolled his eyes. "Mob hits are always fatal."

"Why kill them? Who did they work for?"

Jenny spoke so softly Gabe could scarcely hear her. He sighed. He hadn't meant for her to know how complicated things had become, but now he had no choice. "We haven't discovered yet who did them, or who wrote their paychecks. I don't even know if this player is different from whoever took out DeWitt," he said harshly. Damn, but he hated operating in the dark. He'd been so focused on rescuing her and the cat that he hadn't concentrated on what he did best, dotting i's, crossing t's, and putting together the unmarked pieces of a puzzle.

"But why were they killed?" Her eyes were wide and tear-filled, the skin beneath them bruised-looking.

Gabe gentled his voice. "They'd failed, Jenny." He realized it was only the second time he'd spoken her name aloud. "They didn't deliver for the people who gave them orders, so they had to go. They weren't useful anymore." He took her arm and led her to her seat. Somehow he got her settled into its cushioned depths. When he lowered the cat into her lap, her arms closed around the animal as if she would never let him go.

"At first it looked as if DeWitt had cheated his employer, and the guy wanted his money back. Sterling relates to that, although he wouldn't have stooped to murder. Now we think DeWitt might have been trying to play competing mobs against each other. The second one hired the three brothers, who'd probably worked for our crook. My guess is that whoever wants the account number knows we have it, which is why we're on the run. Can you imagine any other reason these slimy types would be after you?"

Jenny closed her eyes. Her thick dark lashes were stark against her cheeks. She shook her head. "I don't want to talk about this anymore. I'm not dangerous to anyone. I . . . I did what I promised . . ." She lowered the seat back and curled onto her side, cradling the cat against her stomach.

Frustrated, his curiosity dancing the tango after her choice of words, Gabe returned to the cockpit.

The inquisitive glance Will slanted at him as he slid into his seat and took over the controls didn't improve Gabe's disposition, but he swallowed his frustration. The Gulfstream's captain would be better off knowing as little as possible. "Don't fuss over her. It was probably my fault she didn't eat much. If we leave her alone she might get some sleep," Gabe told him. Dammit, what had Jenny promised to do or not to do? And who had she promised?

"Certainly, Mr. Boss Man," Will said. He sat back in his seat and gazed out at the western horizon. "I radioed our ETA ahead. The limo will be waiting."

Two hours later, Gabe made his way back through the luxurious cabin. Jenny was awake, but she didn't acknowledge him. She was still curled on her side around the cat, her gaze fixed on the window of the plane, which showed only the darkening night sky. He thought he saw traces of tears on her cheeks.

Without speaking, he made his way to the queen-size bed in the rear of the plane. An hour of rest, whether he slept or not, would prepare him for Sterling's inevitable all-night grilling.

SEVEN

Diffused sunlight filtered through the blinds. Even diluted, the light had an unfamiliar quality. Disoriented, Jenny turned onto her back, opened her eyes, and surveyed her surroundings.

She was in Palm Springs. The night before, she'd been so stiff she'd felt like an old woman when she stumbled from the limo. She remembered a low, cultured voice giving instructions, being led along a covered walkway . . . then nothing.

She raised the sheet and looked at herself, verifying the fact that she was naked.

Her cheeks warmed. She never slept in the nude. Then she remembered. At least she hoped she did. Clutching the sheet to her shoulders, she sat up and located her clothes exactly where she'd dropped them. In the middle of the tile floor beside an incredible handwoven Navajo area rug. The suitcase and garment bag Gabe's cohort had packed for her stood beside the closet door. Relieved, she sank back onto the luxurious mattress.

Moments later, panic set in. She looked at her watch. No wonder the sky was so bright; it was nearly noon.

Within minutes, she stood beneath the shower in the adjoining bath, luxuriating in the beat of hot water on her stiff, aching muscles. She tilted her face to the showerhead, praying for the needle spray to cleanse her mind of horrifying images from the past two days. Finally, out of desperation, she switched the water to cold. Then to off.

Wrapping her clean hair in a smaller towel, she snatched a thick white bath sheet from the heated rack. Jenny hadn't thought it possible, but this white and crystal bathroom was twice as luxurious as the one on the Gulfstream. Sterling must have a thing for bathrooms. She grinned, aware of the first real amusement she'd felt in days.

The realization was a grim reminder of her situation. She sighed and padded into the bedroom to unzip her luggage. Her spirits sank further as she saw that each contained exactly what she would have packed herself. Annoyance speeding her movements, she pulled on thin white linen slacks and shrugged into a willow-green cotton sweater before blowing her hair dry. Anger at her abduction grew with each moment that passed. Shoving her feet into leather sandals, she dabbed on lipstick and marched to the door.

The short hall led to a small, perfect living room furnished with oatmeal-colored upholstered furniture and gleaming mahogany tables. Yet another incredible handwoven rug in red, black and cream protected the gleaming tile floor. Through an arch she spied a sunlight-filled dining nook. The table was set with woven mats and one of the chairs was occupied.

Knowing full well she was being unreasonable, she demanded, "Why did you let me sleep so late?"

Gabe looked up from his plate of eggs and bacon. "Why don't you go back to bed and try getting up on the other damn side next time." He bit into a piece of jam-covered toast and chewed, frowning so deeply his thick eyebrows nearly met. His dark hair, still damp from his shower, curled at his neckline, and he wore a lightweight tan suit, white linen shirt and brown-patterned necktie. He swallowed. "Maybe I was interested in getting some sleep myself. I didn't get to bed until four." He lifted the tulip-

94

shaped pottery bell next to his plate and rang it once.

Jenny realized she was being unreasonable. "I'm sorry. I'm disoriented." She massaged her temples with her fingers. "Perhaps I'm hungry."

As if in answer to her problem, a pretty dark-haired girl appeared with a tall glass of orange juice and a plate of fruit. Smiling shyly, she set them in front of Jenny and left the room.

"Carmelita doesn't speak much English, so if you want anything different from what you see, let me know. I'll translate," Gabe said.

Jenny was too busy draining the contents of her glass to answer. The frosty juice revived her spirits, and when she set the glass back down she actually found herself smiling. "Right now there's nothing I wouldn't eat."

"Good. You'll need your strength at the main house."

"Main house?" Jenny clutched the stem of a strawberry in midair. "I thought we were there already."

He looked around the cozy nook and grinned. "This is just a guest house. Sterling didn't want you to feel like a prisoner." His mouth widened into the predator's smile she distrusted.

Jenny dropped the strawberry back onto her plate. Her appetite had deserted her; she digested the implications of his presence. "Except you're here . . ."

"I spent the night in the other bedroom, and a couple of armed security guards are posted outside. 'Fraid you're stuck with me for the duration, Ms. Tyler. Sterling's orders."

Carmelita returned with eggs and bacon. Forcing a smile, Jenny pushed the fruit plate to one side to make room and said, *"Gracias,"* then complimented the girl's cooking in fluent Spanish, pretending to ignore Gabe's surprised expression. Finally, feeling merciful, she asked him, "Where's Choc?"

"With Sterling. He welcomed the little bastard like a long-lost grandchild, one that won't give him any back talk." His sardonic gaze lowered to the faxes beside his plate.

The odd comparison struck a false note. "I take it Mr. Thomas isn't particularly fond of children."

"Yeah, he is. Well-behaved ones." Gabe sipped his coffee and pointed at her plate. "Dig in. Today might be another long one."

A similar warning the day before had proved distressingly accurate. Jenny frowned back at him and applied herself to her food. She suspected Gabe treated everyone the same way. Giving orders was second nature to him. Last night, during dinner, he had been different, acknowledging the attraction sparking between them. He hadn't even demanded to know what she had done to draw the attention of one of the "players," as he called them. Was he leaving the heavy questions to Sterling? Was that why he'd predicted a stressful day?

The prospect was enough to make her lose her appetite. Jenny's stomach betrayed her by welcoming every bite she took.

"Finished?" Gabe asked ten minutes later.

Jenny realized with surprise that she'd cleaned her plate right down to the pottery glaze. "Let me get my tote," she said, suddenly desperate to delay the upcoming meeting. She needed time, time to consider a means of escape. Gabe and Sterling Thomas had no right to keep her here, and she intended to leave at the first opportunity.

"You don't need it now that I have your gun. Come on. Sterling's waiting." As she opened her mouth to protest, he grinned. "Don't get in a huff. If it'll make you happier, I'll give you your heat back later."

Rather than using the roofed walkway, Gabe led her through a cactus garden. Warm sunlight fell on her shoulders, and the air was so clear and dry it nearly took her breath away. She spotted a plume of water beyond a natural stone fence to her right. "Can't we go that way? I want to see the fountain." And look for a path to an exit, she noted mentally.

"Damn things are all over the place. There's another one outside the room where you'll meet Sterling," Gabe replied. "See one, you've seen them all."

Jenny made a face at his back and followed him. Minutes later they entered a side entrance of a sprawling, hacienda-style mansion that looked as if it covered half an acre. Peeking into rooms as they traveled the long cool halls, she was struck by Sterling's intuitiveness. She would definitely have felt claustrophobic if he'd kept her in this labyrinth.

Near the end of a tile-floored corridor, Gabe stopped at massive double doors, opened one side, and waited for her to enter. The sound of Mozart filled the room. Through broad, low windows to her left was a breathtaking view of the desert that seemed an extension of the room. Mexican pottery and Indian artifacts were displayed on artful shelves that appeared to grow out of the natural stone walls. Colorful handwoven rugs cushioned the tiled floor.

"Ms. Tyler, how delighted I am to finally meet you."

She'd seen Sterling Thomas on a PBS news show months earlier. The television camera hadn't lied—it had simply been inadequate. The man was larger than life. Clad in a silk broadcloth suit, white shirt and tie, he was nearly as tall as Gabe, and although in his mid-seventies, he was fit and trim, his posture erect. His full head of white hair was flawlessly barbered, his dark glance compelling. His voice was mesmerizing, and as he crossed the floor and extended well-manicured fingers to her, Jenny felt truly captive. She held out her hand.

"Gabe, my boy. Walter said those reports you've been nagging him about are complete. Why don't you go look them over while Ms. Tyler and I become acquainted." He studied Gabe, then asked, "Has your barber gone on vacation?"

Gabe's smile could have soured milk. "No. I fired him." He turned and left the room.

Jenny nearly missed Sterling's small sound of distress. He recovered immediately, and led her to the mission-style sofa upholstered in a warm red. "I imagine you'll be glad to see this delightful rascal in such good spirits." He gestured to Choc, who was sprawled on the floor beside the couch blissfully mauling a catnip mouse. "His recuperative powers are truly amazing."

Jenny knelt beside the Siamese, who, with feline consistency, ignored her. The toy rolled from between his back paws and he extended the uninjured one to hook a claw into it and bring the catnip back within reach. The bandage on the other paw had been replaced. In an attempt to cover her nervousness she said, "He looks wonderful, Mr. Thomas. He didn't deserve what's happened to him over the last week or two."

"We shall do our best to make up for his misfortune. I'm very fond of cats." At her nervous nod, Sterling offered his hand, which she accepted once more. As he assisted her to her feet, he continued, "I feel sure recent events have frightened you. Believe me, I shall do everything in my power to return you to your home as soon as the situation is resolved. By the way, I must compliment you. I've made it a point to acquire several samples of your work. Your illustrations are excellent. You have a remarkable talent."

Disarmed, Jenny replied, "Thank you."

"If you'll give me a list of your needs, I shall have a studio set up so you can work here." He led her to a chair beside beveled glass doors that stood open to the patio. The sound of the fountain ten feet away seemed a part of the room, lulling her senses as she sank into the chair. "Perhaps the desert will inspire you to extend the subject matter of your paintings."

The sound of falling water was hypnotic, and Jenny came back to the conversation with a start. He'd evaded any mention of how long he expected to keep her here. But then that hardly mattered. She intended to leave as soon as she found a way. "I'm sure that would be helpful if I were to receive a commission for a children's book set in the desert," she said offhandedly.

Sterling sank into the chair at right angles to her. "Oh, that, too. But no. I mean the paintings you have in Donhaven."

Her heart skipped a beat. "How did you know about those? They've never been exhibited."

A small, apologetic smile played about his lips but didn't reach his eyes. "Jim Slater, whom I'm sure you met, mentioned them to me when he reported the damage to your home. He's quite knowledgeable about art, and he was impressed. Why haven't you exhibited them?"

Jenny fought to remain calm. Her entire past was an open book to a man with endless resources at his command. He probably knew everything about her marriage and her . . . connections. Aware that lies would only entangle her further, she answered truthfully, "I had one small gallery showing some years ago."

"That was where you met your late husband, was it not?"

He knew. Her lips felt numb, as if she had a mouth full

of lemon slices. Sterling's attention appeared to be focused
on Choc's antics. "You know everything about me, don't
you?"

"Oh, yes, Ms. Tyler. Or may I call you Jenny? I feel as if
I know you quite well." His look was compassionate. "I became aware of your complete history soon after Gabe gave
me your name."

"And Gabe . . . Mr. Daniels. Does he know?"

A small smile tilted Sterling's lips. "Yours is one of the
reports he is reading. After I realized who you were, I . . .
delayed its delivery to him until I could be present to defend you." He gestured toward the hall. "In fact, he should
burst in here any minute. You're a new experience for him,
Jenny. I quite enjoy challenging the boy."

Jenny looked at the double door, and then at the opening
to the patio. If she bolted now, could she . . . ?

The doors flew open and Gabe stalked in. To her surprise, his rage was directed at Sterling. "You old bastard,
you've had this for two days! You left me in that hick town
grasping at straws and building a scenario while you held
the key that would have unraveled the puzzle in minutes."
His shirt had pulled out of his trousers, and his loose
necktie flapped against his lapels. He ran his fingers
through his too-long hair. "What if Ms. Tyler had been
killed?"

"You deduced much of the situation without any reports
to work from, my boy. I'm proud of you," Sterling soothed.
He pointed at the third chair in the little grouping. "Sit down
and compose yourself, then tell me what all this means."

"Don't blow smoke at me, Sterling. Je . . . Ms. Tyler's in
a hell of a position. Did it ever occur to you she's probably
the real target? Even if she's not, maybe she prefers to stay
hidden."

"You told me she wasn't safe there," Sterling reminded him.

Gabe sank into his chair and looked at Jenny, his eyes narrowed in concentration. "Yeah, but I didn't know then that one of the players was her late husband's firm."

"No!" Jenny cried. "Uncle G. swore to me the Travinos had nothing to do with any of this."

"Then he's either lying or he's lost his touch and has a maverick," Gabe declared. He stared at the ceiling thoughtfully, then continued, "Yeah, I really like the idea of a maverick."

"No."

"I fear he may be correct, Jenny," Sterling said firmly. "I've encountered the gentleman in the past, peripherally, of course, and the latter is the only explanation. In most matters, he maintains total control. His attention to detail is admirable."

"But . . . did Mr. Do—DeWitt work for him? Was I set up from the beginning?" Jenny said helplessly. "Uncle G. didn't like the idea of my moving to Donhaven after Trent died. He thought the town was the end of the earth, which was exactly why it appealed to me. The house belongs to a friend from art school. Her husband had accepted a promotion on the west coast. The arrangements were all made through my agent."

"Christ, but you're naive." Gabe rubbed his hand over his face. "Ever hear the saying about coincidence, Jenny? 'There ain't no such animal.' Someone in Uncle G.'s organization was waiting for a chance to get at you. Imagine his delight when he discovered DeWitt running a drug clearinghouse for another outfit in the town where you'd gone into hiding."

He shot Sterling a poisonous glance. "When Uncle G.'s maverick discovered the bastard had his hand in the till, probably about the same time DeWitt's employer did, he probably danced the fandango. Then DeWitt's boss moved, and Uncle G.'s man moved, too. Why not get a fix on DeWitt's stash and wipe you out at the same time? When you turned up to discover the body, whoever it was must have pissed down his leg with joy."

"Gabriel! Your language."

Jenny winced at the censure in Sterling's voice. Without thinking, she leaped in to defend Gabe. "I'm not a stranger to earthiness, Mr. Thomas. My late husband's family and business associates were colorfully accurate. Mr. Daniels only stated the truth." Oddly enough, she was so grateful to see a pattern to what had happened that she'd scarcely noticed his language.

"Thanks for standing up for me, Ms. Tyler, but I don't need your defense," Gabe said, eyeing his employer belligerently. "Sterling takes me the way I am or not at all."

Sterling shook his head in mild exasperation. "What would I do without you, Gabe? You enliven my days." He bent to pick up Choc, who had curled against his ankle in a state of catnip intoxication. "My lawyers will prepare the necessary papers to apply for my money from DeWitt's account. The Swiss refuse to act without overwhelming proof. Documenting his drug trade involvement should serve to verify further criminal activity."

It was Choc's defection to a man who already had everything, including the freedom Jenny wanted so desperately for herself, that made her say, "If they refuse, you could threaten to close down a company or two and sink the Swiss economy. But first, let me go. You don't need me, Mr. Thomas."

"Your suggestion is excellent, Jenny." Sterling nodded approvingly. "However, I'm afraid I cannot comply with

your request. I insist you remain here for your own safety."
Sterling stroked the cat's ears while he turned to Gabe.
"Who was DeWitt working for?"

"Kamanedes. I should have recognized the bastard's
stamp on the hit. His network has an agreement with the
other mobs giving them rural Midwest distribution. The
presence of a second set of players makes it look as if the
Travinos are moving into his turf, making life in the sticks
rough." Gabe got to his feet and paced the room, then
stopped in front of Jenny's chair. Glaring at her, he demanded, "You wouldn't by any chance remember any unhappy Travino campers?"

Jenny had expected Sterling to refuse her request, but
the mention of Kamanedes made escape essential. She felt a
certain guilty gratitude toward the rival don, since she was
secretly convinced Nick Kamanedes was the man who had
made her a widow.

She glared back. "How should I know? My husband han-
dled the company's legal matters. The only time I saw any
of his relatives or co-workers was at family get-togethers.
Few of them bothered to speak to me and not one would
have admitted to me that he was dissatisfied with how the
business was run. They didn't like me."

Recalling those years made Jenny's stomach clench.
During the early months of her marriage, Trent had gradu-
ally distanced her from her friends. At first unaware of her
growing isolation, she'd been embarrassingly eager to become part of a family circle which offered a less than luke-
warm reception. His mother, Rose, had hated her.

By the time she understood the true meaning of family to
the Travinos, it had been too late to reestablish her old ties.
By then she'd given up caring whether or not Trent's family
accepted her, and she'd been alone, except for Tania, the one

cousin who had befriended her. It was Tania who had stood up for her when she asked Uncle G. for her freedom after a pizza had exploded in Trent's face minutes after delivery.

The pain that seized her now wasn't caused by loss, but from remembering the horror of that night. And her guilty joy.

Gabe derailed the memory by commenting, "They probably didn't like your snotty accent."

"What's wrong with the way I talk?" Jenny demanded, leaping to her feet. She saw Gabe's gaze slide to Sterling, saw the older man's slight nod, and realized he'd baited her deliberately. The pain of the flashback must have shown on her face.

"You talk just like some rich do-gooder's daughter who got sent to ritzy boarding schools because her folks were off teaching the natives in Africa how to make banana bread."

Only then did she recognize the compassion in his eyes. Jenny didn't want his help or his sympathy, not now or ever. "I've no idea why you trouble yourself to ask me questions, Mr. Daniels. It's quite obvious you already know everything there is to know about me, but for your information, I had an extremely happy childhood. Go search for your unhappy Travino in my file. I'm sure he must be there someplace."

Jenny's survival was her own responsibility, one she had every intention of handling on her own. She stalked to the door, threw it open, then turned. "I'm going for my luggage. Then I'm leaving. Mr. Daniels, you will kindly return my gun to me within the next twenty minutes." Manufacturing a smile, she turned to Sterling. "Mr. Thomas, although your intentions are well-meant, I must refuse your help. Thank you for your hospitality. Perhaps you can look on Choc's affection as interest on the money his owner appropriated from your funds."

★ ★ ★ ★ ★

After she left, the two men stared blankly at each other for a full minute before Gabe said, "How the hell does she think she's going to get through a locked gate?"

Sterling stroked the cat, who was still collapsed across his knees. "I suspect that will be no barrier for such a determined young woman. Her survival instincts are excellent, if misguided. Are you going after her?"

"She's dead meat if I don't." He headed for the door, then looked back. "Ms. Tyler was right about that damn cat. When I carried him in last night you acted as if I'd brought you Julia Roberts. You wouldn't have cared if he'd had a hula dancer tattooed on his butt instead of a damned account number."

Sterling's chuckle followed him down the hall. Gabe wondered if he were going soft. Normally, he would have been much more insulting. That's what came of allowing himself to become emotionally involved in a situation.

The contents of the report on Jenny Tyler had shaken him. Given her background, the discovery that she had tied herself to a powerful Mafia family must have been devastating. Whatever she felt for the crook, witnessing Trent Travino's face blown off in her dining room would have finished off most women. Then she'd discovered DeWitt's rotting corpse. In spite of all that, she'd survived. Gabe pictured her crooning to the little cat, then spitting like a tiger at his own attempt to intimidate her.

Whatever it took, he intended to keep Jenny Tyler alive.

Gabe scanned the gardens as he hurried to the guest house. Sterling's security included an eight-foot-high perimeter wall armed with motion sensors which notified the guardhouse of anything that got within ten yards. An army of guards patrolled the grounds in the guise of gardeners, but no system was perfect. He knew this better than anyone, which was one reason he had put up only a token argument when told to play guard in the guest house.

Stepping behind a saguaro cactus fifty feet from the guest house, he pulled the communicator that connected him with the security switchboard from his pocket. "Where did she ask to be picked up? . . . When?"

Satisfied, he headed for the house, arriving just as Jenny rolled her suitcase into the small foyer. She released the handle and extended her hand, demanding, "My gun, please."

"Jesus, lady. Give me a chance," he muttered, detouring around her. She followed him into the living room, where he knelt beside the coffee table, a ten-inch-thick slab of imported mahogany. Reaching beneath one corner, he pressed a hidden switch. The end of the table opened, revealing a drawer twelve inches deep. Within lay Jenny's Lady Smith. He picked up the weapon, hefted its weight, then checked the safety.

"Give it to me. Even if you've unloaded it, I have spare clips," she said, approaching him with her hand extended. Her sweetly curved jaw was set, and he saw determination in every line of her slender body. "I have no choice but to leave, Mr. Daniels. You have no idea what it's like to be a prisoner in a velvet cage. After Trent was killed, I swore I would never again let another person dictate any aspect of my life." Jenny took the gun from him and checked the chamber.

Gabe closed the drawer and stood. "Where are you going?"

"Telling you would defeat my purpose, wouldn't it? You might be surprised to know I carry the means to disappear at any time." Her voice broke on the last word, then she said sadly, "Deep down, I never truly trusted Uncle G. to honor his promise."

Resisting the temptation to pull her close and comfort her, Gabe asked, "What's to prevent me from following you?"

"Believe me, I'll do my best to keep you from finding me." She moved close for a moment and rested her fingers on his cheek. "Long ago, before I learned to prize my independence, you and I might have had a chance. Now it's too late. Thank you for everything, Mr. Daniels." Rising on tiptoe, she pressed her lips to his. Her scent made Gabe's senses reel; the blow from the heavy pistol behind his left ear caused a meltdown.

EIGHT

Jenny locked the guest house door behind her, then hooked her heavy garment bag to her wheeled suitcase and seized the handle. She had twenty minutes to zigzag through the maze of unfamiliar paths to the corner of the compound wall where the cab was to meet her. She'd settled on that particular spot by climbing the trellis to the roof for a look at the compound as soon as she'd returned from the main house.

"Piece of cake," she muttered encouragingly to herself, grateful she'd exchanged her light sandals for Reeboks.

A sigh escaped her lips. The memory of Gabe lying unconscious beside the coffee table would haunt her. He'd looked so defenseless that for a moment she'd been afraid she'd killed him. When she'd checked his pulse, the feel of his blood pulsing beneath her fingertips weakened her resolve, and she'd left quickly, before her conscience won out.

Jenny headed down yet another tiled path. The two men planting an azalea covered with buds beside a man-made pond never spared her a glance. She thought it odd no one attempted to stop her. Then it dawned on her that Gabe had been her keeper. Since he wasn't available to issue orders, her path was clear.

When she reached the two-foot-thick wall, she pulled the length of nylon rope she'd found looped on a hook in the guest house laundry room from her tote. She secured one end to her suitcase, then measured off a length and knotted the rope through the handle of her garment bag. "There.

That should distribute the weight," she muttered to herself as she knotted the other end around her wrist. She'd never attempted anything like this before, but during her marriage she'd read innumerable thrillers to while away the lonely days.

Rolling the suitcase to the base of the wall, she propped it against the wall endwise. With her fingers mentally crossed, she rolled the garment bag tightly and set it atop the case. Looping the handles of her tote around her neck, she scrambled up the luggage, clawing at the wall for balance with her free hand. Once steady, she reached toward the top. Please, God.

Stretching onto her toes and fighting to keep her balance, she swung her lightweight tote up on the ledge. Climbing until she was beside it took three tries. Her knees were scraped and bleeding. Her torn slacks stuck to the wounds. She gave silent thanks for Trent's well-equipped exercise room. She'd spent hours down there sweating off her fear and anger.

Winded, Jenny collapsed on the broad wall, savoring the irony of hatred that had kept her in shape. She looked at her watch. The taxi should arrive any minute.

Rising to her knees, she tugged on the rope to bring up her luggage. When an accented voice called, "Lady, you want to drop that to me?" she nearly sent her garment bag back to the ground on the wrong side of the wall. Looking down, she saw a slender man with strong Hispanic features standing beside a taxi.

"You're right on time. Here they come." She pushed the suitcase, and then the garment bag, to the edge and fed the rope until they landed at the driver's feet. Again looping the tote handles around her neck, she lowered herself over the edge.

The shot rang out just as Jenny was about to drop to the sandy verge. Panic made her release her hold, and she landed on all fours, sand working through her torn slacks and into her grazed knees. Rolling into the angle of the wall, she turned her head to scan the road. The driver lay in a crumpled heap beside his cab, her luggage on either side of him.

A second bullet struck the stucco wall a foot above her head. Cursing herself for being an overconfident fool, she threw herself flat and dug for her gun. When the third shot came, she gauged the direction and fired two rounds, although she knew with a sinking heart the effort was as useful as shooting into the ground. She was being held in place by someone with a rifle.

The muted roar of a powerful motor came from her left. A black Jaguar appeared from nowhere, heading in her direction. The darkened passenger window facing her lowered; in the opening she saw the muzzle of a gun braced on the car door. Paralyzed with fear, she couldn't even close her eyes. She couldn't breathe. Each second stretched forever . . .

From above she heard the scrape of a leather sole on stucco, followed by the staccato bark of a semiautomatic rifle. The Jaguar went airborne over the ditch between the road and the compound before hurtling crazily toward the wall. Jenny flinched at the grinding clash of collapsing steel and shattering glass.

"Jenny! Are you all right?" Gabe's urgent shout was accompanied by a scrabbling sound as he dropped from the wall. His highly polished brogans, now scuffed and scratched, appeared next to her head.

"No!" she shouted. "I'm mad as hell." Jenny frowned at the demolished Jaguar. The two gardeners she'd seen earlier stood on either side of the car, pistols at the ready. One of them spoke rapidly into the cell phone he held with his free hand. A third man, cradling a rifle, leaped from the wall and headed in the direction of the sniper.

Gabe's hands were gentle as he clasped her shoulders and lifted her to her feet. "Can you stand by yourself?" he asked.

Jenny planted her feet firmly apart and risked looking upward from beneath her lashes. Gabe's features were taut with suppressed anger; his dark eyes glittered between narrowed lids. His grip on her shoulders tightened. Anticipating retribution for knocking him out, she twisted free and took the offensive. "Of course I can. The taxidriver. Has anyone checked to see if he's alive?" She circled around him to head for the taxi, only to be jerked against his side. This time his grip hurt.

"The bullet got him in the shoulder. The guards will see to him. How many goddamn people have to be killed or maimed just so you can be independent?" he ground out between clenched teeth.

The cords in his neck stood out from his effort to control his anger. Slowly, Jenny lifted her chin until she looked him directly in the eye. "You're not being fair."

"Dammit, use some sense. Sterling's just trying to save your skinny hide."

"And get his three million dollars back. The money always comes first, doesn't it? That's how the Travinos operated." She was everlastingly tired of always being at the end of everyone's priority list.

"What the hell's that supposed to mean?"

"I'm sick and tired of being the second person in line," she snapped. "My parents traveled the world doing good for the downtrodden . . . after parking me in boarding school. We hadn't been married six months before it dawned on me that Trent looked on me as an ornament to trot out every time he wanted people to think he was classier than he was. He even bragged about my work as an illustrator, pretending to be the proud, indulgent husband.

"Now I'm a tool in Sterling Thomas's relentless pursuit of embezzled funds. The perfect accessory, that's me. Another loose end." She stamped her foot, something she hadn't done since she was three, and shouted, "I'm sick and tired of people telling me to sit down and smile. Let me run my own life!"

A limousine purred to the side of the road, and Gabe, his face inscrutable, turned her toward it. Sirens wailed in the distance. "We'll argue about this later. I want you out of here before the cops arrive." Ignoring Jenny's protests, he jockeyed her into the backseat and waved the driver on his way.

Frustrated, Jenny collapsed against the leather upholstery and shed the tears she wouldn't allow Gabe Daniels to see.

After two hours of interrogation and greasing wheels, Gabe's head ached like a broken toe. The Las Vegas police had finally come around to the idea that Gabe had fired in response to an attack. Both the cabbie and the driver of the Jaguar were in the hospital, the latter in critical condition with head injuries. His passenger was dead, of lead poisoning. Their IDs were probably bogus, but Sterling's people had their fingerprints. By morning, he'd know when each of them had cut his first tooth.

He stripped off his clothing and stepped into the shower, wearier than he could ever remember. He lathered his hair, flinching when his fingers met the bruise from Jenny's blow. Underestimating her resolve and initiative could have been a fatal mistake, one Gabe had no intention of repeating. He grinned in admiration. Jenny Tyler was one tough little broad.

Twenty minutes later, shaved and dressed in a linen shirt and suit, he rapped on her door. "Jenny . . . Ms. Tyler. Are you ready?" He'd sent her luggage back with her in the limo, much to the cops' disgust, and she should be dressed by now.

"Ms. Tyler?" He waited the count of ten, then tried the knob, which turned too easily. The room was empty, except for the lingering scent of wildflowers. "Sonovabitch!" Whirling, he strode out the door and headed to the kitchen calling for Carmelita.

In the main house, Jenny mentally dug in her heels in resistance to Sterling Thomas's patriarchal charm. "But I must talk to Tania. She'll tell me why Uncle G. has turned against me. I know she will," she argued.

"We were friends. She stood up for me," she continued, her back to the sliding glass door in the room where she'd met him that morning, her fists clenched tightly, as if the effort might help her convince the industrialist. His polite insistence that she remain sequestered in his compound triggered a near-claustrophobic fear. Caged, with every luxury but freedom at her fingertips. She wouldn't live that way again. Not ever.

"My dear, this afternoon should have made you realize that you will be safer here than anywhere." He stroked the cat stretched at his side on the sofa. "Once this is over, you are welcome to all the freedom you desire."

His voice rang with sincerity, but Jenny had heard sincere promises before. She'd lost faith in them. "You can't guarantee anything. How did the gunmen know where and when the taxi was to meet me? For that matter, how did Mr. Daniels know exactly where to find me when he leaped to the rescue?"

A small smile creased her host's face. "For security reasons, the telephone in the guest cottage was monitored. Gabe knew where you planned to go over the wall before you . . . incapacitated him." His smile disappeared. "Unfortunately, we haven't ascertained how the gunmen acquired that information. My technicians are investigating as we speak."

Jenny smoothed the striped silk of her skirt over her knee with a sweaty palm, realizing that if she'd used her cell phone to call the taxi, she might very easily be dead. She repeated the movement. "Even your unlimited resources can't make the compound one hundred percent foolproof. Besides, you aren't obligated to protect me. I'm . . . quite capable of fending for myself."

"That's a crock of the well-known article." Gabe stood in the doorway of the small parlor. His brows drew together in a forbidding frown as he challenged Sterling. "I thought you and I were going to talk with Ms. Tyler together."

The older man looked at him searchingly. "You were otherwise occupied. I'd hoped you might rest a few hours before dinner. You must be exhausted." Concern filled his voice.

"Crap. You just wanted to try to intimidate the little widow. Your take on her is different from mine. She's a tiger, and you might as well treat her like one."

His unexpected defense threw Jenny off base. When he'd stuffed her into the limo, he had been angry enough to tear her limb from limb. Only the imminent arrival of the police had rescued her.

Sterling stood, his craggy features curiously composed. "Well, then. It seems we must devise a different approach

114

to the problem. But after dinner. I believe my chef has come up with yet another delectable variation on chicken for this evening." He gestured toward the door. "Shall we?"

As Gabe led her to the dining room, Jenny murmured, "Thank you."

"Don't thank me yet. And don't get any half-assed idea that I'm willing to let you take off on your own to zigzag around the country. You'd be dead within six hours," he responded before ushering her into a room flooded with the golden light of the setting sun. Palladian windows lined two sides of the airy room, and she blinked at the reflected glitter of silver and crystal. An arrangement of gold candles of varying heights centered one end of a long, damask-covered table. Three place settings clustered around their flickering light.

"Please allow me." Sterling pulled out the heavy teak chair at one side.

Jenny sat, watching warily as Sterling took his place at her left. Gabe slid into the chair across from her. When an impassive dark-eyed waiter attempted to pour her wine she spread her fingers over the top of the goblet. "None for me, thank you."

"You must try my wines, Jenny," Sterling said persuasively. "These come from my own vineyards in Provence."

Her fingers still sealing the globe of her glass, Jenny said levelly, "You may mean well, Mr. Thomas, but at this point I trust you no more than I trust Trent's family. Since Uncle G. may have gone back on his word, I prefer to keep my mind clear."

From the corner of her eye, she saw a saturnine smile on Gabe's face.

"Then I must make a greater effort to convince you my intentions are benign. And please call me Sterling. Shall we also dispense with Mr. Daniels and Ms. Tyler? Surely you and Gabe have shared enough danger to be less formal with one another." He signaled the servant who stood by the sideboard. "Perhaps you would care for iced tea."

Gabe snorted. "Come off it, Sterling. You're taking all the damn fun out of life. Haven't you figured out we're being sarcastic when we 'Mr.' and 'Ms.' each other? She doesn't like me a whole lot better than she does you." He raised his wineglass in a salute to her. "Do you, Jenny?"

Lifting the goblet of iced tea she'd just been given, Jenny returned the gesture, murmuring dryly, "Gabe." Savoring the single syllable on her tongue, she found herself watching his face for a reaction. His dimple flashed momentarily. Her cheeks grew warm. "Sterling does have better manners."

"There now. We're all friends." Sterling picked up his fork. "This avocado salad is particularly delicious, Jenny. The dressing is made with lemons from my own citrus grove."

Five courses later, Jenny was glad she'd turned down the wine. A different bottle appeared with each course, and Gabe appeared to have no difficulty matching Sterling's consumption. To her surprise, neither man showed any sign of inebriation.

To her greater surprise, Gabe maneuvered his way through the multiple forks and various wineglasses as if he'd been born to them. His perfectly tailored suit remained unwrinkled, but his unruly dark hair curled over his forehead and along the back of his neck. The urge to comb it back from a man's brow was one she hadn't experienced since the first few months of her marriage. The realization made her feel hot all over. She hoped her cheeks hadn't turned pink again.

Sterling sipped coffee from a translucent china cup and sat back in his chair. He looked directly at Gabe. "Now we must address the problem at hand. Have you come up with a plan?"

Jenny opened her mouth to comment, then subsided when Gabe sent her a cautionary look. "Yeah. Let Jenny call her friend Tania tomorrow and set up a meeting. We'll choose the location, and change it at the last minute. Then we'll meet her and see what happens." He looked at Jenny. "As soon as you finish talking with her, we'll be out of there."

"Where do you get this 'we' business?" Jenny demanded.

"Lady, I intend to stick to you like a sweaty shirt."

"I have to be the one to set this up," she said stubbornly. "She won't trust a meeting place dictated by Sterling. And she won't talk openly to me if you're there."

Gabe pushed his chair away from the table and stretched his legs out before him. "Is Tania stupid?"

"Of course not. She wouldn't have made it through law school if she were."

"A lot of people might give you some argument there." His lips quirked in an engaging grin before he continued. "If she's grown up in the mob, she knows damn well you'll want security for a meet. Being suspicious is second nature to her. If you keep making dimwitted objections, I'll begin to doubt your intelligence, and we'll just cancel the whole freakin' deal."

Jenny hesitated. Perhaps she would have to compromise temporarily. "All right. I'll do this your way. For now."

"Such grudging capitulation," Sterling commented gently. "You can do no better than to take Gabe's advice in matters of this sort." He stood, dropped his napkin on the table, then turned to Gabe. "You will keep me informed every step of the way?" His sharp gaze would have intimidated a lesser man.

"Yeah, sure. Don't I always?"

"You might prefer I not discuss that particular problem in the presence of a guest," Sterling said gently. He turned to Jenny. "I bid you good night, my dear. We will make arrangements for your enterprise in the morning."

"Yes . . . of course," she managed to stutter. The man's quick shifts of mood were as disconcerting as Gabe's, but she had little resistance when his kindness was focused on her.

After Sterling left the room, Gabe rose and came round to pull out her chair. "Since we'll probably leave tomorrow, let me show you a few of Sterling's fountains by moonlight. That's when they're at their best." He held out his arm. She ignored the gesture. Jenny had no intention of experiencing the flash of uncomfortable heat she'd felt when his fingers had brushed hers on the way to the dining room.

With a careless shrug, he led the way to the French doors in the center of a bank of arched windows. "Some will probably be new even to me. He changes them every few months. The old bastard's not happy unless he's tearing something down and starting from scratch." Ignoring her resistance, he took her hand and folded her fingers around his forearm.

Helpless to protest, Jenny left her hand in place and willed herself not to feel anything. Still, her arm tingled all the way to her shoulder. "It's disloyal of you speak of Sterling the way you do. I'm surprised he doesn't fire you," she said as they moved away from the house. His arm was hard and muscular beneath her fingers, and her body continued to betray her—she wanted to cling to him. Annoying as he was, in less than a week Gabe had become the only constant in her world. Sadness gripped her at the realization that she would miss him when she set out on her own.

Humor lacing his voice, he murmured, "The dining room is bugged. If I hadn't said something nasty about him, Sterling would think I was sick." He led her through an opening in the hedge to a stone bench beside a whimsical fountain. Four elephant heads with trunks extended, were spaced evenly around the edge of the pool, alternately spraying the statue of a clown in the center. Gabe pulled out his cell phone. "What's Tania's number?"

Jenny sat. "I thought I was calling her in the morning."

"Yeah. So does Sterling. He doesn't know squat about this kind of a deal. He likes to drive a straight route. I run my own operations. I didn't make a scene because you get out of shape about my disrespect. What's the number?"

Jenny recited the numbers. "That's her cell phone, in case she's moved," she told him, accepting the phone after he dialed. There was no advantage to be gained by changing the timing, but Gabe was clawing for independence much as she herself did. He must resent Sterling's orders as much as she hated being shuttled around like a UPS parcel.

Tania answered after three rings. "Jenny! Oh, my God! Uncle G. said you'd discovered a body! I've been going crazy worrying about how that would affect you, particularly after everything that's happened. Where are you?" Concern filled her husky voice.

"I'm safe, Tania, but I'm so frightened. Someone's trying to kill me. Why did Uncle G. change his mind?"

"Terrible things are happening, Jenny. The feud between us and the Kamanedes family has surfaced again. No one tells me any details, but I hear Uncle G. is beside himself."

Her evasion reminded Jenny their call might be tapped, digital cell phones or not. She had no knowledge of technology, but she'd at least learned to be cautious. "Tania, I mustn't talk long. Can you meet me?"

"Tell me where you are. I'll be there as soon as possible."

In the bright moonlight, Jenny read Gabe's lips. "Atlanta. I'm staying with a friend of a friend." True, at least on the surface, she thought. "It's a gated estate north of town, in Buckhead . . ." She passed on the directions Gabe gave her. "You'll be there tomorrow afternoon? Oh, Tania, I can't thank you enough." She folded the phone and handed it to him.

"Good job for an amateur."

Jenny's temper snapped. "I wasn't acting, you ape. She's my friend, and I need her help."

"Yeah." He took her arm and guided her along the tiled path. "You better pack your bags before you hit the sack. Tomorrow will be a long day."

Six hours later, Gabe eased open the door to Jenny's room. Her wildflower fragrance assaulted his senses as soon as he stepped inside. He squashed the temptation to abort their plans and spend the next week or two satisfying his growing hunger for this woman. She'd responded when he kissed her, and she'd tried to avoid touching him the evening before. Surely that meant something. Given the proper setting . . .

Years of discipline, plus his own well-developed sense of responsibility, made him approach the blanketed mound on the bed with the intention of waking her gently. Fading starlight, filtering through the sheer curtains, cast pale, elongated shadows across the white spread.

The sheet was pulled to the top of her head. He estimated where her shoulder would be and patted. Before he could withdraw his hand, her arm struck his shoulder with stunning force.

"Jesus H. Christ!" he shouted as her other fist swung wildly toward his chin. He grabbed her wrist before it made contact, and ducked a second blow. "Jenny, it's me. Gabe."

She fought and screamed when he captured her other hand. Before he could speak again, she erupted from beneath the covers and drew her knees up. Gabe did the only thing he could. He threw himself on top of her before she kicked him. "For God's sake, calm down. Sterling can probably hear you at the main house!"

The tension drained out of her. The dim light allowed him to see her features relax. Her eyes opened slowly, and a shudder shook her body. To his everlasting shame, his groin tightened. "Is it safe to let go?" He had to put space between them. Now.

She nodded slowly.

He freed her wrists and braced his hands on either side of her. Before he could stand she reached up to cup his face with trembling fingers. "I'm sorry, Gabe. I really am. I was having a nightmare about Trent, and when you shook my shoulder, it became part of the dream." She shook her head as if to wake herself.

Gabe couldn't seem to make his tongue work properly. Her eyes were depthless pools in the half-light. Her warm body curved subtly beneath him. Heat spread from where her fingers touched his cheeks. "We're leaving now, so Sterling won't have a chance to come up with last-minute suggestions."

A slight frown creased her forehead. "One of these days he's going to get tired of putting up with you."

Her fingers seemed to move of their own accord, smoothing the cheeks he'd shaved half an hour earlier. Dammit, she had no idea what she was doing to him. He wrenched away from her touch and straightened. "Yeah, that'll happen real soon."

"I envy you. I'd love to be able to ignore people who give me orders." Her voice strengthened as she continued, "I'm so everlastingly sick and tired of doing what I'm told."

"Yeah, you made that clear yesterday. You'd better get dressed. Will's running the checklist and filing a flight plan for the jet so he can take off as soon as we get to the runway. I'll wait outside. Don't take any longer than you have to."

NINE

"Will filed a flight plan for Baltimore," Gabe said as he settled Jenny in her seat. Her listlessness disturbed him. He missed the feistiness she'd displayed during her abortive attempt to escape. "Sterling's place there is low-profile, but the security's the best of any of his homes. You can call Tania in a couple of hours to let her know you've changed plans." If trouble came calling, Gabe thought, he wanted to know exactly what direction the threat was coming from. He had a niggling feeling it would arrive with Tania.

"How can you be so sure the house is safe?"

He buckled himself into the other seat as the plane taxied down the runway. "I set up the system and trained the people. And I test them whenever I get the itch."

She showed her first spark of interest since he'd blocked her attempt to escape. "Just what is your job title?"

"Fire Chief," he answered laconically. The term had always seemed comprehensive enough.

"Is that how you describe your duties on your résumé?"

Her tart reply raised Gabe's spirits. She was sounding all snooty and upper-class again. She must be feeling better. The plane accelerated down the runway, and he braced himself against the jet's pull before replying, "I don't have a résumé."

"Everyone has a résumé. What if Sterling fires you?"

Damned if she didn't sound as if she cared. Gabe realized he was happy, which in turn made him nervous. "He won't. I know where all the bodies are buried."

The jet leveled off and Jenny unfastened her seat belt. She stood. "I don't understand you or Sterling. Whether or not I continue to go along with you depends entirely on what Tania tells me. I might still be better off setting out on my own."

Gabe had been afraid of that very thing. Even before her outburst, he'd realized that Jenny hadn't been able to count on many people in her life. Somehow, Tania had climbed to the top of the pile. Nonetheless, he had a bad feeling about this meeting. "Are you sure she'll be able to tell you anything?"

Jenny shook out the cashmere throw from the end of the sofa before lying down and drawing the soft cream folds up to her shoulders. Her eyes were bleak. "I have to try. Tania's my only friend in Trent's family. She'll help me if she can."

For some reason, Gabe's apprehensions doubled.

Sterling Thomas's Baltimore residence was a redbrick Federal-style home behind a stark matching wall. The midday sun fell benignly on budding trees and shrubs, and daffodils waved from several well-tended flower beds. Although Jenny was sure sensors and wires threaded the length of the fence and grounds, she didn't have the hemmed-in feeling she'd had in the Palm Springs compound.

As the BMW rolled to a stop under the porte cochere she sensed warmth in the house, something she hadn't noticed in a building for a very long time. Their driver, a striking auburn-haired woman wearing sunglasses with big lenses, turned to Gabe, who sat beside her in the front passenger seat, and said, "Atlanta wants you to call immediately."

Jenny recognized the shark's smile creasing Gabe's face, and told him, "Go on ahead. I'll be right behind you." She watched until he disappeared, then grabbed her tote from the backseat. Under the puzzled gaze of the driver, she hefted its weight to assure herself Gabe hadn't taken her gun while she slept.

Jenny turned from the car. "Thanks for the ride," she called airily over her shoulder before ascending the low steps to the side door.

Finding Gabe was no problem. He'd already set up his laptop computer and fax in the dining room. Wires trailed across the exquisite surface of the cherry table toward an assortment of wall outlets. This obviously wasn't the first time he'd used the room as a command center.

He'd pushed the sleeves of his black turtleneck up to the elbow and discarded his thin Swiss watch beside the fax machine, which was spurting pages. A cell phone hunched to his ear, he perched on the edge of a chair like a bird prepared to flee the branch. "How many broke through? . . . How long was he in before you nabbed him? . . . Not bad. Not bad at all. You said all three were local talent. Any names? . . . Now tell me about the others." The fingers of his left hand flew over the keyboard.

Jenny dropped her tote beside the table, pulled out a side chair, and sank gratefully onto its needlepoint-covered seat. All she could think of was a hot shower and a nap to supplement her fitful sleep during their flight. She inhaled deeply. Unless her nose was deceiving her, she smelled homemade vegetable soup. Food appealed even more than the shower and nap. Rising, she followed the scent through a swinging door to a sunny little breakfast room that opened off the kitchen, where a tiny dark woman stood before a restaurant-size range with a teaspoon to her lips.

Without thinking, Jenny demanded, "Is it ready?"

Unsurprised, the woman turned and smiled. "Honey,

from the look of you, you must be starved. Sit down while I get a bowl."

Jenny sank into the cushioned ladder-back chair at the navy blue enameled table. In minutes, the scurrying cook had filled a heavy white pottery bowl with soup and cut two thick slices of homemade bread, which she placed before Jenny along with a butter dish and a pot of honey. The homely fragrances made her so greedy she forgot to say thank you.

"Gonna have words with that Gabe. He's supposed to be takin' care of you and you're about t' die of hunger."

A glass of milk appeared beside her bread plate as if by magic. Jenny swallowed a spoonful of soup. Bliss. "Oh, thank you. I didn't even know I was starved until I smelled this. It's been years since I've eaten anything so good." She tore off a piece of bread and spread it with butter. "Thank you . . . ?"

"Sadie. Just call me Sadie." She sank into the chair opposite Jenny. "I keep track of the house for Mr. Sterling. When I know that baby Gabe's comin', I heat up the range. Been feedin' him since he was a skinny kid. Like to never fill him up. He's partial to my vegetable soup."

"You didn't come out to say hello, Sadie. Don't you love me anymore?" Gabe's voice didn't startle Jenny. She'd become accustomed to his uncanny knowledge of her whereabouts. Sadie leaped to her feet and ran to him. He hugged and whirled the little woman off her feet as if she were a lover.

"Now put me down, boy. This one's a real lady. What's she s'posed to think? You got to behave yourself."

"She hit me on the head with her gun, Sadie. Knocked me out," he said as he lowered the cook to the floor. "Maybe you should go snatch that food from her." Gabe's eyes were clear and laughing as he looked at her over Sadie's head. His dimple was much in evidence, and he was as relaxed as Jenny had ever seen him. She suspected the security system wasn't the only reason he'd made Baltimore their destination.

"You must've been actin' too big for your britches again," the little woman scolded as she opened a cupboard to reach for another bowl. "Sure am glad to hear someone put you in your place." She ladled soup into the bowl and set him a place.

Gabe sank into the chair and favored Jenny with a laughing glance. "Don't you have something to add?"

"I think Sadie expressed everything quite clearly," Jenny replied, her attention focused on dribbling honey over the second slice of bread. "It's comforting to learn I'm not the only one who resents your high-handed treatment."

He dipped his spoon into the bowl and scooped up some broth. "I gathered Tania wasn't pleased when you called her from the plane this morning." His attention appeared focused on his food.

"She likes to sleep late, and she objected to the abrupt change of meeting place. Unlike you, she deals with a travel agent." Jenny sank her teeth into the bread. Honey dripped onto her lower lip. As she licked it off, she saw Gabe staring at her mouth. Light streaming through the bank of multipaned windows struck his eyes, highlighting their intent indigo depths. He didn't speak, just watched her, and she self-consciously licked her lips again. Her heartbeat rang in her ears, and her clothing seemed too tight. Why couldn't she look away?

"Gabe, have you gotten rid of her yet?" The redhead's husky voice preceded her entry from the service door. When she saw Jenny, her lips tightened. "There are several problems we need to go over while you're here. You've been neglecting us," she said. Stopping behind Gabe's chair, she rested her hand on his shoulder and looked at Jenny with challenge in her eyes.

The sensations which had held Jenny captive to Gabe's mesmerizing blue gaze vanished. She withdrew so completely that she nearly missed the annoyed glance Gabe directed toward his watch before answering testily, "I'm in the middle of an operation, Faith. E-mail me a list."

The redhead stiffened beneath her severely cut suit. Ignoring Gabe's terse reply, she persevered. "I'm not sure I can do them justice on paper, Gabe. Intuition is easier to explain in person. And you know how very intuitive I am," she purred.

"So that's what they're callin' it these days." Sadie's voice echoed from the interior of the refrigerator, where she appeared to be searching for something.

Jenny stifled a burst of nervous laughter. It was no business of hers that Gabe and the woman misnamed Faith had more than a professional relationship. She stood abruptly. "You two take all the time you want. I'm going upstairs to find my room. I need to shower and change." She glanced at her own watch. "Tania won't be here for another two hours, so I might even grab a short nap." She hoped her expression was neutral when she said to Faith, "Did anyone bring my luggage in from the car?"

"Bert took your bags upstairs. Second door on the left."

Faith sounded so cheerful that Jenny stole a glance at Gabe. His silence and his scowl as he buttered a slice of bread told her nothing.

Two hours later, Jenny paced the small study, stopping every few minutes to peer out the casement window facing the front of the house.

"If you're walking for your heart, you're not supposed to stop so often," Gabe said lazily from the doorway. He'd shed his turtleneck and jeans for another exquisitely tailored suit. "Besides, the chances your ex-in-laws or one of the rogues in the organization will blow you away are so good that if I were you I wouldn't waste the little time you have left on exercise." He came the rest of the way into the room, took her gently by the shoulders and eased her into the leather chair beside the desk. "Relax."

Jenny pulled away from his touch. Her nap had been a dismaying collage—a lurid scenario in which Gabe Daniels toured Sterling's holdings, using security inspections as an excuse to maintain compliant beauties at each location.

In an attempt to erase the memory, she demanded, "What happened in Atlanta that made you so happy?"

"Lots of visitors," Gabe replied, smiling. "The one guy got as far as the rose garden. They caught two other goons climbing the wall on the other side. The funny thing is, the hits weren't connected. And they were all local talent."

"Who sent them?" Jenny demanded, curling her hands into fists. She had to know before Tania arrived. Whatever transpired during her visit, Gabe mustn't guess how uneasy she was. What if Tania had unwittingly revealed her plans to Uncle G.? What if . . . She looked up to see Gabe watching her closely.

"That's what's so damn interesting. Nobody knows. Each group took on the contract through an intermediary, the traditional 'stranger in the alley.' Christ, some of those alleys could qualify as business offices." Gabe picked up the letter opener from the desk and tested its edge with his thumb. "Hell of a thing to learn the mobs are farming out the bloody stuff now. Where's an ambitious young punk supposed to learn the ropes?"

Two words made Jenny's mind contract. "Bloody stuff?" she squeaked. "Gabe, what were they hired to do?"

Gabe grimaced, as if suddenly aware he'd frightened her. He remained silent.

"Tell me!"

"The sonovabitch who got as far as the roses had enough plastic with him to blow the place to smithereens. The others were carrying a tidy supply of accelerant . . . enough to torch a five-story department store." He paused, then continued reluctantly, "One slime with the accelerant was able to fill in a few blanks after a little persuasion. They were supposed to spread the stuff, then kidnap you before they lit it. They had orders to deliver you to the back room of a local nightspot for pickup. Of course, when my people kept the appointment for them, no one knew anything."

Jenny shrank against the back of the chair. "I can't believe this." Everyone in Sterling's home would have been killed. So much potential death, and all of it connected to her. What had she done to bring this on herself? "Why would they want me?"

"You had the cat. They know you must have seen Dolan's account number."

Disbelief made her stutter. "All this d-destruction for . . ."

A soft chime interrupted her words. "What's that?" Jenny's nerves were strung so tightly that she forgot what she had been about to say.

"The gate just passed Tania." Gabe stood. Gesturing for her to remain in the room, he reached beneath his jacket for his gun before leaving to answer the front door.

Without thinking, Jenny pulled her tote closer, reassured by the weight of the Lady Smith. Would she ever again live in a world where a gun was something she saw only on television or in a movie? Jenny sent up a silent prayer.

Voices came from the foyer, Gabe's baritone flowing smoothly beneath Tania's bubbling pleasure. Standing, she hurried to the doorway to greet her friend.

Tania, her shining dark hair windblown and her amber eyes aglow, appeared in the opening. Gabe, towering behind her, made her look even tinier than her five feet three inches. "Jenny!" she cried. "I refused to believe you were all right until I could see you with my own eyes." She ran into the room and threw herself into Jenny's open arms.

The warmth of her greeting and the presence of someone who genuinely cared for her brought tears to Jenny's eyes. "I was so afraid you wouldn't be able to get away by yourself."

"Ha! Since when does anyone care what I do? To sooth their egos, they throw a few crumbs of paperwork my way when someone thinks of it." Tania's golden eyes flashed with anger. "Trent was the only one who treated me like an equal. The rest are pigs."

Gabe's inscrutable gaze met hers over Tania's shoulder. She nodded, annoyed by the reminder that she was expected to pick her visitor's mind. Jenny released her friend and led her to the sofa that sat at an angle to the fireplace. "I need your help, Tania. Why has Uncle G. changed his mind about me?"

"I'll go scare up some coffee and food," Gabe said.

Tania's hungry gaze followed him from the room. "How did you hook up with him, little one? If I didn't know better, I'd think I was back with the family."

The observation was typically Tania. "He's Sterling Thomas's chief of security," she lied. "Gabe and Sterling have appointed themselves my guardians. Let me tell you everything that's happened. Then you'll know why they're playing nursemaid. You've no idea how desperate I am to be free of them."

In the minutes before Gabe returned with a laden silver tray, Jenny told Tania what had occurred since she discovered the body. She left out several details, such as the amount of money Dolan/DeWitt had on deposit in his Swiss account, or even that Gabe had accessed the bank's records, but she'd included Gabe's educated guess that the accountant had been embezzling from whoever had employed him. As she spoke, she evaluated the expressions flitting across Tania's face. Could her friend have betrayed their meeting place?

"It couldn't have been the Travinos," Tania exclaimed, shaking her head. "We ceded that part of the country to the Kamanedes family years ago in exchange for territory in Florida. We'd both wasted too many resources elbowing each other back and forth. The rivalry was interfering with profit." Confusion was written across her features. "But that could explain . . ." She absently accepted the thin Lennox cup and saucer from Jenny.

From the corner of her eye, Jenny noticed Gabe lean forward in the chair he'd taken behind the desk. She shook her head, cautioning him. "Explain what?" she asked, realizing she, too, was leaning toward her friend. Perhaps Tania had the key.

"Uncle G. called a meeting yesterday. You can bet your life I wasn't invited, but Larry said Uncle was really angry." Tania grimaced, then continued. "My brother doesn't usually tell me anything about what goes on, so this in itself was unusual. Apparently, Kamanedes claims we broke the agreement. He's accused Uncle G. of muscling in . . . and Uncle G. doesn't know anything about it. He's furious, and he ordered everyone to take a closer look at their people. Your name came up as a possible leak."

Jenny poured coffee for herself and left the saucer on the

tray. Wrapping fingers that had gone ice-cold around the cup, she asked in a steady voice, "Surely Uncle G. can't think I've broken our agreement. I . . . . Trent never told me anything."

Tania reached over to pat her knee reassuringly. "That's exactly what I told Larry, but my opinion doesn't mean zilch. It's what they think that counts." She stared into her cup briefly. "Jenny, I'm your friend, and I believe you, but the fact is, several older council members still think you had something to do with Trent's death. And those people have Uncle's ear."

"Oh, God." Jenny set her cup on the table and stood. Trent's shattered features flashed across her mind. Her love for him had died with her discovery of what he really was, but she'd never hated anyone so violently as to wish them a death like that. She walked to the window where she'd watched for Tania's arrival and leaned her forehead against the cool pane. "They must think I'm as cold-blooded as they are. Why would I arrange for the assassination to happen in my own dining room? Do they think I enjoyed watching?"

"If only you hadn't been the one to find that old man's body," Tania sympathized. "That must be why they suspect you of being in league with Kamanedes. The dealer was one of his."

With surgical precision, she forked a bite of cake from the slice on her plate and chewed thoughtfully. "I think the best thing would be for you to let me go back and plead with Uncle G. I'll reassure him that your involvement was a coincidence. Then I'll get Larry aside and remind him of the favors he owes me. If he makes a strong enough case for you, maybe Uncle G. will go along. You need the inner circle on your side." She set down her plate and fork. "You really have no idea why you've become a target?"

"None whatsoever. Tania, when I walked away from the family, I didn't ask for anything but my freedom. I meant it when I swore I would never do anything to hurt any of you." Jenny thought of the intruders with the accelerant and explosives. Who had they worked for? "Why would I go back on my word?"

Tania looked at her pityingly. "I know you're innocent, and you know you're innocent, but we're talking the future of the family here. Uncle G. had no hand in DeWitt's death or in taking out those three locals. He told the council he'd never in a million years hire such amateurs to do his errands. But the accusation has angered him. He intends to punish whoever caused this insult to his honor. I'm afraid he suspects you're to blame."

Gabe flinched at Tania's implications. Jenny's pale skin tightened over her cheekbones, and he saw the desolation in her expression. He moved out from behind the desk.

Tania's careful recital of recent events at the Travino head office aroused his suspicions. Jenny was so intensely focused on her own problem that she must have missed the reference to the three locals. Tania shouldn't know anything about that. He'd specifically asked Jenny not to mention them. "I never heard such a can of crap. The old man must be losing it if Jenny's the only suspect he can come up with, and you can tell him I said so."

He almost laughed at the horror on their faces, as if he'd uttered the f-word at a tea party. Tania broke the silence. "No woman would dare pass on such an insult. You know Uncle's prejudices. The only reason he let me speak up for Jenny was that I'm a lawyer." She laughed ruefully. "And he'd still rather think I earned my degree by sleeping with the professors than because I have a brain."

"Then I'll get the message to him myself," Gabe growled. He surprised himself further by adding, "By God, I'll even offer to finger his broken link for him." Sterling's reaction to such a plan was predictable. The old man would blow his top. Gathering proof that DeWitt had fattened his Swiss nest egg by illegal activity had already grown to babysitting an innocent bystander. A side trip such as he'd just proposed increased the risk factor by 500 percent. He wondered if Kamanedes would be interested in a similar offer in exchange for the documentation Sterling needed.

Tania eyed him speculatively, then stood and held out her hand to him. When he took it, she said, "I have to get back to New York. I'm sorry I couldn't be more help, but I can't thank you enough for arranging for us to see each other. I've missed my friend." Her eyes held a message, one he'd never misinterpreted, when she looked up at him. She squeezed his hand before releasing it. Gabe smiled back, masking his distaste for her blatant offer.

Jenny hugged her. "You'll never know how much your friendship means to me. I'd ask you to give Trent's mother my regards, but I don't think she'd welcome them."

"Aunt Rose is more bitter than ever since Trent's death. I . . . I moved in with her, thinking it would make her feel she has family again. Now I've begun to dread going home at night." Tania scooped up her shoulder bag and walked toward the door.

Intrigued by her smooth performance, Gabe followed. He wouldn't be comfortable until the Mafia princess was off the premises, so under the guise of courtesy, he accompanied Tania to her rented Lexus, opening the driver's door and assisting her inside. He closed the door and stayed to watch the car pull away.

The explosion behind him knocked him face first onto the grass, leaving him breathless. "What the hell!" Gabe scrambled to his feet, peering through the smoke and flames. The front door and the narrow leaded windows surrounding it had blown inward, so the explosive had been outside. Had Jenny followed him to the foyer? Ignoring Tania's screams, he ran toward the ruined entry. "Jenny!" he shouted as he leaped through the flames.

Just inside the door, he nearly stumbled over a crumpled female figure. "Jenny!" Without a thought for his own safety, he bent and scooped the deadweight into his arms. Once past the blazing perimeter, he set her down gently, even though he already knew two things—the woman was dead, and it wasn't Jenny.

He'd never have to fend off Faith's advances again.

For one brief moment he felt guilt. The security officer had been one of his first hires, and she was superb at her job. She had simply never been able to accept his refusal to become personally involved with Sterling's employees.

Bert and two other security people were focusing industrial fire extinguishers on the blaze. As explosions went, this one had been small. But where was Jenny? Slapping at his singed left sleeve, he peered through the haze in what was left of the foyer and ran toward the study. "Jenny, are you all right?" he shouted. His throat, irritated by the smoke, was raw. Gabe scarcely recognized the ravaged voice calling her name as his own.

TEN

He heard her soft whimper before he saw the limp hand extending from the threshold of the study. When he reached the opening, he found Jenny curled in a fetal position against the open door. Kneeling, he clasped her hand and squeezed gently. She looked so small. "Jenny," he murmured, "where do you hurt?" She moaned and rolled onto her back. "Don't move until I check to see if anything's broken!"

"Not . . ." she protested as she slowly uncurled. "Don't . . . think anything's . . ." A racking cough broke off her sentence.

Swallowing tightly to keep from echoing with his own hack, Gabe peered through the smoke to see what progress the security team had made. They appeared to be gaining on the flames. In the distance, sirens wailed. Deciding quickly, he slid Jenny back into the study and shut the door. Like the doors in all of Sterling's residences, the room was air-sealed once the door was closed and locked. Haze filled the room. Jenny coughed again.

"Stay down on the floor where there's less smoke. I'll let in some fresh air." Striding to the casement windows, he cranked the frames wide open, then did the same with those on the other side of the room. A breeze from the back kept the smoke at the other side of the house, and fresh, untainted air flowed in. Gabe sucked in several lungs full before returning to Jenny and running his hands over her body. She coughed again. Finding no obvious injury, he knelt beside her and peered into her eyes. "Did you hit your head when you fell?"

"Didn't," she managed. Exercising great care, he lifted her and headed for a window. He positioned a cushioned Windsor chair, then sat so the late afternoon breeze struck her face. "Breathe deep, Jenny. And keep coughing. Bring up the crap." Her slight weight sagged against his chest. For the first time he became aware of his heart thumping wildly against his ribs. He swore viciously.

"If I'm about . . ." Jenny paused to cough, "to die, I'd prefer those . . . not be the last words I hear."

Her voice was raspy, but Gabe heard the growing strength behind the sound. And she was feeling well enough to bitch. His relief was so great that he forgot the fear that had nearly paralyzed him. "What do you want, a goddamn lullaby?"

When she struggled to sit upright, he pressed her face back against his shoulder. "Don't get too energetic too fast. There'll be medics with the firemen, and I want them to look you over."

Using his free hand, Gabe reached into his inside pocket and pulled out a tiny two-way radio. He depressed the switch at the bottom. Several minutes passed before Bert answered. He sounded harassed. "You got things under control out there?"

"The locals just took over. The cops are here, too. Gabe . . ." Bert's voice broke.

"I know. Anyone else?" Gabe kept his voice noncommittal and his eyes averted from Jenny's.

"All accounted for. That woman who came to talk with Ms. Tyler . . ."

Inwardly cursing his own stupidity, Gabe broke in. "Took off through the gate like a scalded cat when it opened for the fire truck, I bet. Don't tell the cops about her. And have someone run a trace on the plates. Try to have her picked up when she turns in the rental. I want to talk to her." He suspected a total stranger would return the car to the agency, but they had to go through the motions. "Ms. Tyler was hammered by the blast. She seems all right, but someone from the squad better check her out. Tell them to knock on the study door and I'll let them in." He released the switch and replaced the radio in his pocket.

Jenny struggled free of his hold. "Tania. Was she hurt? I'll never forgive myself if she . . ." She broke off, as if unwilling to believe what she read in his eyes.

Hating what he had to say next, he decided the news was best delivered bluntly. "Your friend tucked that little package under the doormat on her way out. I think she counted on being gone before it went off. Sometimes that stuff's not dependable." He suspected that Tania had counted on Jenny following them to the door. If she had . . . "My fault. I should have been suspicious when she made such a show of walking out of her shoe and kneeling to put the damn thing back on." He rubbed at a soot smudge on her cheek with his free hand.

"Oh, my God." Jenny sank her face into her hands. Tears, gray from the residue on her cheeks, seeped between her fingers.

The dejected set of her shoulders shook Gabe more than the tears. Sighing, he wrapped his arms around her and held her close, rocking gently. "You couldn't have known," he murmured. When a cough, triggered by her tears, racked her body, he loosened his hold but continued stroking her back, all the while cursing himself for being a lecher. The soft body beneath the simple silk shirtwaist dress was affecting him more than it should under the circumstances.

He shifted his position on the chair. "I'll get to the bottom of this, Jenny. I promise." He pulled her shaking body closer. A sharp rap sounded at the door.

Gabe cursed, shifted his hold and crossed the room, still carrying her sob-racked body. Using the hand supporting her legs, he managed to turn the knob to admit the medical technician.

The heavyset young woman took one look at Jenny's tears and gestured toward the couch. "Shock?" she inquired.

"Probably. And some heartbreak," Gabe replied enigmatically. He settled his burden as carefully as possible, then stepped back as the medic wrapped the blood pressure cuff around Jenny's arm. Mentally, he sorted their options. His priorities had just been shuffled. Sterling's insistence on retrieving his money would have to take a back burner; preventing Tania and Uncle G. Travino from eliminating Jenny took stage center.

Jenny cooperated listlessly with the technician's exam. Beneath a coating of grime, her fair skin was nearly colorless with fatigue, but her answers were coherent. Gabe thought they were out of the woods until she asked, "Was anyone hurt?"

"Just the one casualty," the technician replied calmly. She peered into Jenny's left eye, moving her penlight back and forth.

Before Gabe could intervene, Jenny pulled away from her and sat up very straight, her hands shaking in her lap. "Who?"

"The police were establishing her identity when I was sent in here. One of the staff, I believe." The technician's gaze swung to Gabe, as if hoping for confirmation.

"It was Faith." Saying her name out loud was hard enough. The spasm of pain that crossed Jenny's face knifed through him, and he felt the sorrow of his discovery all over again. He sank onto the sofa beside her. "She must have stood in the doorway when I walked Tania to her car. Jenny, she knew the risks when she chose her career."

"But she's dead," Jenny moaned. "If I hadn't insisted on meeting with Tania, none of this would have happened." She buried her face in her hands.

Gabe frowned at the EMT, who was watching them with avid curiosity. "Are you finished here?"

She mumbled an apology and gathered up her equipment. "She appears to be all right, but you might want to have her see her own physician." The door swung shut behind her.

Once again, Gabe gathered Jenny into his arms. How could he make her see that Faith's death wasn't her fault? She'd seen so much death in the last year. So much violence. Love had a lot to answer for, or at least the love that had thrust a gently raised artist into the heart of a syndicate family rife with infighting and jealousy. He'd bet his bottom dollar that dear cousin Tania had once held high hopes of giving a new meaning to family ties. Elegant little Jenny had dashed those hopes when Trent married her instead, and apparently Trent's cousin intended to make her pay. With her life.

Although Gabe's embrace was impersonal, a forgotten heat spread through Jenny's body. How long had it been since a man had held her, simply held her, sharing his strength and warmth?

Gabe had an abundance of both. Despite the horror of the last few hours, she felt surrounded, secure. His tender embrace dispelled the inner chill caused by the series of physical and mental shocks she had undergone.

Moments passed. She allowed herself to relax against him. His heart beat solidly against her shoulder and his even breathing feathered her temple. Giving in to her growing awareness, she burrowed her face into the angle of his neck. Her lashes brushed his skin and she felt his heartbeat quicken. He must think . . . "Gabe."

"What?"

His voice was husky, intimate. She wrenched her thoughts away from the delicious heat curling in her midsection and drew back, away from the seduction of security . . . and attraction.

Forcing herself to sound in control, she raised her gaze to his face. "Hadn't we better plan what we're going to do next?" Dear heaven, even the burgeoning stubble on his cheeks appealed to her. She fought an urge to run her fingers over his cheeks.

He expelled a gusty sigh and stood. "First, I'm going out to blow smoke at the cops. They'll queer everything if they barge off after Tania. Then we're going to get our luggage. Everything probably smells like smoke, but at least the clothing upstairs is undamaged." He looked at his singed jacket and complained, "This is the second suit I've ruined this week. Damned if I don't put in an expense voucher for both of them." He turned his head away as if avoiding eye contact.

"Then what will we do?" Jenny said patiently. An annoyed Gabe was easier to keep at a distance.

"Then we're going to a hotel where we can take showers, get a decent meal and a good night's sleep. Will you be all right on your own for a little while?"

When she nodded, he turned toward the door. Jenny called to his back, "Please make sure Sadie's all right."

"Where do you think I'm going first?"

Jenny stood cautiously, picked up her tote and looked around her. Except for the acrid smell, the room was as it had been when Tania arrived. Sadness etched Jenny's heart. How had she been so oblivious to Tania's hatred? Hurt at the loss of a friendship that had never existed nearly made her cry out in pain. Anger at her own stupidity propelled her to the door and up the stairs.

Repacking drained what little energy she had left. Jenny wanted nothing more than to stretch out on the flowered comforter and sleep until the horror of the day was a vague memory. When sudden dizziness made her sink onto the chaise, she leaned forward, resting her head on her knees. "I'm frightened," she whispered. "More frightened than I was when Trent was murdered, more than I was in Donhaven. I trust Gabe, but I hate people making decisions for me. Six years. For six years I allowed Trent to control every aspect of my life. For six years I counted on Tania as my friend. Oh, God, I wish I knew what to do."

"If you're finished with your prayers, we can get the hell out of here. I made reservations," Gabe said from the doorway.

In spite of his flippancy, Jenny saw compassion on his face. She managed a weak smile. "I'm afraid I was a little dizzy."

He crossed the room and held out his hands. "Not surprising. You were knocked on your butt."

She grabbed hold and let him pull her to her feet.

"All right?" he asked. When she nodded, he picked up her garment bag with one hand and put his other arm around her. Warmth radiated from his body, enveloping her and dispelling the chill. "Bert will bring your other case to the car. Sadie's downstairs waiting to say good-bye. She's taken a liking to you."

When they reached the kitchen, the little cook's calm amazed Jenny. Was she accustomed to such attacks?

"Take care of this one, Gabe. Don't let anythin' happen to her," Sadie said as she rose on tiptoe to kiss Jenny's cheek. "We'll fix things up here. When you come back you won't know anythin' happened."

With a pang, Jenny realized the little woman misunderstood her presence. Rather than explain, she leaned down to return the kiss.

Gabe hugged Sadie, then led Jenny out the back door to the service porch. The car Faith had driven from the airport, its motor running and doors open, was parked at the bottom of the narrow steps. Haze from the explosion hung low. Jenny shuddered, then straightened her shoulders and stepped into the passenger seat. Bert gave her a thumbs-up and closed the door.

As Gabe got behind the wheel, she heard the other man say, "I'll give Sterling your message." Gabe grunted in reply and slammed his door.

They were half a mile from the house before Jenny inquired, "What kind of a message did you send Sterling?"

Gabe flashed her a wolfish smile. Tendrils of curling hair fell over his forehead, and he looked like an unrepentant ten-year-old with a streak of soot on his cheek. "Just my notice that I'm slipping my leash for however long it takes."

"What does that mean?"

He glanced into the rearview mirror, then changed lanes. "Just what I said. You and I are going to disappear from his damn radar screen. Our first move will be to see how many tails we can pick up at the hotel." He reached over to brush her hair back behind her ear. The gentle touch revived Jenny's physical response to him that afternoon. Her clothes felt too tight. "As soon as I find out who to look for, we'll ditch them and leave. Until then, we're tourists. If you know what you're doing, the best places to get lost are big hotels and tourist attractions."

An hour later, Jenny luxuriated in the needle spray from two showerheads pummeling her body. She knew full well that by morning she would ache like a quarterback after the homecoming game, but at least this glorious heat would stave off the consequences of the blast. She reached for the little bottle of shampoo she'd liberated from the basket beside the sink and lathered her hair a second time. The odor of smoke lingered in her nostrils, a reminder that an innocent person had died in that senseless explosion. She leaned her forehead against the tiled wall, water sluicing over her shoulders and tears running down her cheeks.

The shower door opened.

She whirled, striking out wildly. Before she could scream, strong arms turned her around and a hand closed over her mouth. A vision of Janet Leigh at the Bates Motel appeared in her mind, and she threw her elbows backward, then doubled over in an attempt to catch her assailant off guard.

"Christ, woman, are you trying to cripple me?" Gabe murmured, his amused voice just loud enough to be heard over the sound of the shower. "I'm not here to kill you. I didn't even come for fun and games. Unless you insist."

Jenny wondered giddily why that should reassure her. She was gripped in a ruthless embrace against his naked chest, achingly conscious of the hardness thrusting against her hip through the towel wrapped around his waist.

"Promise to be quiet, and I'll take my hand off your mouth."

Jenny nodded, her body instinctively shrinking away

from him. When he freed her lips, she demanded, "What are you doing in here?" She tugged at the hand around her waist.

Gabe trapped her fingers and spoke close to her ear. "Someone got here ahead of us. There's a bug in the flower arrangement on the console. I purposely called for our reservation from the land phone at the house, and it worked. I just wanted to warn you before you gave away the game."

She tore free. "Oh, God!" she said, her forehead resting once more against the tiled wall. "Are there more?"

"One's enough. We'll talk about it in the elevator." With that, he released her and unlatched the shower door before saying, "Nice butt, Ms. Tyler." With that he was gone.

Jenny was sure the anger surging through her raised the temperature in the shower at least ten degrees. Even more annoying was the knowledge that the heat wasn't entirely from anger. What was happening to her? Her delight in the shower had vanished, so she rinsed her hair, stepped out onto the mat and reached for a towel.

When she had finished blowing her hair dry, she wrapped herself in the thick white robe furnished by the hotel and padded into the living room of their suite. Outwardly, the decor was nearly as elegant as the rooms in Sterling's house, except that the silk-appearing upholstery was synthetic fabric and the figurines and paintings were copies. A knock sounded, and she moved toward the door.

"Jesus, woman, get back in your room." Gabe, his hair damp but combed, clad in a robe that was a mate to hers, strode out of the second bedroom, his gun at the ready.

Instead of leaving, Jenny retreated only as far as the doorway of her room. Surely he didn't think . . .

After squinting through the peephole, Gabe cracked the door a scant inch and peered into the opening. Closing the door, he unhooked the security chain, tucked the hand holding the gun into his robe pocket, and admitted the bellboy.

"The concierge believes the cleaners have removed the smoke odor, sir." The white-coated man held out two plastic-covered hangers. "If this isn't satisfactory, please let us know."

"Thanks. I appreciate such quick service." Gabe laid the clothing over the back of a chair and reached his free hand into his other pocket to remove a bill. "Will the rest be ready in the morning?"

After a discreet glance at the denomination on the bill, the bellboy smiled broadly and gushed, "Definitely. Just call when you want the garments delivered."

"Good, because we intend to sleep in." Gabe closed the door.

"I still don't understand . . ." She had been about to protest once again his insistence on eating in the elegant Hampton's Restaurant when she remembered the bug.

His eyebrows lowered in warning, he separated their clothing. "You deserve an excuse to dress up and go out for a decent meal, sweetheart. You've had a tough week." He hooked the bag containing her dress over her arm.

Jenny wanted to strangle him with the hanger. Instead she turned her back on him and stalked to her room.

Gabe couldn't repress a smile as he dressed for the evening. It had been a long time since he'd had a real puzzle to solve, and this one had as many twists and turns as the maze at Sterling's manor house in Sussex. The bonus was the presence of Ms. Jenny Tyler. He'd joined her in the shower with the purest of intentions. Or so he'd thought. Instead, the moment he'd touched her water-slick skin his hormones had gone on red alert.

Beneath the prim, tailored clothing she favored was the toned, subtly sexy body of a swimsuit model. Classy swimsuits, he decided—none of those cheesy string bikinis.

He buttoned the neck of his silk shirt and slipped a discreetly patterned necktie beneath the collar, frowning as he concentrated on the intricate knot he favored. Jenny Tyler also had a discouraging tendency to shrink away from him every time her body began to warm up. Gabe's experience with women was wide and varied. He liked women, and women liked him. Only once before had he encountered that built-in withdrawal. The woman had been a rape victim.

Not for the first time, he wondered what kind of a life Jenny Tyler had lived with Trent Travino.

In spite of Gabe's glib assurance that they would be safe in the hotel restaurant, Jenny was a mass of nerves. She dropped the pale blue, silk knit dress twice as she attempted to slip it over her head. Shock carryover from the explosion, she told herself. All right, admit it, the encounter with Gabe in the shower had shaken her. Even more disturbing was his stated intention of sticking with her until he untangled the web of danger that became more intense with every hour. Common sense, and the internal response of her body each time he touched her, told her that at some point . . . What would she tell him when the time came?

Inspecting herself in the mirror, she realized even generous application of blusher and eye shadow failed to make her eyes appear anything but haunted. She drew in a deep breath and sent up a real prayer, not the garbled pleas she'd fashioned after the explosion. Then, reassured by the weight of her gun in her tote, she stepped into the sitting room. A harsh sound greeted her, as if the breath had been forced from Gabe's chest.

"Ms. Tyler. You should have warned me."

Puzzled, Jenny looked down at herself. The neckline of her sleeveless sheath was wide, catching at her shoulders and swooping modestly in front and back. The ankle-length skirt clung, but respectably, or so she thought. She took another step, then remembered the slit which bared her left leg to above the knee. Even then . . . "You're exaggerating," she protested.

"Christ, everything else I've seen you wear has been buttoned to your chin and practically zipped at the ankle."

The heat in his eyes disconcerted her. Although aware every word they spoke was overheard, she took refuge in counterattack. "If you'll recall, your operative selected this from my closet. I would never have packed anything so dressy, but you told me to look my best, and this was the only suitable thing in my luggage." She looked accusingly at his immaculate silk suit and shirt. "Or would you rather I dressed like your poor relation from out of town?"

He shrugged and reached for the doorknob. "You just surprised me, that's all. You clean up real good, Jenny."

"I'm overwhelmed by your approval," she said as they stepped into the hall. A small corner of her heart smiled.

As the elevator doors opened, Gabe glanced at his watch. "We're right on time, our reservation's for nine-thirty." He rested his arm casually around her waist while they descended, then leaned close to her ear as they exited. "Check out every single person you see this evening. If anyone looks familiar, I want you to point them out to me. Can you be subtle about it?"

The question pricked at Jenny's temper. "You mean I'm not to leap to my feet and wave my arms? Really, Gabe, I'm not completely ignorant." She tried to pull free of his hold, but his fingers tightened against her hipbone. "Of course, if you continue to stay this close, all I need do is jab you with my elbow."

"Just being cautious is all. I don't want some lowlife to peel you away from me in this crowd."

The smile that accompanied his low-voiced explanation showed his dimple, and Jenny gritted her teeth. When he decided to employ it, Gabe Daniels projected a devastating amount of charm. Dismayed by the prospect of being the object of his public attention for the evening, Jenny tried to bolster her spirits by reassuring herself that she had been immunized to masculinity.

Their table was in a corner opposite the door. As they wove their way between the tables, a distinguished, white-haired man rose from a chair to their right. "Miss Tyler?" he said questioningly. "Jennifer Tyler?"

Jenny paused and said hesitantly, "That's my name, but I don't believe . . ."

Cheeks reddening, he apologized. "Of course. It was so long ago. You accompanied your parents when they spoke to my church about their mission trip to Iraq. I'm Reverend James Whitehead of First Universalist Church in New Haven." He held out his hand. "Your family made an immense impression on me that day, and we were talking about them just last week, so when I saw you . . ."

Jenny took his hand and squeezed it reassuringly. "Of course. I should have remembered." She turned to her right. "This is my . . . friend. Gabe Daniels."

"Glad to meet you, Daniels," Whitehead said, extending his hand. "Will you folks be in town long?"

"Oh, a week, anyway. We want to see the sights, maybe make a trip to the track," Gabe said vaguely.

Jenny glanced over her shoulder at the host, who stood drumming his fingers against the menus in his hand. "Our table's ready, we'd better go. So nice to see you again, Reverend Whitehead."

When they were seated and alone, Gabe scowled and hissed, "Iraq, for God's sake. Your parents must be loony tunes. It's a wonder they weren't thrown in prison."

"Children there were starving, Gabe," Jenny reminded him as she picked up her menu. "You might like to know one other thing, however. I never accompanied my parents when they spoke in churches. If he heard Blanton and Irene Cartwright speak he must have the memory of a cucumber. Tyler is my mother's maiden name. Believe me, I've never seen that man before in my life, any more than he's seen me."

ELEVEN

Gabe pretended to scan the nineteenth-century decor with appreciation. "What happened to that guy? I don't see him."

"He and his party are gone," Jenny informed him. "They left while we were being seated."

He reached inside his jacket, fumbled at the pocket, and pulled out a hammered silver cigar case.

"You can't smoke in here, Gabe."

"I don't intend to. I just wanted to show you my birthday present from Sterling." Gabe flipped one end open and began sliding the case around the surface of the table. "Pretty thing, isn't it?" He reached for her hand and squeezed her fingers tightly. When she nodded, he said, "See how the light changes the surface of the silver?" He held the gadget up so she could see it. The strip of tiny jewels, part of the design, pulsed.

"May I see it?"

He gave her the miniature bug sweeper and she moved the heavy silver case cautiously across her side of the table. Then he took it back and hitched the tablecloth over his knees while he swept beneath the table. A tiny beep sounded.

"Might I be of any assistance?"

Gabe looked up into the waiter's face. The young man's eyes implied that although he'd already seen everything, the two of them had just made the top ten. Gabe frowned and said, "It felt as if I might have snagged my suit pants when I sat down, and I was checking for a rough place on the table."

"I'm so sorry. Perhaps you would be more comfortable with different seating." The waiter gestured toward a table farther along the wall.

Jenny was already gathering her tote. "Let's not take any chances, Gabe. You've had such ghastly luck with your suits lately."

Settled at the new table and their drink order taken, an unfamiliar sound caught Gabe unawares: Jenny's laughter. "Do that again," he ordered. Light sparkled in her eyes, which reflected the blue of her dress. "I've never heard you laugh before."

Her expression sobered, but a ghost of mirth lingered in her eyes. She shook out her napkin, spread it across her lap and picked up her menu. "I used to. Laugh, that is. After today, I would have said I'd never laugh again." Her lips quirked in an irrepressible smile. "But if you'd seen yourself with your arm beneath the table . . ." Laughter shook her slender shoulders.

"The waiter thought I was trying to cop a feel," he replied, dazzled. Her smile stole his breath. The fear and sadness had disappeared from her blue-green eyes, and her whole face lit up like a child's at the circus. Her sleek blonde hair, shifting color in the candlelight, swung forward along her elegant jawline. He wanted to plunge his fingers into the shining silk and hold her face still, capturing all that light and happiness.

Jenny giggled again. "That wouldn't have shocked him half so much as if you'd admitted what you were really doing."

"I was just being cautious." As if to back up his statement, he checked their new table. "I made the reservation at the same time I booked our suite. I wondered if the line was tapped."

"Not everyone carries a cigar case that . . . secures an area. Did I use the right word?"

"Close enough." He leaned to one side as his single malt, with cubes on the side, was set in front of him. When they were alone again, he said, "Watch the room." His libido was running wild, as it had since he'd surprised her in the shower an hour earlier. Gabe pulled himself together. The next few days were going to be hazardous enough without sexual complications. The lady deserved better than a randy knight for protection. Looking up, he saw her watching him. Regret filled her eyes as she moved her head slowly from side to side. Without thinking, he asked, "Do you read minds?"

Jenny sipped her vodka and tonic before answering. "No, I read your eyes." She rested narrow fingers on his sleeve. "I apologize for being so difficult the past few days. You can't imagine how desperately I wish none of this had happened, that we had met under different circumstances. This afternoon made me realize the extent of the risks you and Sterling's people have taken on my behalf." She sipped her drink once more, as if to fortify herself. When she spoke again she stared at a point somewhere over his left shoulder.

"I'd be dishonest if I didn't admit I'm attracted to you, Gabe. Unfortunately I don't think I'm fit for any man. Not ever again."

A sick feeling clutched at Gabe's stomach. "That sonovabitch didn't . . ."

"No. No, I was never physically abused." She clasped her hands around her drink. "He . . . I . . . in spite of everything, I enjoyed that aspect of our marriage. But then I came to hate myself because I did. Particularly since my love for Trent died before we'd been married a year. Even more so because he knew and didn't care. He considered me a possession. This doesn't make sense, but hating myself made me hate him even more."

"He was your husband," Gabe said harshly. "You loved him when you married him. And you're a healthy young woman." As he reached for her fingers to warm them, he saw her features grow taut. "What is it?"

"A man just came in. I can't think of his name, but he came to Sunday dinner at Uncle G.'s several times." She shrank back into her chair, as if hiding from the newcomer. "He's sitting at the table to the left of the door. And he's staring at us."

Satisfaction made Gabe smile again. He patted her fingers. "Good. I'll look him over shortly. Then the other one was probably a Kamanedes plant. All present and accounted for. Now that I know both sides have picked us up, I'll figure out a way to ditch them so we can be on our way." He opened his menu, then looked up. The corners of her mouth had drooped again.

"Jenny, you have me on your side, whether you sleep with me or not." Her troubled, blue-green gaze swept up to meet his. "I can read eyes, too. I wasn't completely honest with you. Sterling told me to do whatever was necessary to settle this for you, but he made a point of saying he'd have my ass if I hurt you. That's his way of telling me to keep my hands to myself." He was rewarded with a small smile. "But Sterling never said I couldn't tell you I want you. Bad."

He ran his index finger along her jawline. Her skin was like satin. "Relax. I won't lay a finger on you unless you ask." Refusing to look away, he watched her eyes widen. Satisfied, he picked up his menu. "What looks good to you?"

Waking early the next morning, Jenny padded to the window and pulled back the drapes. A tentative sun was rising on the eastern horizon, but the sky overhead was filled with moody clouds. The day ahead looked the way she felt—edgy and apprehensive. Gabe's words last night had swirled through her subconscious, haunting her dreams each time she dozed off.

Gabe. Since Trent's death, she'd felt such guilty delight in her freedom that the last thing in her mind was the possibility of another man. She'd had her art, and her entire being had been consumed with expressing her joy on canvas after canvas. At some point, she knew, she would plunge back into exhibiting, allowing art critics to pass judgment on her work. That knowledge, rather than stressing her, hovered in her future like a treat. Her only concern had been healing the scars of her emotional imprisonment.

Now she'd been thrust back into the world of violence she'd fled with such relief, and into the company of a man.

Gabe Daniels possessed traits she despised—roughness and arrogance—but he'd become her protector. And God help her, she was attracted to him. The more time she spent in his company, the more she sensed the value of the person behind his facade. But he demanded too much control. She wondered if there was some flaw in her makeup, a flag that made dominant males attempt to ride roughshod over her.

Gabe had promised not to take their relationship any further unless she asked, but a part of her wanted to do just that, and Jenny despised herself for being so hungry for affection, no matter what form it took.

She wrapped her arms tightly around herself and looked out over the Inner Harbor. Boats of all kinds and sizes were setting out from the dock for a day of pleasure or of work.

Others rode at anchor. The scene was alive, just as her body was coming alive. She watched the dawn, and wondered how long she would be able to resist asking Gabe Daniels to make love to her.

An hour later Gabe rapped on her door. She wrapped her robe more tightly before admitting him. "Breakfast should be here in twenty minutes, sweetheart. Our clothing just arrived."

She accepted the plastic-draped bundles and pasted a saccharine smile on her face as she replied, "I'm nearly ready, love. Did you order me any fruit?" She hated the false endearments nearly as much as she hated the situation in which she found herself.

"Hell, I ordered the whole damn menu. If you're going to insist on seeing every museum and gallery in town, we'll both need our strength," he replied.

Jenny hung the clothing in the closet and surveyed the heap of belongings she'd collected on her bed. The night before, Gabe had instructed her to pack her tote with whatever items were indispensable to her comfort, in case the opportunity to disappear presented itself during the day ahead. The flat zippered case containing her change of identity hid beneath a change of underwear and her deodorant. Her gun and the extra clips of ammunition fit nicely alongside the "indispensables" after she had packed the bag. As an afterthought, she jammed a thin black turtleneck around the pistol.

Selecting camel slacks and a gray-and-white-striped shirt, she dressed quickly. Her gray blazer lay over the back of a chair.

Gabe knocked once more. "The food's getting cold, sweetie. You don't have to scour the tub and make the damn bed. This is a hotel, for God's sake."

She pulled open the door. "You're such a lovable slob. I suppose you left towels all over the floor of the bathroom and the bed in shambles. Just like home," she said in the direction of the bug on the coffee table.

"Why not? This place is charging enough to pay for three maids up here," he said, arching his left eyebrow in her direction. "I'm ready to get on the road. The concierge promised to have a cab for us in less than an hour."

"Gabe, you don't have to go to the Museum of Art with me. I'll probably want to spend the whole day. You can go to the Aquarium, or something else you'd enjoy more," Jenny teased, beginning to enjoy the farce they were acting out. She walked to the room service table and lifted a carafe of grapefruit juice.

Close behind her, Gabe said sunnily, "You insult me, sweetheart. You know I'm looking forward to seeing the Picassos."

Unsure whether he was teasing or serious, Jenny poured a glass of juice and removed the domed covers. "You're a big fan of his, are you?"

Their gushing discussion of art continued through breakfast. When they stepped into the unoccupied elevator an hour later, Gabe growled, "If whoever was listening knows anything about me, they probably think I've gone around the bend."

"I thought we did quite well." Jenny eyed Gabe's briefcase of communications equipment. "I assume all that is more necessary to you than a clean shirt."

The elevator door opened and Gabe waved her out, his eyes dark with laughter. "Damn straight."

Jenny realized he was enjoying the cat and mouse game. When he assisted her into the taxi, he flashed her a delighted grin and pointed to the driver's photograph and license. "This makes my day. What do you bet he doesn't speak English."

She attempted to pronounce the collection of consonants that made up the driver's name, then said, "I give up. Where is he from?"

Gabe flashed a look behind them, smiled even wider, said, "Syria," and then addressed a series of questions to the driver in a foreign tongue.

Amazed, Jenny listened as the driver unleashed a barrage of words, frequently pausing to smile at Gabe in the rearview mirror as he navigated the cab north through the traffic.

Ten minutes into the trip Gabe sat back with a satisfied expression on his face.

"What on earth was all that about?" Jenny demanded.

Gabe's eyes were shuttered. "Harry, as he's called now, is an old friend who's going to make arrangements for us. We'll take off late this afternoon."

A stutter of fear bubbled in Jenny's throat. Even though she'd known they would leave at anytime, she couldn't suppress her apprehension. "Where are we going?"

Gabe's expression was shuttered as the cab gathered speed on its trip north on Charles. "Where the wind takes us."

"How poetic," she snapped. Once again she had been put in her place. Do as you're told, when you're told, and ask no questions. She was all too familiar with the drill. Fine. She'd look at pictures. And she wouldn't ask Gabe Daniels for anything.

Four hours later, Jenny decided she couldn't pretend to appreciate one more painting. Not with her nerves jumping each time anyone came near. Gazing around longingly, she promised herself to come back someday when one half of her mind wasn't frozen with fear and the other half burning with anger. Gabe had never left her side. Nor had he set down the soft-sided black briefcase. She wondered if his shoulders were as stiff from its weight as hers were from her tote. "Surely we're not still being followed," she protested as Gabe steered her toward the exit.

"That broad in the Budweiser shirt and jeans and the weedy-looking twerp with the ponytail have been as close to us as lovers ever since we left the cab," he said, speaking from the side of his mouth. "They should team up. They're a match made in heaven." They rounded the corner and approached a row of taxis. "Maybe they'll get together after we leave them in our dust."

Suddenly Jenny wanted to throw herself on the sidewalk and kick her heels. He still hadn't shared one hint as to their destination and how they were to avoid being followed. "I'm hungry," she said petulantly, hoping to goad him into anger.

Gabe selected the third cab from the front and jockeyed her into the backseat. "I told you to eat that last brioche this morning," he said reproachfully.

"Where are we going now?" Jenny demanded.

"Inner Harbor," Gabe told the driver.

Her stomach growled, and she realized hunger really was part of her problem. "You're going to feed me when we get there, aren't you?"

He inclined his head warningly toward their driver. "Can't have you fainting on me, can I?"

Recalling her earlier worry that she might not be able to resist asking the man to make love to her, Jenny formed a new resolve. She would kill him and feed him to piranhas before she allowed such a thought to enter her head again.

From the corner of her eye she caught the tail end of a self-satisfied grin curving his lips. Biting back an insult that would lower her to his level, she pretended to be absorbed in the passing buildings.

Her feelings mellowed somewhat when Gabe led her into Harborplace. Beset by the aromas of foods of every description, Jenny's stomach rumbled again. Under pretense of tucking his shirt collar back beneath his coat, she murmured, "How much time do I have?"

Beneath her fingers, his chest heaved with laughter as he whispered, "An hour or two. If you're lucky. Don't eat too much junk. I don't need you puking your guts all over the car."

Jenny pulled away from the path of his warm breath along the side of her neck. She smiled as if she'd just been given a preview of the Second Coming. "You're disgusting," she cooed.

An hour later, revived by a cup of hearty soup and a Greek salad, Jenny dragged Gabe through the shops, playing the role of an obsessive shopper insistent on inspecting every item. "I have such a wonderful time looking, but my shelves and closets are full," she confided to an elderly clerk. From across the shop, she saw Gabe nod toward the door. "Oh, dear. I think I'm being hurried along." She returned the silk scarf, patting the woman's hand as she did so. "You've been patient. I appreciate it."

She wove her way through the crowd to Gabe and followed him, making a show of describing every piece of merchandise she'd inspected as they exited the shop and left the pavilion. Jenny's nerves jumped at every sound. The random appearances of both of their tails in the crowded tourist trap had made her feel like a teenager in a carnival fun house.

A picture of casual indifference, Gabe took her arm. At the curb, a nondescript gray car with its motor running lingered beneath a No Parking sign. Moving swiftly, he opened the back door, tossed his briefcase on the seat and thrust her inside. As he crowded in behind her, Jenny shoved his case to the floor and edged away from the brush of his hard thigh.

Harry, their taxi driver from that morning, pulled away from the curb and merged with the late afternoon traffic.

"Don't look back," Gabe ordered, his grip on her nape directing her face forward. "Anyone behind us, Harry?"

In perfect English, the Syrian replied, "Just two ill-dressed tourists standing on the sidewalk looking stupid."

After they pulled into the seemingly derelict warehouse and the huge overhead door rumbled closed, Gabe grunted with satisfaction. In the dim light of two bare overhead bulbs, he could see the dark blue BMW sedan parked along one wall. "You do good work, Harry." He hefted his case and eased out of the car, then turned to help a shaken Jenny join him. "I thought I knew the city, but I've never seen some of those alleys."

Harry's only answer was a white-toothed grin before he disappeared into a derelict office. When he returned he handed Gabe a large manila envelope. "The keys and a new identity, if you need it, are in here. The maps are in the glove compartment. Watch your temper. There are orange barrels everywhere."

"That figures. Damn bureaucrats tear up roads all over the country as soon as the snow melts," Gabe grumbled.

"Do you think you'll require a new identity?" Jenny demanded.

"Sure. I didn't want you to be able to disappear by yourself." He watched her expressive features for the explosion.

She didn't disappoint. "You searched my tote, you . . . you lowlife!"

Gabe winked at Harry, who was watching the exchange and wearing a wide grin. "I just checked to make sure you didn't have a switchblade in there to go with your gun." He held out his hand to the Syrian. "Thanks for everything. We should be clear now."

"Glad to help out. I'll raise the back door for you, then leave the way I came in. Give my regards to Bill."

Gabe set out for the BMW. "Come on, 'Tess.' How in hell did you come up with that name?" A thought struck him. "Who made up that paper for you? Don't tell me it was a friend of Cousin Tania."

"What a silly idea. My agent procured them for me a year ago through a cousin of hers who is a computer nerd."

He smiled down at the neat part in her shining hair as he helped her into the passenger seat. She was so self-sufficient it was difficult to imagine her living as a gangster's trophy wife. How did she intend to escape? "Travino's execution kind of made all your planning unnecessary, didn't it?" He closed the door and rounded the front end, removing his suit coat and tie as he went.

Tossing his jacket into the backseat, he unbuttoned his top shirt button with one hand, pulled a bulky turtleneck from a plastic bag on the driver's side and tugged it over his head. He then retrieved a gray beret from the bottom of the bag and handed it to Jenny. "Put this on so it covers the right side of your head and shields your profile."

He settled into the driver's seat and twisted the key in the ignition. While the motor idled, he squeezed the contents of a small tube onto his fingers and massaged it through his hair. After several quick swipes with a pocket comb, he glanced in the rearview mirror before turning on the headlights. Gabe grinned. He looked like a tight-ass stockbroker on dress-down Friday.

When the metal door clanked upward, he eased the car out onto the street and headed west, following a series of residential streets until he was clear of the city.

"Would you please be so kind as to tell me where we're going?" Jenny inquired.

"New York." The steel in her voice told him she was furious, but Gabe could come up with only five or six things he'd done recently to annoy her. "You might as well unload why you're so pissed off. Don't pull that woman crap and simmer while you tell me I should be able to guess."

A feminine version of a growl erupted from her throat before she demanded, "Woman crap! Are you accusing me of trying to manipulate you?"

Her indignation delighted him. Jenny hadn't lost her spirit, and she'd need it in the days ahead. "Damned if you're not. Back at the Harborplace, when you were pretending to be normal, you jabbered like a twit. Now I'll probably have to turn on the heater to melt the frost on the windows." Gabe selected a cross street that led to a state highway. "Spit it out. You'll feel better. Start with screaming about me searching your tote. Just don't pretend you wouldn't have broken into my computer if I hadn't locked the case."

"You undoubtedly have your files protected with obscure passwords anyway," she said dismissively. "All right. I tried. But I couldn't open the case."

"I know. The lock records unauthorized attempts."

"That's what infuriates me," Jenny said stonily. She lowered the visor against the setting sun. "You're Mr. Control Freak. Back at the hotel, you ordered me to take only what

I could pack in my tote, because we might leave unexpectedly. Does it occur to you I might be concerned about where I'll sleep tonight? At the museum, you couldn't be bothered to confide where we were headed. You took it for granted I'd ask how high when you said 'Jump!' "

With a clenched fist, she scrubbed at a tear which had escaped her brimming eyes and rolled down her cheek. "I spent six years being manipulated and coerced into doing whatever someone else dictated. I refuse to live like that again. I'd rather die."

Gabe remembered his overwhelming frustration when his freedom had been taken from him. He had responded with rebellion, not tears, too caught up in his own misery to recognize the lifeline dangling in front of him. Somehow, he had to convince Jenny he was her lifeline—and then he had to prove it.

Anger, disappointment and fear consumed Jenny in equal parts. Tears she'd denied herself when she was in much direr straits now flowed steadily, and she couldn't stop them.

So immersed was she in her misery that she didn't notice the car pull to a stop behind a deserted gas station, nor did she feel the tug of her seat belt as it released. The enveloping warmth of Gabe's embrace as he pulled her against his chest was shocking, but welcome. "Christ, Jenny. I didn't mean to make you cry." His big hand cupped the back of her head and pressed her face beneath his chin. He rocked her gently. Beneath her cheek, his turtleneck was damp from her tears. She snuffled against her fist, which still rested against her cheek, trapped between them. "I'm . . . so angry . . . and so frustrated."

"You're having a perfectly normal reaction." Gabe released her, freed her trapped arm and drew her back against his chest. "I know I promised to keep my hands off you, and if you tell anyone who knows me I said this I'll have to kill you . . . but you need a big-time hug right now."

His blatantly out-of-character statement banished her tears. A hiccup of laughter gathered in the back of Jenny's throat. The warmth gathering in the region below her stomach sent out tentacles, vanquishing the hiccup. True to his words, Gabe's hands were impersonal where they rested on her back, but his heartbeat beneath her cheek had accelerated. Laying one hand on the side of his neck, she felt the tension in his muscles.

Curving her fingers around his nape, she turned her face into his and rubbed her forehead against the whiskers which had been visible since shortly after noon. Their softness surprised her. "Gabe. What would be your reaction if I asked you to put your hands on me? And not with the intent to comfort, the way they are now."

Gabe was silent for a moment. The expression on his face when she glanced up at him startled her. He looked as if he were in pain. Then his lips parted and he said only one word: "Shit."

TWELVE

Gabe felt as if he'd just been punched in the gut. He knew his reaction showed when Jenny's features closed. She pulled away. Good job, Gabe. Reaching for her, he cupped his hands around her face—Jesus, they looked like hams next to her delicate features!—holding her still in spite of her determined struggle to retreat to the far corner of her seat.

"Let me go."

"Not until you listen to me," he gritted through clenched teeth. Now wasn't the time to tell her he'd planned to stash her away safe until he'd eliminated the threats to her life and safety. Or should he just bite the bullet and admit the truth, that he didn't think a one-night stand or an affair with her would ever be enough for him? The damn woman had gotten under his skin like a chigger. Her response to their kiss still lingered in his senses.

Gabe looked at her closed expression, and his heart turned over. He should have known she'd cry efficiently. A slight puffiness below her closed eyes was the only remaining sign of her tears. Long, dark lashes spiked with moisture fanned across her high cheekbones. The last of the sunset cast a glow over her fair skin. She sniffled. Reassured she was at least human in that respect, he dug in his back pocket for a handkerchief, which she accepted gratefully.

When she finished patting her eyes and blowing her nose, he tossed the crumpled linen on the dash and captured her face again. He wanted her, here, now. And he couldn't have her. Not without telling her the truth. Hell. Someone was bound to let the snake out of the sack, one way or another. He was still surprised she hadn't picked up on Sadie's slip in the kitchen of the Baltimore house. "We should probably get out of here before I do something stupid, like take you up on your offer," he said. The words sounded feeble even to him.

Concentrating carefully on the task, he settled Jenny in her seat and refastened her seat belt. When she didn't respond, he rested his hand on her knee, massaging gently. "Don't look so embarrassed. I know you didn't make that offer lightly. And I wasn't turning you down. It's just that there are things you'd better know about me before we turn that page."

Jenny retrieved his handkerchief from the dash and worried it between her fingers. "You don't have to . . ." Her voice dwindled. Her gaze remained fixed on her hands in her lap.

Gabe shifted into drive and turned back onto the highway. "Oh, yes, I do. You grew up sheltered. Then you fell in with the front man for a mob. There's nothing to be ashamed of for making that mistake; his stock-in-trade was fooling people who'd been around a hell of a lot more than you had. Now maybe you're thinking that since you've already trashed your future, you might as well give in and sleep with another gangster type."

From the corner of his eye he saw her flinch. Maybe he'd hit closer than he realized. "Sterling's my grandfather. The old bastard saved me from the juvie tank when I was twelve."

"How . . . how did that happen?"

From the disbelief in her voice, he could tell the idea had never crossed her mind. "When my mother was seventeen, she ran away to marry a motorcycle junkie. At the time, Sterling hadn't made it big yet, and he didn't have the resources or the savvy to track her down. As soon as he'd come up in the world, he did. My old man had ridden off with his friends when I was five, and until he found us, my mother worked two dead-end jobs to keep us in a tenement in Chicago." The memory hurt, even now. His mother had been so exhausted each night she'd cried herself to sleep, and he'd repaid her by sneaking out to roam the streets with the most degenerate types he could find.

Her voice held confusion when she asked, "Why didn't she go back home?"

"Stubborn pride. She hated to admit she'd been foolish. As you might have noticed, I inherited a fair share of that little commodity. Anyway, after my third arrest for petty theft, a judge decided I was incorrigible, and sentenced me to a juvenile detention center." He risked a sideways glance to gauge her reaction. She didn't look horrified, so he continued. "My mother had run out of choices, and she fell all over herself apologizing to Sterling when he showed up and bargained with the judge."

"I suppose he offered to finance the judge's next reelection campaign," Jenny said wryly.

Her quick, cynical reply amused Gabe. "Yeah. Sterling also promised him that if he couldn't shape me up, the state of Illinois could have me back . . . in a box. Then he sent me to military school. That first year was pure hell. Reform school couldn't have been worse. Sterling even planted his own man on the staff, to keep tabs on me. I couldn't break a pencil point without the ax falling, and I hoarded resentment like chocolate bars. By the second year, I'd learned to go along with everything. I planned to sucker Sterling into thinking I'd seen the light, figuring he'd let me go to a regular school."

"One where you could get back to your old routine."

Not really surprised by her insight, Gabe asked, "How did you know that?" A faint smile curved her lips. She'd removed the beret, and her hair glowed silver-gold in the streetlights. His mouth went dry at the thought of disrupting the tidy chin-length cut with his fingers. He swallowed.

"My parents are do-gooders, remember? Whenever I was with them, they'd discuss their project of the moment. For two years during my teens, they attempted to set up a rehab program for juvenile delinquents. Resistance like yours was one of the pitfalls they had to overcome. When did you see the light?"

Gabe hadn't talked about Lowell Friedel to many people, but he found himself opening up. "The school had an assistant commandant who read me like a book. One day, when I was brown-nosing in a big way, he called me into his office and explained the facts of life. Said he'd rather deal with me as a bad-ass than watch me turn into a manipulator. He challenged me to grow up to be somebody I could live with. He beat it into my head that I was the only person I'd always have with me." He smiled at the memory. "Not terrifically profound, but I was such a dirtball I'd never thought beyond the next scam, and he got through to me."

Jenny rolled her eyes as the light dawned. "So now you're respectable, but you keep in practice by going out of your way to drive your grandfather crazy."

Gabe grimaced. "Every chance I get. Keeps him on his toes. Anyway, I did everything the old man wanted. I went to law school and I learned how the government works. Spent ten years with the DEA. When I realized Sterling wasn't getting any younger, I resigned and took the job he'd been dangling ever since I'd gotten out of law school. He signs my paycheck, and I damn well earn it. He tells me what to wear, and where to be. But I'm still a tough Chicago street kid. And I never let him forget it."

He smiled, suddenly remembering Jenny's expression the night the Donhaven police chief had taken him to her home. "Hell, all he has to do is look at me. I may wear a two-thousand-dollar suit, but I still look like a gangster. When he took us in, he insisted that my mother change our name. He didn't like having a grandson named Danieli. It reminded him of my no-good father."

Jenny looked at him shrewdly. "You haven't changed at all. You manipulate him constantly, don't you."

Uncomfortable with her perception, Gabe kept his gaze focused on the highway ahead. His next admission surprised him. "Yeah, I suppose you're right. Except that I actually love the old goat. I just haven't told him yet."

He laughed shortly, then continued, "He knows my game. I conform just enough to make him happy, and every once in a while he reels me in, just to let me know he's on to me. I enjoy my job a hell of a lot more than I would have liked a life sentence in a penitentiary. Even so, when the old bastard dies, I'm changing my name back to Danieli. Before my mother died ten years ago, I promised her I would. And Sterling knows it." He grinned as he recalled his grandfather's response to his announcement.

"Perhaps he enjoys the game as much as you do."

Gabe shrugged, then decided he might as well tell her the complete truth. "Since I'm into honesty, I have to tell you what I've planned next. We're heading for my place in New York. My friend Bill and I rehabbed an old warehouse, and we each have apartments on the top floor. Most of the first floor is leased out, but the middle floors are empty.

The security is as good as it gets. I intended to stash you there, then go tackle Uncle G. myself." He was afraid to risk looking at her.

"You really are a son of a bitch, aren't you."

Gabe winced, although coming from her lips, the curse sounded elegant. Her voice had lowered, not risen, and every finishing school inflection had been intact. "Probably. Dammit, we're treading a high wire between the Travinos and the Kamanedes. It's going to be dangerous as hell."

"And of course the poor little woman must be protected. Has it ever occurred to you I might be helpful?"

He'd had a vision of furnishing her with painting supplies and leaving her in his loft to wallow in creativity while he killed every dragon that threatened her. And in the back of his mind he'd nurtured a nebulous dream of the form her gratitude would take. With a sense of foreboding, he recalled the outrageous plan Bill had laid out for him in his last scrambled E-mail. The plan he'd rejected out of hand. In spite of its effective simplicity, the scheme was so fraught with danger Gabe had nearly taken Jenny back to Palm Springs and left her there.

Now he was on the horns of a dilemma. If he stashed her, she'd hate him forever, but Bill's scenario would put her in grave danger. The thought of using Jenny that way made cold sweat break out on the back of his neck.

If Gabe hadn't been driving sixty-five miles an hour on the Pennsylvania Turnpike, Jenny would have hit him with her gun a second time. How had she ever allowed herself to feel anything for such a clod? She thought back over the past few days. Until yesterday, he'd reported their every move to Sterling. Now, with the industrialist out of the picture, Gabe was free to devote himself to protecting her.

Although he gave all appearances of having taken charge, he suffered from a severe case of male hysteria. The idiot planned to lock her away while he went out to play macho games. Unable to resist, she said, "After the way you were forced into the straight and narrow, I suppose my complaints about having no control over my life struck you as pretty funny."

"Your life with Travino was more like captivity. At least Sterling took me out of jail and turned me into something. I was his salvage project. You don't need rehabilitation, you need protection. I just want to make sure you survive."

"Which means doing exactly as you tell me."

He shifted uncomfortably, then sighed. "Exactly how much do you want to be involved?" he demanded.

Jenny's heart leaped into her throat. "I'll do anything. I don't care how dangerous it is," she said steadily.

"That's what I thought you'd say. Damn!" He massaged the back of his neck. "Yesterday I turned down an idea Bill came up with because it would send you right back into the lion's den. Dammit, if you want the honest truth, the thing scares the hell out of me. Everything hinges on luck, and on you doing exactly what you're told. Your ass would be on the line," he said savagely, pounding his fist on the steering wheel.

His voice was emotionless as he continued, "I don't want to talk about it anymore. We'll settle this later."

She looked at the grim set of his jaw and pushed aside the questions clamoring for answers. "I hope you know I'll do anything . . . anything, to get out from under this."

His reply was a surly grunt.

"Are you sure no one will know where we are?"

He glanced in the rearview mirror. "We got away clear. They didn't have enough people to box us in. By the way, how were you going to use that fake ID?"

Unnerved by his sudden change of subject, Jenny said, "My agent suggested the idea a year before Trent was killed." Alice Darnley had always been someone she could count on.

The thought made Jenny think of Tania; she pushed aside the memory of her naive trust. "Trent mistrusted my visits to her office to conduct business. He always sent two goons with me to make sure I didn't try to escape, and it enraged Alice."

Gabe swore as he accelerated around an eighteen-wheeler.

Jenny smiled. "Those were Alice's exact words. She encouraged me to grab the first chance I could to leave him, and mentioned her cousin who . . ."

"Dabbled on the wrong side of the law? For a nice girl, you don't seem to have skipped many chances to deal with criminals."

"Actually, the cousin is quite reputable," Jenny replied primly, determined not to respond to Gabe's delighted smile. "I hid a decent nest egg from my royalties under my new name. By the time Trent died, Alice had already arranged the lease on the house in Donhaven. My only problem was to get Uncle G. to release me. If anyone had known what I already had in place, they would have suspected me of murdering Trent and . . . I wouldn't have gotten away." She didn't want to think of the terror-filled weeks following the funeral. Pushing the memory from her mind, she settled more comfortably into the seat and leaned her head back.

"Don't tell me Alice gave Uncle G. an earful."

"No." After Tania's betrayal, she didn't want to relive what came next, but she had no choice. "Tania did. She reminded him that she and he were the only ones in the family who actually liked me, and asked him if he wanted me to be happy. Knowing what I do now, I can't imagine why she did that. Maybe she wanted me away from the family, where she could get to me."

Reliving that terrifying time had exhausted her, and whatever lay ahead would require all her resources. Jenny realized she had operated on adrenaline ever since she'd discovered DeWitt's body. Now Gabe was taking her back to New York, where she'd been imprisoned and unhappy. To New York, where she intended to put herself at risk. "I can't talk about this anymore, Gabe. I simply have to sleep," she said, closing her eyes.

Rainwater flushed the streets early the next morning when Gabe pulled into his garage on New York's Lower East Side. His Porsche and a battered Ford pickup truck shared the brightly lit space with the black limo parked in one corner. If Jenny went along with this crazy scheme, they'd need the variety of wheels. He activated the door behind them and switched off the ignition.

Then he turned in the seat to watch Jenny sleep. Lines of concentration creased her forehead; even in her dreams, she appeared to be fighting for control of her life. A segment of his heart he'd never known existed contracted.

They'd stopped only once, for gas, the bathroom, and a quick snack. He'd had to wake her to accompany him, and she'd sleepwalked through the entire break. Otherwise, her sleep hadn't been peaceful. Her restless movements indicated terror so deep she'd cried out, interrupting his detailed instructions to Bill over the cell phone. He'd nearly stopped the car to comfort her.

Leaning over, he brushed his knuckles down her cheek,

rested his hand against her shoulder and murmured, "Jenny. We're here."

She stirred beneath his touch, then came awake with a start. Her eyelids rose jerkily and she struggled to sit up straight. "Where are we?" Knuckling sleep out of her eyes, she peered out the window.

"New York, remember?" As he went around to help her from the car and guide her into the ancient freight elevator, Gabe prayed the plan he'd put in motion wouldn't self-destruct. He pulled the metal grill closed and pressed a button. The open cage inched noisily upward.

"A bachelor's pad for your wild flings on the town?"

"Yeah. I'm a real sonovabitch when I hit the bright lights," he growled.

The elevator stopped, opening into a small, brick-walled inner courtyard. Driving spring rain pounded on skylights high overhead. Gabe released the grill and ushered her across the brick floor to the heavy steel door of his loft. He pressed his hand on the screen beside the frame. The door swung open. Even with rain sluicing down the broad windows reaching nearly to the roof, entering the room gave him a sense of peace. "How do you like it?"

Jenny looked up at the double skylights in the ceiling. Then she moved like a sleepwalker to the wall of glass and peered out. "This looks like an artist's studio," she said. "Can people see in when it's not raining?"

"We're eight stories up, but there are automatic shutters. Just in case." Gabe gestured to the computerized panel beside the door. He set his bulging briefcase on the floor and announced, "I'm going up to bed." He gestured to the left of the wrought-iron stair curving up to the balcony that fronted the second level. "There should be food. Bill's cleaning service was supposed to stock the kitchen and get things ready."

Jenny wandered into the kitchen, opening doors and checking the contents of the freezer and refrigerator. After scanning the interior, she took out a gallon of milk and filled a goblet from the rack above the sink. "There's certainly enough food here. You really did mean to lock me away, didn't you." She drank thirstily.

Still struggling to clear his fatigue-blurred mind, Gabe was in no mood to argue with her accusation. He plunged his hands through his hair, breaking down the gel that had held it flat until now. "Dammit, I've worked things out. You're going to get the chance you wanted to risk your cute little fanny. While I'm asleep, use your superior mind to figure what you want to ask Uncle G. when you see him. And stay away from the phone."

Gabe jerked the sweater over his head by the time his feet hit the third step. His shirt, which was already out of his trousers in back, came off by the seventh tread, rewarding Jenny with a mouthwatering view of his muscular shoulders before he disappeared into the farthest of two doors opening on to the landing. She was so full of conflicting emotions her thoughts reminded her of a whirlpool. Foremost at the moment was an almost irresistible urge to follow him upstairs and run her hands over the smooth skin that stretched tautly over his back each time he moved his arms.

Mortified by her own thoughts, she realized he had neither accepted nor rejected the offer she'd made him. Her old feelings of inadequacy came rushing back. She was too thin; even Trent had said so. She'd cried down the front of Gabe's sweater, whining about the way life had treated her. And then she'd thrown herself at him. How pathetic she must seem.

The door to Gabe's room slammed open and he appeared in the opening, his big body covered only by the towel draped around his hips. "Forgot to tell you. Bill Gates is coming over at five to help me do a computer search and get us set for tonight."

"Bill Gates?" she gasped.

He scowled as if she'd just said something stupid. "Yeah. One of probably two or three thousand in the country. You look like hell. The bedroom and bath next to mine are all yours. Use them." With that he disappeared.

Narrowing her eyes at the closed door to his room, Jenny mouthed all the curses she'd sworn she would never use. Earlier, she'd felt justified in swearing when Gabe had pushed her too far, and now he deserved all the other obscenities she had learned during her marriage. Take a nap? I just might surprise you, you . . . Unable to think of anything strong enough, she crossed the room to his briefcase. Just as before, the computerized lock refused to open.

Other than the wall of windows and the refrigerator, she'd paid scant attention to her surroundings, so she looked around the loft. The walls were flat white, the gleaming walnut floor covered with jewel-toned area rugs. On a sunny day, the room would be ablaze with light and warm color. Even the sumptuous black leather couches and chairs clustered sociably around the rugs wouldn't absorb enough of that brightness to matter. The sheer space of the room intrigued her. She walked around the waist-high glass block wall that defined the dining area.

Four padded chairs on rollers sat around the circular glass table. A tall, flat, paper-wrapped parcel was propped against one chair. Beside it sat two cartons which had been opened but not emptied. Jenny peeked at the contents—paints, acrylics and oils, and brushes and . . . She ripped the paper from the parcel. An easel. She looked around the room once more. Any idiot would know a bachelor owned this place. He had no pictures on the wall.

Jenny shrugged out of her wrinkled blazer and kicked off her shoes. She'd always thought better when her hands were occupied.

Six hours later, she heard a rush of water in the shower. Scurrying across the room, she trashed the core of the apple she'd been nibbling and pushed the last of her paints back into the carton. She scrambled upstairs and slipped into the queen-sized bed, pulled the ticking-striped duvet up around her shoulders and buried her face in the pillows. She knew she wouldn't sleep. Although she'd been exhausted for the last three hours, she'd been unable to stop. Ideas had flowed from her fingertips to the brushes. She yawned. Maybe she could sleep. Painting was so relaxing . . .

Gabe tried to stop laughing as he sent the elevator down in response to Bill's ring. He'd spent the last twenty minutes looking at the mural covering the bottom section of one-third of the longest apartment wall. His loft now sported a flower garden. Wicked caricatures of the faces of all the people he and Jenny had encountered together were embedded in suitable blossoms. The sharp portrait of Tania as a black widow spider vied with that of Sterling peering out from a surround made of chrysanthemum petals as his favorites, although the segmented worm with DeWitt's face had a certain charm. Only Choc appeared as himself, a graceful stretch of cream and dark brown reaching for a fuchsia blossom caricatured in Will's likeness. He wondered what she planned for the remainder of the wall.

Bill stared at him through the elevator grill. "You don't look like the grim soul who woke me out of a sound sleep at midnight with a list of life-and-death errands that absolutely had to be accomplished immediately. Help me out of this thing. My hands are full."

"Were you able to find what we need?" Gabe demanded as he opened the grill.

"Gigi did the honors." He handed Gabe a shiny shopping bag. "I wouldn't be caught dead in one of those boutiques, and I wouldn't recognize hot rollers if they came in a Tiffany box."

"I owe Gigi dinner, then," Gabe replied. He rolled his eyes. "Maybe this is my big chance. I've been trying to convince her to leave you for two years." He sniffed, then lowered his face to the bag in his hand. "Got carried away at the perfume counter, didn't she?" he said before leading the way to the loft.

"You said you wanted something a high-class tart would wear. Gigi really enjoyed . . ." Bill stopped dead in his tracks, his guileless blue eyes round with inquiry.

Gabe wondered if any of the Gates Closed, Inc., employees, or the people who hired him to design their security systems, appreciated the truly devious mind that lurked behind Bill's open, youthful features. With his crew-cut blond hair and perfectly proportioned five-foot, eight-inch body, he looked more like a college cheerleader than a veteran of the government's drug wars. Right now he resembled a stunned ten-year-old. "My house guest was madder than hell at me this morning. I'd had only about eight hours of sleep over the past three or four days, and I crashed after we got here," he explained.

Dropping the two ungainly dress boxes he'd been carrying, Bill walked closer. "Christ! Don't ever let Sterling see this. Is that a Venus flytrap she's painted around you?"

Gabe set down his own burden. "Yeah. When you meet

Jenny you'll understand. She's probably hiding upstairs. I'll go get her."

Stepping as heavily as he could on each tread, Gabe climbed the stairs, calling, "Jenny, you can come out now. Bill's here to protect you."

Jenny burrowed her head beneath the pillow to shut out the vibrations of the staircase and Gabe's shouts. She'd just enjoyed an hour of the deepest sleep she'd had in a week, and her body craved more. Suddenly the meaning of his words sank in. Oh, God, what have I done? She curled into a self-protective ball just before the door opened.

"Your new clothes are downstairs. Don't you want to see what Bill brought you?" He approached the bed, then seized the corner of the mattress with both hands and heaved.

Desperately afraid she would roll to the floor, Jenny let loose of the pillow and grabbed for the edge of the mattress. She glared at him. "I'll come down when I feel like it."

Gabe dropped the mattress back in place and gave her a smile that made her want to wipe the smugness off his face. "Better hurry. You've an assignment tonight, and you need to be bright-eyed. I'll bet you're hungry, too."

With that he turned and left. "If he wants me to swear at him again, I just might oblige," Jenny mumbled to herself as she stripped off her clothes and headed for the shower. At the same time, she was excited. Gabe was keeping his promise.

Fifteen minutes later, her hair blown dry and her wrinkled silk turtleneck tucked into her travel-worn slacks, Jenny descended the staircase calmly, concealing her curiosity behind the mask of poise she'd learned as a child.

Gabe was bent over the shoulder of the collegiate-looking man seated at the computer. As she approached, the stranger said teasingly, "See? They have an extra path in here that shunts an average hacker like you off into space."

"Average hacker, my ass. I got into that Swiss bank's records."

"Banks are too stodgy to protect themselves with anything creative. That's why you got in. Successful crooks, on the other hand, think they're really clever, so they're more of a challenge. What they forget is that some of us law-abiding citizens are even more devious."

"I've always heard it takes a crook to catch another one," Jenny remarked frostily, peering at the screen over the stranger's shoulder.

Neither man acknowledged her for a moment, then Bill added a few scribbled notes to the pad at his left and pressed a key. Jenny glimpsed the name "Kamanedes" just before the screen went blank. The stranger stood and turned toward her. His open features inspired trust, and he could be anywhere between twenty-five and forty. She wondered how he and Gabe had gotten together.

"Glad to meet you, Ms. Tyler. I'm Bill Gates." He extended his hand. "Gabe didn't do you justice when he described you."

His quick squeeze of her fingers was reassuring. "I'm quite sure he referred to me as a 'snooty, tight-assed broad,' " she replied dryly.

"As a matter of fact . . ."

Gabe broke in. "You two can gossip later. We have a lot of ground to cover before ten o'clock. Bill, show her the stuff you and Gigi collected while I thaw something to eat."

Ten minutes later, Jenny struggled with growing misgivings. She held up a sequined tank top that looked scarcely big enough to encircle her thigh. "I . . . This will never fit."

Bill's eyes twinkled lecherously, much the same as Gabe's did when he was trying to intimidate her. Her first assessment had been wrong. He was every bit as venal as Gabe. "It stretches. Gigi assured me that wearing this would put you into character."

"And precisely what character is that?"

"Uncle G.'s having one of his private parties tonight. He's contracted for a half-dozen call girls to entertain him and his guests. I've made arrangements for you to be one of them."

THIRTEEN

"A what?" Jenny felt the color drain from her face. Gabe's laughter ran from the kitchen area behind her. "You can't possibly be serious."

A tentative smile crossed Bill's features. He shrugged. "The maverick is monitoring his phone calls from within. Gabe's candidate is Tania, but we don't know what her motive is. If you approach him by phone, she'll find out you got to him. If you go to his home, the same thing applies." His enthusiasm grew, and he continued persuasively, "The whole setup tonight is in your favor. You'll be the only blonde, and my sources say he has a weakness for platinum of any shade, which probably explains why he let you go in the first place. This might be the only way you can talk to him without the whole chain of command knowing about it."

He eyed her skeptically, then continued, "Gigi says once you get into the outfit, you'll feel more like a tart."

Every fiber of Jenny's being rebelled. "What if he . . ."

Gabe's voice came from directly behind her. "You know him better than we do. Would he put a serious move on you? Besides, you said you're willing to do anything necessary to get your life back. Are you chickening out?"

Beneath the harshness in his voice she detected complacency, as if he were thinking, I told you so. He thought she was going to back out. Jenny's spine stiffened. "Of course not. The Uncle G. I know wouldn't harm a hair on my head. I don't know what Tania is up to, but it's hard for me to accept her hatred. What did I ever do to her?"

"You want me to explain, Gabe?" Bill's voice shook with laughter.

"Can it, Gates. Let me be the one to tell her. While we eat." He took Jenny's arm and led her to the glass table, where he'd arranged plates and flatware on woven place mats. By the time she and Bill seated themselves, Gabe appeared with a lasagna casserole, which he set in the middle. "Sorry about salads. This will have to do." He scooped a wedge onto her plate.

Jenny picked up her fork. "You may explain now," she ordered.

"Bill's done a little historical research since Tania dropped the bomb, if you'll pardon the bad pun. Remember when you and Trent met?" Gabe asked.

"At my exhibit."

"Tania was with him that night, wasn't she?"

"Well, yes. They were very good friends, as well as cousins. They'd grown up together, and they shared an interest in art," she explained.

Gabe snorted. "They shared a hell of a lot more than that. They'd been banging each other since Tania was fourteen." He lowered his gaze to his plate, adding disgustedly, "And they were probably lovers after Trent married you." He looked up, his eyes dark with compassion. "I'm sorry, Jenny. Tania hated your guts from the start."

At the realization of her naivete, Jenny's fork fell from suddenly numb fingers. How could she have been so blind? All the signs had been there. At first, dizzy with infatuation, she'd overlooked Tania's constant presence. Later, she'd interpreted Tania's overtures toward her as a sign of compassion for her own misery, gestures of friendship she'd seized hungrily. "I should have . . . if I hadn't been so . . ."

"Lonely. Trusting. Watching your parents do good deeds and a sheltered life in private schools didn't prepare you for life with a Travino. In all fairness, not many backgrounds would."

Gabe picked up her fork and wrapped her fingers around it. "Eat. You have a busy night ahead of you."

Bill chose that moment to interject, "The way I read the background, Uncle G. knew all along. He probably felt sorry for you. When you wanted to cut your ties with the family, he let you go for your own safety, before Tania could arrange a little accident that might prove fatal. Since she and Trent had been getting it on, he probably never thought to suspect her in connection with your husband's death."

Something inside Jenny unraveled. Each time she learned to live with one revelation, another piece of information altered her viewpoint. Would she ever be able to put behind her the repercussions of her infatuation with the first handsome man to express interest in her? Or would she spend the rest of her life suffering the consequences of one monumental act of stupidity?

She studied the faces of the two men watching her. Bill probably doubted her ability to carry off the masquerade ahead. Gabe's expression was harder to read, but she didn't think he had much faith in her ability to inject herself into the role. Well, he's wrong, she told herself. She'd insisted on being part of this operation, and now that the time had come, she refused to change her mind. Jenny wondered if he'd ever watched someone's head blown to bits. Gabe Daniels was in for the surprise of his life.

"In that case, it's even more important that I talk with Uncle G., isn't it?" Jenny picked up her fork, cut into the melted cheese and through the noodles. Meaty tomato sauce ran from between the layers, and she thought only of her hunger as she forked the lasagna into her mouth.

Hours later, Gabe paced the loft, too wound up to watch as Bill printed hard copies of the Kamanedes files. "How the hell long is she going to take? We're running short on time."

"Never been married, have you." Bill swivelled in his chair to face Gabe while yet another file appeared on the screen.

Gabe said irritatedly, "You know damn well I haven't. What's that got to do with . . ." Bill's eyes rounded, and his mouth went slack. Gabe turned to see what had prompted his friend's glazed expression.

The vision descending the stairs made sweat break out at the back of Gabe's neck. His stomach tied into knots. "The deal's off. No way in hell you're going to that party. Go back upstairs and put on a pair of my sweats or something." Never in his wildest dreams had he expected Jenny to go through with this. But then he'd never suspected she could transform herself into anything so blatantly sexy.

Bill laughed.

Reaching the bottom of the stairs, Jenny came to a stop and turned slowly, her hands planted on hips encased in an emerald green satin miniskirt so snug it cupped her rounded buttocks. The hem brushed the lacy tops of black thigh-high stockings covering slender legs that seemed entirely too long for a woman who couldn't be more than five feet five. Gabe recalled Bill telling her earlier that the sequined tank top would stretch, but he hadn't realized how the tiny glittering disks would quiver at each breath she took, at every movement of her sweetly rounded breasts. "You're not even wearing a bra!" he complained.

Her body undulated with each step she took on four-inch heels of shoes which seemed to consist of two narrow thongs across the instep. Drawing closer, she said throatily, "The straps would show, Gabe." She batted darkened, curled, fake eyelashes and purred, "Besides, in my line of work, a bra is a definite inconvenience." All trace of her private school accent had disappeared. The musky fragrance of the "slut" perfume Gigi had selected surrounded her. And him.

Bill laughed again, harder this time. Gabe felt his blood pressure rise above his ears. "What have you done to your hair?"

Her blonde blunt-cut was curled and swept up into a cluster atop her head, with artfully careless tendrils falling around her ears and her slender neck. She patted one particularly fragile ringlet and batted the false sable lashes a second time. "Bill seems to like it," she breathed.

Gabe's erection grew so painful he sank into the chair. "I won't let her do this. There has to be another way."

Jenny stepped in front of him and stood with her feet planted apart, her hands once again on her hips. "I'm the one taking the risks, not you. I have to talk to Uncle G., so I'm going to that private club in exactly . . ." —she lifted the glittering lavaliere from where it nestled in cleavage Gabe had purposely refused to think about since he'd surprised her in the shower, and glanced at its jeweled face— "one hour. And I won't allow you or anyone else to stop me."

"I do believe she can pull it off, Gabe." Bill's laughter subsided, and he leaned back in his chair and gazed at Jenny appreciatively. "I wouldn't have thought it possible, but no one will ever recognize you. You're the exact opposite of your real self. What do you intend to do? Sidle up to

Uncle G. and whisper a few pure vowels into his ear so he recognizes you?"

His friend's grin reminded Gabe of a proud father. He wanted to punch him in the mouth.

Jenny looked down at herself as if aware of her body for the first time. "I'll have to play it by ear, but Gigi was right. Once I put on the outfit, I knew I could make this work. The clothes make me feel . . . I don't know, like a different person." She tilted her hip provocatively.

"Like a high-class hooker," Gabe growled. Up until now, he'd snickered inwardly at Jenny's prim buttoned blouses and shirts. Seeing her like this made him realize he preferred her prissy way of dressing. The thought of Uncle G.'s corporate thugs seeing her tarted up made his insides churn. "Christ, I can see all the way up . . ."

"A gentleman wouldn't look."

Jenny's finishing school voice sounded obscene coming from her cherry red lips. And when had her lower lip become so full and pouty? Gabe wanted to put his fist through the wall. "I told you what I was. Remember?"

"Stop bickering, children."

Gabe swung around to look at Bill, who appeared to be enjoying the whole setup entirely too much.

"We still have logistics to coordinate." Bill grabbed a sheet of paper. "The party's at The Stuffed Olive. Uncle G.'s used the place on its dark night before, which was how I got a line on the . . . ah, the agency he uses to supply the ladies. I'll deliver you in Gabe's limo, Jenny. One of the Travino boys might recognize Gabe, especially if one of them is in league with Tania. Gabe will follow in another car."

"No dice. I want to be in the limo," Gabe interjected.

Bill sighed. "All right, but you have to stay out of sight.

Jenny, once you've completed your mission, I want you out of there. The limo is too noticeable to hang around in, so one of us will stay there on foot while the other comes back for the pickup truck. There are six steps up to the entrance, and the door has lights on either side. When you come out, pause at the top of the steps to make sure we see you."

"If you're in trouble, don't bother looking. Just scream and run like hell," Gabe ordered. "We'll be there for you."

Her voice wobbled on the first syllables as she asked, "Gabe, what if we're wrong? What if Uncle G. is behind all of this? I'll be putting myself right into his hands. Literally."

For the first time, he realized Jenny was terrified. Until now, her determination to seize control of her life had consumed her so completely that she hadn't taken time to consider the possible consequences. His own experience as a rebellious teen who'd been jerked to the straight and narrow wasn't comparable. He'd been a dirtball to start with. Instinct told him to cancel the caper, send Bill home, and scrub every speck of makeup off Jenny's face. He wanted to hold her through the night. Hell, he wanted much more, but if that was all she would allow, so be it.

"I don't think that's a problem. While you were getting gussied up, Bill weaseled E-mail out of Uncle G.'s files. The old guy's been pulling out all the stops to discover who initiated the war with the Kamanedes. Your name never came up. Tania undoubtedly has a partner in all this, but whoever it is has covered his tracks as well as she has. What we don't know is whether he's inside the family." Gabe paused, staring at her as if he'd never seen her before. He frowned. "Bill, we have another problem. Half the turkeys at this little affair must have met Jenny at one time or another. Her eyes will give her away."

Bill patted the pocket of the black uniform jacket he'd

just donned. "Whoops. Gigi'd kill me if I forgot to give Jenny the most important part of the costume." He held out a contact case and a tiny bottle of solution. "Ever used colored lenses?"

"Once, for a costume party while I was in art school. I went as a black cat, and turned my eyes green. What color are these?"

Gabe looked at his watch. "Don't get picky. We leave in fifteen minutes."

When Jenny vanished into the lavatory off the kitchen, he turned to Bill. "She's so scared her guts are eating her from the inside. Should we tell her she's wired?"

Bill shook his head. "She'd have one of two reactions: inhibition or overconfidence. We've told her enough." He grinned. "It'd be a shame to take the 'cha-cha-boom' out of that walk."

"She terrifies me. That 'cha-boom' could put her up against a wall before she ever makes it to Uncle G."

Forty-five minutes later Jenny stepped from the black limo onto the sidewalk in front of The Stuffed Olive. Her ankles wobbled, whether from fear or from the unaccustomed high heels, she wasn't sure. Remembering Gabe's warning that the doorman would be watching for her, she reached into the pocket of the fox fur jacket Bill had furnished and closed her fingers around the brass identification token he'd given her. Drawing a deep breath, she tossed her head and made her way up the steps.

Throughout her marriage, Trent had enthused about Uncle G.'s "reward parties." In her innocence, she'd pictured masculine versions of the awards banquets she'd attended during her college years, naively assuming the entertainment at a gang version would consist of a stripper or two.

Now, with a whole new frame of reference, she knew nothing could possibly have prepared her for the next few hours. Gabe's last advice rang in her ears: "When it's time to leave, run like hell."

I'll just pretend this is happening to someone else, she told herself. She felt like someone else. Gigi hadn't exaggerated the effect of the clothing on her inhibitions. She'd been raised conservatively, even to the design and fabric of her underwear. With each item she'd donned, her body had become progressively aware of heat and texture. She'd felt liberated. Jenny wondered if she would ever again be comfortable with her old wardrobe.

The thought made her smile. She believed she would like her own panties back. The thong she wore left her virtually naked beneath the silky satin of her skirt. If it weren't for the fur jacket, she was positive she'd have frozen her . . .

"Identification, lady."

The hulking doorman's demand interrupted her thoughts. Summoning what she hoped was a come-hither smile, she presented the token. "The Travino party."

His gaze swept her from head to toe. Jenny quaked inwardly under his lascivious glance, a direct contrast to the horrified, but attracted, expression on Gabe's face when she'd come down the stairs. Gabe had stroked her feminine pride; the doorman made her feel dirty.

"Party room at the top of the stairs to the right. You're late," he said, intimating she might not be allowed to enter.

"A girl has to make an entrance if she wants to be the star attraction," Jenny replied, scarcely recognizing her own voice. She swept past as if he were beneath her notice and sashayed up the stairs, burningly conscious of his hot gaze on her bottom. Swallowing nervously, she realized that soon she would have to remove her jacket. Dear God,

192

please help me carry this off.

The carved door swung open, revealing a short, swarthy man of about forty. This would be her first test. Danny Travino was yet another cousin of Trent's, and they'd attended numerous affairs with him and his sullen wife. She'd disliked both of them. Danny's dark eyes were little and cruel, and moved constantly. His wife had treated her with contempt.

"Well, well. What have we here?" Danny pulled her in the door and reached from behind to remove her jacket. His right hand cupped her breast while he pretended to search for the edge of the lapel.

Jenny nearly gagged, but kept a half-smile in place as she slid skillfully free of the fur and his touch. "Naughty naughty. The way I heard it, the merchandise isn't available until later."

"Christ. You're as uptight as the last two broads!" he complained. "Go on in."

Her knees watery with relief, Jenny crossed the anteroom and tugged on the polished brass handles of the double doors, the only other exit, before he could rush to help her.

Her senses were assaulted on all sides by the fragrant smoke of expensive cigars, the sultry tones of the singer performing on the little stage to the mellow accompaniment of a three-piece combo, and the occasional burst of feminine laughter punctuating the rumble of masculine voices.

The only lighting came from the subdued spotlights on the performers, frosted glass sconces at intervals around the room, and candles in the middle of each of the tables around a postage stamp–size dance floor. Even in the resulting gloom, she could pick out a half-dozen familiar faces. Her stomach did a triple somersault. This was never going to work. Where was Uncle G.?

A warm hand clasped her upper arm. The backs of strong fingers pressed against her breast too firmly to be accidental. "The missing hostess! And I'm the lucky one to find you first. Let's dance."

Before Jenny could reply, the stranger's hand shifted from her arm to her back, where he rested his open hand just below her waist. He guided her purposefully toward the dance floor and took her in his arms. Groping for something to say, she giggled playfully as she pushed against his chest to widen the distance between them. "Have I met you before? My mother told me never to dance with strangers."

For some reason, her remark amused him. He chuckled and tilted her chin up with one hand. "We won't be strangers for long. Is this your first party with the Travinos, too?"

Jenny gulped as she looked up. He was blond, with the perfectly sculpted features of an angel. She knew her eyes had rounded with appreciation, so she managed a throaty laugh and nodded. "I hear the pay is the best. What's your name?"

"Dave Lassiter. I'm on the legal staff. And you must be the missing Mitzi. I cheated and looked at the list," he confided. He pulled her close and released her chin to entwine his fingers with those of her free hand. As they swayed to the seductive rhythms, he asked, "Do you know how these things are set up?"

Her breasts pressed flat against his broad chest, and his legs bracketed her scarcely covered thighs. The glittering watch pendant Gigi had selected pressed into her chest. "Actually, no. One of the girls who's come before raved about what a wonderful time she had, but she wouldn't tell me what actually happens."

She managed to pull back and survey the room. Perhaps

thirty men, all wearing tuxedos, were seated or standing. All were drinking. One woman held sway at the table in the far corner of the room, another claimed the attention of five men at a closer table. The other three hostesses present partnered dark-suited men on the dance floor.

The party reminded her of the few nightclubs Trent had taken her to, except for the disparity of numbers between men and women. What made this different?

"From what I hear, we dance a little, drink a lot, eat a little, brag, and at the end of the evening, Uncle G. draws six names from a hat." He twirled her around so suddenly she nearly lost her balance. "You, my dear, are one of the door prizes."

Pasting an eager smile on her face, Jenny cooed, "Oh, good. I hate those 'who gets her first' parties." She wished she hadn't eaten the lasagna. Could she keep it down?

During the next half-hour, Jenny danced with four other men, two of whom she knew, but neither made any connection between the amber-eyed blonde and the late Trent Travino's cool, reserved wife. Each made explicit suggestions and gave her their cards. One even asked for hers. None could understand her refusal of a drink. She'd become adept at looking up from beneath her false eyelashes and diverting their advances with breathy responses and regretful giggles.

Just as she had given up on Uncle G.'s arrival and begun to search her mind for a way to escape, the double doors opened and he entered.

The head of the family was a tall, imposing figure. His silver hair gleamed above his handsome features in the flickering candlelight; although Jenny knew he was in his late sixties, he looked fifteen years younger. His shoulders were square and powerful-looking beneath his hand-tailored tuxedo. He looked like what he was. A leader.

As he made his way around the room, shaking hands and administering masculine hugs, Jenny heard Danny Travino's voice close to her ear. "Now that I'm off the door, it's my turn to sample the merchandise." The words were followed by a damp kiss at the juncture of her neck and shoulder. Jenny couldn't hide her shiver of revulsion. He swung her around and pulled her against his bull-like chest. "Maybe I'll find a way to diddle the door prize drawings," he said, squeezing her left buttock. "I have a weakness for blondes, particularly blondes who aren't willing."

"Let me go. You're hurting me." Jenny pushed against his shoulder.

He pulled her closer. "You'll like it that way."

Jenny fought back tears of frustration. She'd been frightened before she set out this evening. Now she felt pure terror. "Please . . ."

"Danny!" Uncle G.'s voice boomed across the room over the singer's sultry rendition of "Stormy Weather." "Bring the young lady over here. You know I always order a blonde dinner partner."

Danny's anger fairly radiated. His piggy dark eyes were filled with such fury that for a moment Jenny thought he would disobey the good-natured command. Then his hold on her loosened and he swore beneath his breath. She nearly fainted with relief.

Silence fell over the crowded room; Danny's angry reaction had drawn attention. This sign of rebellion left him open to punishment, and Uncle G.'s ruthlessness was legendary. As they crossed the dance floor, she felt as if she were under a spotlight.

"Lovely. A fresh face is always welcome," Uncle G. enthused as he stood to pull out a chair for Jenny. "Mitzi, isn't it?" When she smiled brightly, he told Danny, "You show good taste, my boy. But you must learn to share more cheerfully." The menace in his soft voice was unmistakable.

Jenny held her breath in anticipation of Danny's response to the veiled reproof. When he grasped his uncle's hand and mumbled an apology, she nearly crumpled with relief. Uncle G. sat again, calling for a waiter. "What will you have to drink, Mitzi?"

"Cranberry juice with a shot of Southern Comfort," Jenny said, naming the obscure drink which had been a private joke between them ever since she had seen it in a Southern Comfort brochure. She kept her eyes averted.

"And I'll have my usual," Uncle G. said. "So, Little Mitzi, where are you from?"

Relief flooded Jenny. He had always called her "Little Jenny." And he hadn't given her away. Remembering her role, she batted her eyelashes, leaned toward him and said seductively, "Where would you like me to be from?" Why was this harder to do when the man beside her was treating her like a lady?

As if taking her cue, Uncle G. put his arm around her shoulders and drew her close. He whispered in her ear, "Play up to me. Then I'll take you where we can talk."

Jenny managed one of the breathy giggles she'd been substituting for intelligence ever since she arrived. She patted his cheek and said playfully, "Naughty man. You have to wait until the drawing like everyone else."

Danny Travino, who had lingered nearby, grumbled bitterly, "Uncle G. makes the rules, Mitzi. He can break them if he wants. He's the boss."

"Thank you for reminding me, Danny. Ask the band to play 'Stormy Weather' again. I like that song." Keeping his arm around Jenny, Uncle G. chucked her under the chin and murmured, "Danny has his eye on you. If I'd arrived any later, he might have broken the rules and spirited you away."

Jenny heard the distrust in his voice. Had Danny been disloyal in other ways? Maybe he was Tania's partner. She looked into Uncle G.'s sad dark eyes and patted the big hand cupping her shoulder. "I need to talk with you. Privately," she whispered.

With a suddenness that caused heads to turn, Uncle G. stood and pushed back his chair. Command radiated from him, and Jenny was reminded once again that the man was a consummate leader. His voice rose above the sudden hush. "Please accept my apologies. Tonight there will be only five door prizes. I've decided to claim this one for myself." He held out his arm to Jenny, and only she saw the twinkle in his eyes. "Be assured, gentlemen, that this discrepancy will be compensated for in the future."

Mortified by the avid lust written on the faces of every man in the room, Jenny turned toward the double doors. As a lackey leaped to swing them open, Dave Lassiter stepped forward, then stopped, as if remembering his newcomer's status. His jaw was set with anger. Surely he knew better than to question Uncle G.'s authority so openly. Why would he make such a mistake?

FOURTEEN

"Jesus. She's better than I expected!" Perspiration soaked Gabe's black turtleneck. The transmission from Jenny's lavaliere had swept him from apprehension to panic to relief.

Ever the technician, Bill fretted, "If I'd had more time to prepare, I'd have remembered the bug could be smothered when she danced." He fiddled with the controls of the receiver on the console between them. "Holy crap! Cranberry juice and Southern Comfort. The woman must have a cast-iron stomach."

Squashing a vision of Jenny being manhandled by the hoods inside, Gabe spat, "Quiet. They're leaving. Where in the hell is he taking her?" Slouched down in his seat, he peered cautiously from beneath the baseball cap pulled low over his forehead. "They're not coming out the front door, and they're not talking, either. Upstairs?"

Uncle G.'s voice came as if from a distance. "You surprise me, Little Jenny. If you had exhibited a small part of this talent for . . . well, let me just say your years with poor Trent would at least have been more . . . entertaining."

"I don't think so, Uncle. I have a very real affection for you, but your way of life was never acceptable to me. You've always known that. Is that why you want me dead?"

Gabe's heart nearly stopped at Jenny's direct approach. She was pushing too hard. He reached for the door handle.

The Mafia don's reply froze his fingers on the cold metal. "Never!" Uncle G.'s voice rang with sincerity. "As I reminded you when you called, you left with my blessings. I

199

took great care to inform everyone that you were off-limits, a free person. Anyone who ignored my order will be punished." His voice came and went, as if the man were pacing. "What has made it necessary for you take such risks to talk with me?"

The bug magnified Jenny's sigh of relief into a whooshing sound. "I was afraid Tania was acting on orders from you. After everything that's happened, I was afraid you'd changed your mind about me." Her voice firmed. "She met with me at one of Sterling Thomas's homes the day before yesterday. Uncle, I wasn't sure who to talk to, and Tania had been my only friend in the family, besides you. She told me several of your people thought I was responsible for the problems you're having with the Kamanedes family.

"Before she left, she planted a bomb on the doorstep. One of Sterling's security people was killed. Uncle, I know about Tania and Trent." Jenny's voice wavered on the last sentence.

Gabe heard a rumbling string of curses. "My niece grew from a sweet child into a bitch with no morals. I had hoped you would never discover that. Start from the beginning. Tell me everything."

Jenny launched into a recital of the events following her discovery of DeWitt's body, but her voice broke when she reached Faith's death. She gathered her composure and continued the narrative, finishing, "There was a man in Baltimore. I couldn't remember his name, but I'd seen him at your home."

"Describe him."

When Jenny finished her description, he said, "Vinnie Torinelli. He wanted a joint venture with the Travinos, and for a short time, I considered it. He was most unhappy when I decided not to take part. Tania must have heard about him." A long silence followed, then, "Little Jenny. Even though you were unhappy with us, you kept your vows." Uncle G. chuckled. "I must admit I was annoyed by your agent's efforts to help you leave Trent, but under the circumstances, you could be excused. I would never have permitted you to succeed, however."

Once again, Jenny's gasp was magnified, and Gabe couldn't repress a smile of appreciation for the old don's wiliness.

"Then Trent died. He had promise, that boy. No one has yet paid for his death, but the day will come soon. Your story convinces me the murderer is the leader of the nest of worms within my own family." Uncle G.'s voice held venom. "I have waited, pouring rain into the soil, hoping each worm will come to the surface, but now I know. It saddens my heart to know one of my own blood has acted against me."

"And the war with the Kamanedes firm?"

This time it was Uncle G. who sighed. "A diversion designed to draw my attention away from them. Obviously, Tania hoped to revenge herself on you while she stirred up this feud."

"Uncle G., when I called, you cautioned me about Gabe Daniels. You said he was dangerous. Why?"

The old man's bitter laughter came closer. "He is dangerous . . . to anyone who offends his code of honor. I warned you because I didn't want to draw his attention to my business enterprises. Although he's no longer with the government, he still has influence. This rebellion within my organization I can handle. If Daniels decides to encourage an attack on us from the outside at such a time, we will be badly damaged."

Gabe laughed. "The old dragon. What would happen if I turned in that whole outfit?"

Uncle G. continued, "But if I had a daughter, he is the man I would choose to protect her. What is he to you? You aren't lovers, or he would not have allowed you to do this foolish thing."

"Of course not," Jenny protested.

Gabe snorted, pretending not to notice Bill's curious stare.

"I . . . I think 'partners' would best describe our relationship. At least for now," Jenny said. "Sterling Thomas wanted me to go into hiding until the danger was past. When I refused, Gabe helped me set up the meeting with Tania. Then I discovered he only wanted to put me into another prison while he approached you. I convinced him otherwise. Never again will anyone 'allow' me to do anything. I'd rather be dead."

"Ahhh." Gabe heard the amused cynicism in the drawn-out sound. "Sterling has molded a model creature, has he not? And you, my dear, have become formidable."

"Gabe gave Tania a message for you. He offered to help you with your problem."

Uncle G.'s short bark of laughter erupted. "She delivered no such message. Thank him for me, but I still have people I can trust. What you tell me about Tania saddens me, but it fits well into the puzzle I have been working. The rest of her small circle is known to me, but I hadn't suspected she could be the leader. I shall act quite soon. Tell me, where do you go next?"

"Now that I can assure him you weren't behind Tania's attack on me, I must talk with Nick Kamanedes. Two sets of people were following us in Baltimore, and Gabe is sure the other is Nick's. He wants the Swiss bank account number Gabe and I discovered."

The sound of rustling clothing crackled through the receiver. "You must go. I assume your dangerous friend is outside, prepared to rescue you from this den of iniquity after a reasonable period of time. You must resume your masquerade. I'll see you to the door before I slip away." Gabe heard the sorrow in his voice as he added, "To be truthful, I will be glad to leave. I have no heart for celebration tonight."

Gabe sat up straight. "Pull up in front, Bill." He slid his Beretta from its holster, tucked it beneath the seat, and leaned forward to grasp the edge of the dashboard. "When she hits those stairs, I want to be ready to rumble."

The souped-up engine of the truck idled smoothly as Bill maneuvered into an opening between a Jaguar and a Porsche. Gabe watched the club's doors. When they opened, he frowned at the tender kiss Jenny bestowed on Uncle G.'s cheek before sauntering down the concrete stairs, her head turning left and right as if looking for a taxi. The old guy may have treated her fairly, but he was responsible for more human misery than Gabe cared to think about. Since his token offer of help had been refused, he had half a mind to call his old agency while the old man was vulnerable. Even as he swung the door wide, an inner voice told him he'd never betray Jenny's trust. He called, "Over here."

The sound of her nervous breathing came to him through the bug around her neck, and he flicked the switch and stowed the mechanism beneath the seat, murmuring to Bill, "Don't mention what we overheard." A small corner of his mind wanted to hear Jenny's version of her talk with the Mafia don.

As she came alongside, Gabe reached out and pulled her

inside the truck, tumbling her onto his lap. Before the door closed, they shot away from the curb. Even her garish perfume smelled good to him as he tucked her into the curve of his shoulder. Profoundly relieved to have her safe, he warned, "In five more minutes, I'd have barged in that door, guns blazing."

Her voice, thin and strained, was muffled against his shoulder as she answered, "That's what Uncle G. suspected."

"Did you have any trouble getting close to him?" Gabe inquired innocently. He hated himself for testing her, but the whole impersonation had been almost too smooth. Loosening his hold, he pulled Jenny upright on his lap.

She shook her head in the negative. "Gabe, he didn't know about Tania. And from what Uncle G. said, I'm almost positive Trent's murderer is someone within the family. None of the Kamanedes could have had anything to do with it."

Bill swore ripely, interrupting them. "Sit tight, gang. We've picked up a tail." He lurched the truck to the right, down a one-way street, and switched off the headlights. The city's overabundance of light offered more than enough visibility for anyone familiar with the streets.

Gabe seized Jenny's shoulders and forced her to the floor between his legs, then pushed her head beneath the dash. "Stay down. If there's any shooting, you'll be safer." He retrieved his gun and turned to look out the rear window, resting the muzzle on the back of the seat. "I'll wing whoever it is if he pulls too close," he reassured his friend.

Bill laughed as the truck bucketed into an alley. "That'll never happen. I can lose them in a heartbeat."

The next twenty minutes succeeded in breaking Jenny's composure. The high-speed ride through alleys, over curbs and through obstacles she could only guess at while curled within the safe haven of Gabe's powerful calves and the underside of the dashboard, was like a roller-coaster trip, out of her control. The tension-filled hour she'd spent in The Stuffed Olive replayed itself on a large screen in her brain like an unpleasant dream. By the time she heard Bill's satisfied, "Lost the bastards! Told you I could," she was a quivering mass of nerves.

Gabe's hands closed around her shoulders. He pulled her into his lap, then enveloped her in a close embrace, pressing her head beneath his chin. "You're shaking. Are you cold?"

Unable to speak, she turned her head from side to side. His body heat warmed her, but Jenny's inner core was freezing, so cold she feared she would never be warm again.

Regret filled Gabe's voice as he folded her closer. "You've had a bad evening, and it's my fault. There was no reason for you to be frightened while you were in the club, Jenny. I should have told you you were wired. We heard everything, including your talk with Uncle G. The reason I didn't tell you ahead of time is that I was afraid you'd be self-conscious. I'm sorry. We wanted to be able to rescue you if someone blew your cover." He held her away from him long enough to pull the pendant over her head and throw it into the backseat.

Surrounded by Gabe's warmth and scent, Jenny tucked her freezing hands between their bodies. If—no, when—she felt stronger, she would probably kill him for that admission. But not right now. She couldn't even find the words to describe how tired she was of living on the edge of a precipice. And this evening had been the worst. She pretended she hadn't heard him.

"How much longer until we arrive home?" Calling their

destination "home" wasn't accurate, but the isolation of Gabe's loft promised something she'd decided she wanted very much. A place that was hers, a haven where she knew the rooms would welcome her and nourish her. She'd felt that way since halfway through the mural she'd put on the wall.

"Coming right up," Bill said cheerfully.

Jenny pulled her face free and looked at Gabe's friend. "I'm so pleased someone is having a good time this evening."

He looked at her briefly, a delighted smile creasing his face, then turned his attention back to driving. "Things always liven up when Gabe's in town." He nudged the turn signal and reached above his head to punch a code in a tiny keyboard.

Ahead, on the right, Jenny saw a garage door rise. Dim light spilled a spreading rectangle across the street. "I'm going to take the longest shower in history. I feel as if I've been in a sewer." She mentally reviewed each place on her body Danny Travino and the others had brushed against or pawed, and wondered if enough soap and water existed to decontaminate her skin. She wasn't sure she would ever cleanse her soul.

Gabe's arms tightened protectively. Bill eased the truck into the garage and switched off the engine. Before the overhead door closed behind them, Gabe stepped out, still holding her in his arms. "I'm taking her up, Bill. Bring Gigi for lunch tomorrow, and we'll work out the next step."

Jenny struggled to lower her feet to the ground. "I'm perfectly able to walk."

"Yeah. Maybe you can break your damn ankle while you're showing me how tough you are." He pushed open the elevator grill and punched in his code. "That would put the frosting on a perfect evening, wouldn't it?"

Was that disgust in his voice? Jenny reared her head back and stared at his unhappy face. "Now what did I do wrong?"

He closed his eyes, shielding his thoughts. When the elevator bumped to a stop, he looked at her apologetically, "You did everything right, even though you were scared shitless. Do you mind if I wallow in a little guilt for letting you do it?"

Jenny was too stunned by his apology for speech. She stared at his solemn features the whole time as he carried her through the little courtyard to the door, then across the main floor of the apartment, lit only by the glow of dim track lighting on the inside wall, and up the wrought-iron stairs. He kicked open the door to her room with one foot and pressed the switch with his elbow, flooding the room with light from the two bedside lamps.

When he continued to carry her, she said, "You needn't grovel. I was the one who insisted on doing this. Put me down."

"In a minute." He headed for the bathroom.

Jenny struggled against his hold. "You're forgiven, I tell you." Surely he didn't intend to . . .

Gabe set her on her feet. Turning her, he slid the fur jacket from her shoulders and tossed it through the door onto the bedroom floor. With surprisingly gentle hands, he pressed her down to sit on the closed lid of the toilet. "Hold still."

He reached for the cleansing cream on the cluttered vanity. "I can't argue properly with someone wearing this much makeup."

His fingers patted the fragrant cream on her skin, meticulously smoothing it to her hairline. Jenny sat quiet beneath his ministrations, silenced by this abject display of guilt for allowing her to degrade herself. She understood why he felt that way, but no one had forced her to take part in the dangerous masquerade. She'd made the decision on her own.

When he had patted her face clean with tissues, she looked up into his eyes. "You didn't send me out at gunpoint, you know. I just didn't realize how . . ."

"How disgusting some of your late husband's relatives really are?" he interrupted savagely. "And they were gentlemen tonight. I knew! I just didn't think you'd go through with it. Then, like a fool, I convinced myself that you knew what those parties were like, that you could handle yourself. Jesus! I sent you in there like a lamb to the slaughter."

He slammed the jar back onto the vanity. "God knows how you ever carried it off. That gathering you attended was pretty tame for a boys' night out in Mafia Land. Did you know that?"

His vehemence stunned Jenny. Throughout her life she'd constantly been flung into new situations, situations she learned to confront with a semblance of outward calm. Protesting yet another boarding school and new friends would have been fruitless, just as pleading with her parents to take her with them would have been.

When her impetuous choice of a husband had thrust her into a frightening situation, she had adapted, then waited, hoping against hope for a way out. When Trent was murdered, she had wondered if her yearning to be free had made the thought into a deed.

This evening she'd accepted the tawdriness of her masquerade and the surroundings in much the same way—as the price she had to pay to reach Uncle G. "I'm not that naive, Gabe. I have an excellent imagination."

Jenny stood, pushing at his chest with both hands. It was

like trying to move a wall. "Now get out of here so I can wash the filth off." She glanced upward into his eyes, saw their threatening glitter, and pushed harder. As his arms came around her, she tried to back away. Her calves encountered the unyielding toilet seat. "You wouldn't."

"Oh, yes, I would."

Before she could protest further, his hands moved to her waist. The waistband of the silky skirt loosened and he tugged it down over her hips till it dropped to the floor. Then he rolled her hose down from her thighs. Jenny, standing perfectly still, wearing nothing but the indecent thong on the lower half of her body, thought she detected a tremor in his fingers, but they worked efficiently, as if they'd performed the task many times.

She kicked off the ridiculous spike-heeled sandals as he reached her ankles. His gaze was locked on the bottom of the sequined top, and, looking down, she saw that the scalloped edging provided an erotic border above the flat band of her thong panties. "Stop! I . . . can do the rest myself."

His heavy-lidded midnight eyes were half-closed, focused on her body, and she had no problem interpreting his thoughts. "No. Please. I have to do this myself. Gabe, I was once part of that . . . what I saw tonight. I chose to confront it. Let me get rid of the stench myself."

Gabe looked up into her eyes. Without a word, he held her hands beneath the faucet and handed her the soap. "Wash your hands and remove the damn contacts. I hate talking to you when you don't look like yourself."

While she did as he ordered, he turned and threw open the shower door. Reaching inside, he adjusted the showerheads and turned on faucets until the spray from the nozzles crossed in the middle. "We'll talk in the morning." With that he turned and left.

Jenny sagged with relief. She'd seen the desire in his eyes, but her very soul felt tarnished by the role she'd played tonight. The lust written on Danny's face had made her feel naked and somehow—fallen. With an angry twist, she shrugged the gaudy top over her head and tossed it toward the wastebasket, then struggled out of the tawdry panties and pitched them on top. Leaning close to the mirror, she peeled off the mink eyelashes.

Steam filled the shower compartment by the time she entered it. Jenny stood, the water pounding her head and shoulders, until warmth reached her frozen core. Then she scrubbed her body until her skin felt raw.

Afterward, she threw open the medicine cabinet door in search of something to help her sleep. Finding only aspirin, she downed three and padded into the bedroom, where she slipped into the batiste sleep shirt Gigi had sent, turned out the light and crawled into bed.

The rumble of traffic on main arteries several blocks away was broken by the insistent wail of a siren. The two-note warning of an emergency vehicle reaching an intersection speared into her brain, reinforcing the fears which had mushroomed after she crawled into the safe cave made by the fluffy duvet.

Uncle G. had seemed so different, still powerful and still in control, but there had been an aura of sadness about him. Could the aging don have lied to her? Who had followed them tonight? Perhaps one of the men inside had recognized her and slipped out to see who picked her up outside The Stuffed Olive. To see where she went.

Well aware she was creating monsters that might not exist, Jenny struggled to relax, starting with her toes, as she'd been taught years earlier. By the time she reached her knees her feet had knotted again, and her hands were clenched tightly beneath her cheek. A chill seeped along the back of her neck, and she shifted the duvet, drawing it closer around her ears. The cold continued to spread until shudders shook her whole body.

Earlier that evening, Gabe's arms had banished the iciness which had overwhelmed her. His body heat had flowed from the strength of his embrace, entering her pores. For once in her life, she'd felt safe, as if the person cherishing her genuinely cared. She shuddered again.

No longer capable of logical thought, she threw the bedding aside and set out to find Gabe.

Even a frigid shower hadn't taken the edge off the desire that possessed Gabe while he cleansed Jenny's face. He'd begun the task as personal atonement for allowing her to degrade herself, then found himself drowning in the depths of her eyes. The amber contacts hadn't detracted from her appeal, but they were part of the disguise, and his guilt had multiplied.

The brush of her sequined breasts against his thighs had been the final straw. He'd experienced a surge of lust that nearly knocked him off his feet. Damn. He shifted beneath the lightweight thermal blanket, unable to discover a comfortable position for his aroused body.

When he'd carried her to the loft she'd looked so vulnerable beneath the layer of makeup that he'd have given anything to erase her memory of the evening. What an ass he'd been to allow her to go ahead with the masquerade! The woman had no sense. She'd probably need a bodyguard for the rest of her life.

That thought implied permanence, an idea which should have damped his libido as nothing else could. Instead, the possibility acted like a tranquilizer on his exhausted body.

At peace, he found a comfortable position in the bed and dozed off.

Not an hour later, his instinct for survival registered a drifting movement in the doorway. He awoke fully alert, stretching so his right arm burrowed beneath the pillow, toward where his Beretta lay ready.

"Gabe?" Jenny's voice sounded thin.

He started to sit up, then lay back down. The moonlight streaming through the double skylight overhead would reveal his nakedness. Not that he cared, but he couldn't rid himself of the need to shield her from reality. "What's wrong?"

"Gabe, I'm so cold."

The memory of her compulsive shudders earlier that evening was accompanied by the feel of her curled against him. Now she was asking for his warmth again. Gabe sighed, well aware the night's torments were just beginning. Promising himself he'd behave like a gentleman or die in the attempt, he raised the edge of the blanket and growled, "Come on. I'll warm you."

Before he'd finished speaking, Jenny dived beneath the covers and plastered her back against his chest, then settled the soft curve of her bottom against his groin. She reached back as if to pat him. "I'll never be able to thank you . . ."

He felt her stiffen when her hand encountered his bare hip. Gabe's heartbeat danced a polka. He fought to ignore the pleasure-pain attacking his loins. "Want me to find some pajamas?" Or maybe an athletic cup.

Six heartbeats later, she replied, "No."

Gabe nearly swallowed his tongue. Moving carefully, he tucked the sheet and blanket snugly beneath her chin. He left his arms around her, one hand flat against the sharp line of her collarbone, the other around her waist. She took a deep breath, and her breast pressed against his arm, falling away as she exhaled. Her hair, still slightly damp, brushed against his nostrils, the biting fragrance of his shampoo smelling foreign.

Ten minutes later, her shudders subsided. Just as suddenly, Gabe was too hot. "Jenny, I don't think this is a good idea."

She turned within his arms, her foot sliding down his calf as she fit herself against him. "Gabe, I think it is."

FIFTEEN

Jenny had never been so sure of anything in her life. She turned her head against Gabe's shoulder and inhaled, savoring the subtle fragrance of soap overlying the musky scent she'd come to associate with him.

His body stiffened against her. "Jenny, you're having a perfectly normal letdown after a traumatic experience. Don't do anything impulsive." He shifted nervously on the mattress. "Let me get up and find some sweats. Then I'll . . ."

"Make me a nice cup of hot tea?" she interrupted. The strain in his voice, combined with the evidence of her effect on him prodding her, gave her confidence. Turning, she slid her arms around him and flattened her hands against his back, luxuriating in the feel of taut muscle and sinew quivering beneath her touch. She pressed her lips against his throat, seeking the pulsing vein she'd felt against her cheek. His quickened heartbeat seemed to surround her. She needed him. Now. And if she had to beg, she would. "Please, Gabe." She shifted her lower body closer.

He caught her hips with his hands and held her a heartbeat away from him. "God knows I've tried to do the right thing here. No matter what you think of me, I don't take advantage of women."

The man was much too chivalrous. "Fine, then I'll take advantage of you," she said, tilting her head to nibble his chin. The remembered softness of his day's growth of whiskers brushed against her lips. When he still didn't move, Jenny nestled her breasts against his chest. She felt his muscles contract. Everything about him felt so good she wanted to drown in him. "Gabe, you have no idea how much I need this. Need you."

For a moment Gabe made no response, rigid beneath her fingertips. Then his arms swept around her, clasping her tight as he rolled onto his back. A rumble of laughter vibrated against her. "All right, woman, but if anyone should ask, the whole thing was your idea and you were in charge."

Jenny lifted her head to stare into his eyes. The pale moonlight sifting through the skylight mixed with the glow of the city and revealed only shadowed pools. His expression was impossible to read. Did he mean it? Trent had always insisted on being the master, the supreme being conquering his woman. Ever since she'd known him, Gabe's behavior had led her to believe he would demand the same role. His hands moved gently along her sides, the slide of his callused fingers unbearably erotic. She shuddered with pleasure. "Don't play head games with me, Gabe."

His grin was a mixture of pain and encouragement. "I'm giving you to the count of ten to get on with it, woman. After that I won't be responsible for what happens."

A bubble of joy rose in her throat. Laughter at a time like this was out of her realm of experience. She turned his words back on him. "If anyone should ask, I'll assure them you fought for your honor every inch of the way." She arched upward, reaching for the buttoned placket of her sleep shirt. "Help me get out of this thing first. I want to feel you against me."

To her delight, he obeyed her first order with such enthusiasm that her arms became hopelessly tangled in the sleeves. Laughing, she freed herself and leaned forward to kiss him, sliding her tongue between his lips just long enough to gain his cooperation. As soon as his arms rose to draw her close she pulled away, pressing his arms back to his sides. "Not yet. I want to explore all of you first."

She rose to a sitting position, her knees on either side of his lean hips. Calling on every shred of her willpower to ignore the sensations where their bodies touched, she concentrated on the wedge of dark curling hair on his chest. Leaning forward, she slid her hands into the silky pelt. His skin was hot, and beneath it his heart beat against her palms, the pulse matching her own, as if their bodies were already one. Need exploded inside her.

"Jenny . . ."

The yearning in his voice nearly sent her over the edge. She slid her hips toward the erection which had been nudging at her backside. Her thighs quivered as she lifted to take him inside her. "I'm afraid the explorations will have to wait," she murmured.

Hours later, Gabe awoke and shifted cautiously beneath the slight weight sprawled over his left side. Jenny's torso felt fragile and boneless between his hands as he eased her to the right until her breasts pressed against his rib cage and her face was buried in his shoulder. Her soft breaths raised goose bumps on his skin. She was so deep in sleep he doubted anything short of a three-alarm fire would wake her. The moon had waned, but the reflected light of New York still poured through the skylights, highlighting the contrast between her tousled cornsilk hair and his tanned skin.

Gabe fought to tamp down the blazing need which had brought him to wakefulness. The easy explanation was that any man with a nude woman sprawled partially atop him would awake in the same condition, but he wasn't buying that. Two hours earlier, Gabe would have sworn Jenny's passion had drained him so completely that he'd been sure his libido wouldn't revive until noon.

He tightened his hold, marveling at the way she fit against him and reveling in the silky flesh of her hip beneath his hand. Who would have thought the rather prim, reserved woman beside him had so much passion buried within her?

And she had given it to him. Gabe's objective side argued that her unself-conscious ardor was a natural psychological release after her stress-filled masquerade the evening before. His impractical side, where his dreams resided, remembered her offer on the outskirts of Baltimore. At the time, he'd put her off, because even then he knew without reservation that a one-night stand with Jenny Tyler would never be enough.

He'd been right. Now he wanted the whole enchilada. If it wouldn't have wakened Jenny, he would have indulged in a hearty horselaugh at his response to any mention of permanence only a week earlier. In spite of her buttoned-to-the-chin blouses and cool private-school voice, she filled a void in his life.

He'd never realized anyone with so many factions working against her could fight so valiantly. Jenny was a survivor in the truest sense of the word, a woman a man could count on no matter what life threw at him. If he lost her now, Gabe was desperately afraid he would never again be complete.

She stirred, dragging her knee up the side of his thigh, and Gabe's body disgraced him by reacting even more violently. When her questing fingers sifted through his chest hair, he covered them with his hand. God. Even sound asleep, she was going to make him go blind.

"Gabe?"

Her sleepy voice caused him to lose his place in the internal lecture he was delivering to his unruly body. Beneath his light grasp, her fingers continued to wander.

"Gabe, I know you're awake," she murmured huskily. She shifted her knee higher.

Sweat broke out on his forehead. "You're insatiable, woman."

Her fingers wandered lower. "And you're cooperating so beautifully," she purred as she found him.

The hell with restraint, he told himself as he rolled her beneath him. Her breasts seemed to rise to meet his touch, and he was lost.

Jenny stretched lazily, her mind still clouded by sleep. Her feeling of well-being deepened when she recalled the night before, and she reached out for Gabe's solid warmth. The sheet beneath her fingers was rumpled but empty. Disappointed, she forced her eyes open. Rectangles of sunlight dotted the plush carpeting of Gabe's otherwise spartan room. She heard traffic in the distance, but no sounds within the loft. The covers were tucked snugly around her shoulders.

Where was he? She'd hoped to wake in his arms, to luxuriate in the feel of his big body against hers—in the complete trust she'd come to feel for him. In the love for him that had carved out a secret place in her heart. Love that had nothing to do with the fact that last night, for the first time in her life, she had enjoyed such sanity-destroying sex that the memory of it made her blood heat. She groaned.

Did Gabe think she was some kind of nymphomaniac? Or would he distance himself because he considered her uninhibited response a type of psychological therapy?

Jenny buried her head beneath the pillow at the embarrassing possibility.

A soft click sounded. Cautiously, she edged her face free and opened her eyes. Gabe, sweatpants riding low on his lean hips, crossed the room and set a tray on the bedside table. The fragrance of coffee rose from a thermal carafe. "Good morning."

The warm rumble of his voice danced over her nerve endings. Unable to meet his gaze, Jenny closed her eyes. After a moment the side of the bed sagged beneath his weight and he whisked away the concealing pillow. She forced her eyelids to open. His face was inches from hers; a teasing smile brought his elusive dimple into play. Freshly shaved and bare-chested, the man was devastating. "Hi," she forced out. Her voice sounded squeaky.

"Are we having a case of buyer's remorse this morning?" he inquired. Devil lights danced in his eyes.

"What do you mean?" Jenny clutched the sheet beneath her chin.

"I figure you have two ways to go," he said reasonably. "You're either trying to convince yourself I was just being kind to you because you'd been through a traumatic experience, or you suspect I think you're an oversexed nymph disguised as a Sunday School teacher. I plead guilty to planting the first idea, but that was only an excuse to put off what was going to happen eventually anyway. Which one have you decided on?"

Jenny groaned and attempted to shrink into the mattress. "I don't know," she wailed. "I've never been like that before."

The sight of Gabe's satisfied smile this close made her breath hitch. His lips when he kissed her were warm and seeking, with a promise of much more. He pulled away and cupped her cheek in his callused fingers. "Neither have I, and it scared the hell out of me. We lit some pretty big fires."

Without thinking, Jenny blurted, "I didn't know making love could be like that."

"Kind of like knowing how to drive your old Ford, and then getting behind the wheel of a Porsche for the first time," he said solemnly.

Jenny swallowed her sigh of relief and smiled at his male arrogance. "That's quite the nicest thing anyone has ever said to me." If she'd been standing, her knees would have given way. Then caution intervened. Once before, she had leaped into love, and the results were disastrous. Jenny prayed she had learned her lesson, that this time would be different. But she had to be sure. "Gabe. I might be out of my depth."

He surprised her by responding seriously, "I'm not." He kissed her softly. "Let me keep you afloat till you learn how to swim, okay?" With that he reached to the foot of the bed, picked up a short terry-cloth robe and threw it to her. "I fixed breakfast. Bill and Gigi are coming for lunch."

"Prompt as ever," Gabe said two hours later. He bussed Gigi on her lips. Catching Bill's disapproving glare, he winked at him and stole another kiss. "And pretty as ever," he added, gazing appreciatively at her mane of shining copper hair.

Gigi Gates was one of the few females Gabe considered his friend. In his experience, most women manipulated relationships to their advantage, when all he had ever demanded was honesty. Bill never tired of telling him his wariness bordered on a phobia, but Gigi, her bright blue eyes sparkling with humor, had told him he was elusive, a natural challenge for any ambitious woman. After reminding him that she'd already achieved her own ambition, she treated him as if he were an inept younger brother.

"You can take your hands off my wife now. She's in a delicate condition, and she doesn't need her hormones disturbed any more than they are already," Bill ordered.

"No kidding!" Gabe stepped back and looked at Gigi's tall, willowy figure with narrowed eyes. "When did that happen? Last week?" He rolled his eyes suggestively.

Gigi laughed, and Bill replied, "If she weren't already seven weeks pregnant, we would have done the deed two nights ago after I told her what kind of an outfit you needed for Jenny. We got turned on, planning the particulars." He cast a glance around the big room. "Where is she? Still recovering from last night?"

Even though Bill was referring to Jenny's experience at The Stuffed Olive, Gabe's cheeks warmed. Positive his sated state was written on his face, he turned toward the kitchen to hide his expression. Over his shoulder, he said, "She should be down anytime. You want a drink before lunch?"

"This is a workday for me, remember? My clients prefer me sober and respectable." Bill followed him into the kitchen, while Gigi headed for the caricatures Jenny had painted on the walls. "Have you told Jenny what the next move is?"

Gabe handed him a big bowl of salad, then turned to the oven and peered in at the chicken casserole. "I refuse to allow her to take any more risks like last night, and this caper will be tougher to pull off. Don't bring it up while we're eating."

"Back to Plan A, are we? Lock the pretty widow in your apartment while you do the dirty, then present her with the results after you've slain her dragons yourself. Big, macho hero man," Bill teased.

"The widow intends to be with him every step of the way," Jenny said from the bottom of the stairs.

Gabe straightened, wincing when he encountered her accusing gaze. "We'll talk about it after lunch."

"We'll talk about it now. How dare you even consider such a thing?" Jenny demanded, glaring at him.

Ignoring Bill's delighted grin, Gabe glared back. "Last night you at least had a fifty-fifty chance going in. You also lucked out because Uncle G. apparently has some kind of father fixation for you. Nick Kamanedes is mine. DeWitt stole from him, too, and he's willing to kill to get his share of the money that little weasel stowed in his Swiss account. Since Sterling and I have the number and a legitimate claim on the contents, I hold all four aces." He softened his voice. "Tania shoved you into their line of fire, hoping to get you eliminated. I'm just doing my d . . . best to keep you safe."

If she appreciated his substitution, she made no sign. "Nick Kamanedes thinks I'm a party to this awful scheme. So I'm the obvious one to convince him I had no part of anything that's happened. And that Uncle G. didn't, either. I owe him that."

"Fat chance. This job will take muscle." Gabe turned and reached for an oven glove. "We'll talk about this after lunch. A civilized lunch. Gigi's eating for two."

"I certainly am, and two is just as hungry as one is," Gigi said as she entered the kitchen. She eyed Jenny, then held out her hand. "Hi. I'm Gigi Gates. Those slacks and that knit top suit you, although picking out the call-girl outfit was more fun than I've had in years. I'm sorry I missed the show. Bill said you looked terrific."

"You didn't need to rescue me, Gigi. I'm capable of protecting myself," Gabe protested.

Gigi grinned at him. "I never gave rescuing you the first

thought, sweetie. You got what you deserved. I agree with Jenny, you know. She has every right to see this through to the end. If I were in her shoes, I'd face the devil myself. It would be the only way I'd ever feel completely safe." She turned to Jenny. "Men are so thickheaded about understanding how women feel."

His head spinning from such tilted logic, Gabe carried the casserole to the table with Bill's laughter ringing in his ears.

Buoyed by Gigi's unexpected support, Jenny ate heartily. No further mention was made of Nick Kamanedes, but she knew Gabe was busy concocting unassailable arguments against her accompanying him to confront the head of the Kamanedes family. The man was so full of contradictions! Last night, he had given her control of their lovemaking. Certainly a man intuitive enough to guess her need to exorcize her sexual demons couldn't be this thickheaded about her need to clear the air with Kamanedes personally.

With a sinking heart, she acknowledged to herself that Gabe Daniels wasn't a good prospect for permanence of any kind. If she told him she was falling in love with him, he'd probably take her along in the hopes that she would be killed, then run like the wind in the opposite direction.

Gigi's voice broke into her thoughts. "Those caricatures you did on the wall are great. I've met only Sterling and Will, but I feel as if I'd recognize any of the others as soon as I saw them. Would you be willing to do a mural for our nursery? I can't even visualize flowers and cute animals with human faces, much less create them. I'd pay you, of course," she added hurriedly.

"Then you better have a one-day pregnancy," Gabe grumbled. "That's about her life expectancy if she goes with me to confront Nick Kamanedes. Those goons of his don't ask questions. They just shoot. And it doesn't matter what the target is."

Jenny felt a surge of anger so intense she hurt. How dare he be condescending and negative? Clenching her fists until her nails cut into her palms, she said scathingly, "Your faith in me is touching. Last night you apologized for allowing me to undertake such a disgusting masquerade. After, that is, you complimented me on my performance. Now you act as if I can't take care of myself if I go with you. I'm not a weak sister, Gabe. I was married to Trent Travino for six years, remember?"

"Yeah, and he kept you on a short leash," he said flatly.

"You're a man. You have no idea what it's like to have no freedom, to be treated like an ornament . . . to be cut off from all your . . ." Her voice broke as she struggled for control, then she finished, "friends."

Jenny pushed herself unsteadily to her feet. She'd hoped never to find it necessary to share any of the details from those awful years. "Three months after our wedding, Trent ordered our gardener's legs broken. While I watched. That was Pedro's punishment for speaking to me." She felt the tears coursing down her cheeks and tried to control her shaking voice. "It wasn't even his fault. I'd asked him about his family. All the poor man did was answer my questions."

"Jesus!" Gabe surged to his feet and tried to pull her into his arms.

She pushed him away. "Don't you tell me I have no experience with violence, Mr. Daniels. I let myself be intimidated and forced into silence all those years, but never again. And don't you dare tell me I'm not to go through with this, because I can and I will. Risks be damned!"

Nearly blinded by her tears, Jenny fled up the spiral

staircase to her bedroom. She'd been stupid. After one night with Gabe, she'd allowed herself to trust him. Was she so hungry for closeness that she'd interpreted his concern for love? Only a fool would fall into the same trap a second time.

She picked up her tote and dumped it on the bed. Swiping away tears as she worked, she repacked it with the few things she would need until she'd found herself a place to stay. The Lady Smith went in last, cushioned between the extra underwear Gigi had purchased for her and the side of the tote, where she could reach it quickly.

That finished, she went into the bathroom to repair her face. She could hardly set out on the streets of New York with puffy eyes and tearstained cheeks.

The ice-cold washcloth felt like heaven against her burning eyes. Opening the floodgates of her past had dredged up painful memories of Trent's mind games. She began to cry again, warming the cloth with hot tears. She reached blindly for the faucet.

Warm fingers wrapped around hers and took the cloth from her. "Let me do that."

Squinting through swollen lids, Jenny glared at Gabe's reflection in the mirror. "Leave me alone."

Ignoring her order, he wrung out the folded cloth before giving it back to her. "You win, Jenny."

"I never win. I'm the biggest loser in history. And stupid along with it," she said bitterly, pressing the blessed coldness over her eyes. At least her tears had stopped flowing.

"I'll take you with me. We'll confront Kamanedes together." He lifted her, turning her around so she sat on the vanity.

His hands lingered at her waist, and his voice was low and apologetic. "I should have guessed what you've been through. I should have noticed that you avoid mentioning Trent in anything but general terms. The report on him mentioned his reputation for brutality. Any idiot should have realized he created situations for the purpose of controlling you." His voice faltered. "Something in me wouldn't believe you'd been terrorized."

Jenny shuddered. "He waited until the honeymoon was over, until he was convinced I was so besotted I'd be intimidated by his temper tantrums. They got worse after the first year, when I hadn't become pregnant."

"He was a bastard."

"Literally," Jenny said, lowering the cloth.

"What?"

"His mother is Uncle G.'s sister, Rose. His father was an enforcer who was killed in a drug deal gone bad before they had time to tie the knot." Jenny wondered why that hadn't turned up in his background check, then reminded herself that Gabe's primary interest had been in her, not Trent.

Gabe's hands had tightened around her waist, and he stared at her intently. "Go on."

"Rose was obsessive about Trent from the day he was born. He once told me that when he was little, he was never allowed to get dirty, much less do anything the least bit dangerous. Rose was the one who insisted he go to law school, so that he wouldn't be in the front line, so to speak. When Trent was killed, she nearly went mad with grief." Jenny wondered what she had said to make Gabe's eyes darken, as if his thoughts had turned inward.

His fingers absentmindedly caressing her waist, Gabe said, "When Tania was there, in Baltimore, you mentioned Rose."

A vast wave of sadness rolled through Jenny at the reference to Tania. She said falteringly, "Rose's hatred of me wasn't a secret. Before . . . back when I thought Tania was my friend, we joked about that."

"While she was humping him," Gabe pointed out.

Wrenching free of his hold, Jenny cried, "Why must you keep rubbing my face in that? To remind me that I was such a cold fish I couldn't hold his interest? That I was so unacceptable his family hated me? That I was so stupid I married into the whole ghastly mess in the first place? All right! I was all those things. I was naive and blind and ignorant and . . ."

Gabe buried the rest of her tirade against his shoulder. "I wasn't trying to make you look stupid. I'm trying to show you how foolish it is to go on believing such crap. The Travinos did a number on you. Apparently Uncle G. was the only one who didn't go along with it. Maybe I owe him more than I realized."

Jenny pushed against him, loosening his hold. She looked up into his intent face, at his beautiful mouth tilted in a tight, crooked smile.

"You survived all that. Only a tough lady could have carried off that little scam last night the way you did." He touched her cheek tenderly. "But even while I was admiring your ability to play the part, I was so scared my guts nearly ate me and spit me out in little pieces. I hated myself for letting you be there."

He closed his eyes and rested his forehead against hers. "Dammit, Jenny, I understand how Trent's mother felt about him. I feel the same way about you. I want to wrap you in velvet and put you in a nice safe cage behind locked doors. I don't want you close to the filth we're dealing with. I hate taking a chance on your getting hurt."

Jenny thought her heart skipped a beat. Gabe wasn't really playing the macho, controlling male when he insisted she stay behind. He was genuinely concerned.

Her cautious inner voice warned her this was a long way from loving, but she ignored the voice. She couldn't remember any time in her life when someone had offered to fight her battles for her. Cupping his face with her hands, she moved his head far enough away to look into his eyes before she said, "All Rose's care didn't keep Trent alive. You could lock me up here until you've killed all my dragons, or you could send me back to Donhaven. I still might get hit by lightning."

"I've heard that crappy philosophy a million times, and I never did buy it. Besides, you might as well know right now that you'll return to Donhaven only over my dead body." With that he lifted her and carried her to her bed.

Just before midnight, Jenny pulled close-fitting black slacks over her trembling legs and tried to steady her nerves by reliving the ecstasy of the afternoon. The intensity of Gabe's lovemaking had both drained and exhilarated her. Still wary, she'd allowed her love to fill her heart, but hadn't given it voice. Love had no place in their next undertaking.

Jenny pulled the black turtleneck over her head and folded the collar with nervous precision, then surveyed herself in the mirrored bathroom door. The reflection, a slender figure in black, didn't reveal the tremor in her knees nor the fear in her heart. She looked competent and trim. On the bed lay a black silk stocking cap and gloves. She felt like a cat burglar.

"Very nice."

Gabe's voice came from the doorway. The mirror reflected his body, garbed just as hers was, except his big, muscular frame looked tough, almost predatory, as opposed to her own slender silhouette. He approached her from behind. She forced her suddenly stiff lips to move. "At least you don't need to wear a silly cap."

His reflection merged with hers as Gabe wrapped his arms around her. "You're trembling."

"I can't help it," she said. Her face felt as if she'd had an injection of Novocain. In the mirror, she saw the wide grin that split Gabe's face.

"What's so funny?"

His chuckle tickled her ear. Bending his head, he brushed his lips over the skin just above her collar. "Last night you wiggled and bounced your way into a private Mafia party dressed like the party girl of the year without so much as the flicker of an eyelash. And tonight you're nervous. Sweetheart, all we're going to do tonight is break into Nick Kamanedes's home and have a little private talk with him."

They'd been over all this before. Jenny gave an exasperated sigh and pulled away from him. "Gabe, there was nothing illegal about my taking the place of one of the . . . ladies last night, but housebreaking is against the law."

SIXTEEN

Half an hour later, brakes squealing, Gabe turned Bill's unobtrusive Honda into a short alley. He doused the lights until he reached the next street, where he turned left before swerving into a parking space at the curb. When Jenny opened her mouth to speak, he covered her lips with his hand while he watched the alley exit in his rearview mirror and listened intently. When no one followed, he turned his lights back on and pulled out into the street. The driver of the taxi he cut off hit his horn and his brakes at the same time.

Convinced their pursuers of the night before were Kamanedes henchmen, he'd left the pickup in the garage and commandeered one of Bill's cars to cut the risk of telegraphing their arrival. By leaving from his friend's garage on the other side of the building, they had diminished the possibility of a tail, but Gabe had no intention of taking chances.

He headed for New Jersey, hoping to God their information about Kamanedes's habits, as unbelievable as it was, was accurate.

As if picking up on his doubt by thought transference, Jenny demanded, "Do you truly believe a Mafia don stays up half the night in his own guest house watching Three Stooges movies?"

"Bill's sources are excellent. According to them, Nick's also fond of the Marx brothers," Gabe said, blending into the heavy flow of traffic over the Hudson River.

Jenny shrugged. "I suppose that's just bizarre enough to be true."

"My own take is that he's depressed by his useless sons and the rest of the goons who work for him, so he watches slapstick to remind himself things could be worse." Gabe sensed a loosening of the tension that had gripped her ever since he had explained exactly what lay ahead. Once again, he'd thrown subtlety out the window. He intended to breach the security of the Kamanedes compound during the only chink in Nick's schedule that hinted he might be alone. Jenny's insistence on coming along was the only hitch in the plan. If there was trouble . . .

Gabe consigned that possibility to the file containing things he had no control over and continued, "The man is so paranoid that he names two different bodyguards every morning. They're joined at the hip with him every minute of the day. Even when he goes to the john."

Jenny chuckled. "I've heard about the guards. Uncle G. once said that they scratched when Nick scratched. I was so naive I thought he was making that up simply to be insulting."

Directing his concentration toward merging onto Route 80, Gabe said, "Uncle G. must have cleaned up the story for you. Bill's source quoted much more colorful examples."

"I've sufficient imagination to supply those on my own, thank you," she reminded him.

God, he loved it when she turned prissy. At least now she was relaxed. He dug beneath the seat, pulled out a leather pouch, and dropped it into her lap. "Here. A little present from Gigi."

From the corner of his eye, he watched her loosen the flap and stare at the contents. "It's an ankle holster and a two-shot .45. She thought you'd feel better carrying that, since you can't hide your gun in that outfit."

Jenny fumbled with the holster, then drew her left foot up onto the seat and rolled up her pant leg. "There's enough room if I turn up a cuff . . ." Minutes later, she stretched out her leg as far as she could in the cramped interior, flexed her knee, and practiced bringing her hand to the inside of her ankle. "It's perfect, Gabe. You've no idea how comfortable I am knowing I have this." Jenny settled back into the seat. "Now I have an excuse to do Gigi's nursery murals for free. She's a nice person, Gabe."

"Yeah." Something in Jenny's voice made Gabe wonder how long it had been since she'd had a woman friend who bothered to do her a genuine kindness. Tania's false friendship didn't qualify. "You do realize," he said, pointing to her ankle, "that thing is only for an emergency. You only have two chances to drop your target. And you'd better be real close." He paused, then added with forced optimism, "Of course, this drop-in tonight is a slam dunk. You probably won't even need that little piece."

Jenny leaned down to test the gun's accessibility. "I know," she mimicked. "Do what I'm told and stay out of your way. You'll keep me safe. You are carrying a gun, aren't you?"

"My Beretta's in a holster at my back, and I'm wearing a toy just like the one you have. Would you mind telling me why Trent armed you and taught you to shoot?"

"It's very simple. We'd been married only a month, and he wanted to impress me with how generous he was. He also knew I was incapable of killing him, even after I learned to hate him." She turned away to stare at the traffic beside her, but not before he saw the anguish on her face. "The gun and the shooting lessons were part of his game. After . . . the really bad lessons, like poor Pedro . . . and several other incidents, he would treat me coldly for several weeks, to teach me my proper place."

Her slender fingers contracted into fists, then relaxed. "When he decided I was sufficiently cowed, he would lavish me with attention." She grimaced. "I'm so slow. I'd stopped loving him after the first year, but it took me another whole year to recognize the pattern. His changes of mood were used to control me, sort of like in that old movie, *Gaslight*. Remember how Charles Boyer tried to convince Ingrid Bergman she was crazy? Learning to counter Trent in little ways kept me sane."

Gabe's foot pressed so hard on the gas the car accelerated, nearly ramming the car in front of them. He took the rest of his anger out on the brake pedal. "Dammit! He was the unstable one."

"Someone else must have thought so, too, or he'd still be alive," she responded quietly.

The remainder of the trip to the Kamanedes compound took place in silence.

After guiding the Honda onto a quiet residential street with widely spaced houses, Gabe checked his watch. "One-thirty, right on schedule. We'll hoof it from here. It's less than half a mile. Even as bad as his security is, one of the goons might notice a car parked too close to the property." He removed the car key, placed it in the palm of her hand, and closed her fingers around it. "Put this in your pocket. There's another key beneath the rim at the top of the right rear fender in case you lose this one."

Not giving Jenny a chance to respond, he got out and hurried around to the passenger side. When her door swung open, she demanded, "What was that all about?"

"Shhh. We don't want the people who live here calling

the cops," he warned softly. "If we get separated, or if any-thing happens to me, get out and run like hell." He hooked his arm through hers and began walking away from the car.

"You told me this afternoon the whole caper would work like a charm, that it would be routine," she protested in a half-murmur, running to keep up with his long strides. "You were lying, weren't you. You're afraid there'll be trouble."

Gabe stared at the walkway ahead of them as he an-swered, "Of course I was lying. This thing could blow up in our faces, and there's no fallback. You're the one who wanted to be included." He stopped abruptly, drawing her behind an immense blue spruce, out of the illuminated circle cast by a wrought-iron light post at the corner of a driveway.

She felt the tremor in his hands as he pulled her close. "Shit. I sound like some kind of nutcase." He kissed her, hard, his fingers digging into her ribs. "I've got a rotten feeling about this. Jenny, if anything should happen to you . . ."

"Nothing will go wrong," she said, praying she was right. Then she added more confidently, "Nothing will happen to either of us. We'll talk to Nick and then we'll leave. I'm sure he'll believe me." She mentally crossed her fingers. "Anyone who puts up with such clumsy sons has to have some goodness in him."

Gabe's response was an uncommunicative grunt. His hold tightened, and he kissed her once more, this time as if he would never let her go. With a sigh, he tugged her back to the walkway. "You've shot my focus all to hell. Just re-member what I said to do if things go sour." He lowered his voice as they reached a decorative brick walk. "We better not talk anymore. This leads through a communal park that backs up on Nick's place. Just a green space, really, but teenagers sometimes sneak in to . . ."

"I've heard about drugs, booze and sex, Gabe," she reminded him in a soft whisper. "The place appears deserted tonight."

Fifteen minutes later, after traversing a path that wound through shrubs and trees, they arrived at a deep brick wall. Leaning close, Gabe whispered, "Same kind Sterling has in Palm Springs, only this time you'll be breaking in, instead of out."

Jenny suppressed a spurt of laughter. If nothing else, the reminder relaxed her.

The extent of Bill's research fascinated her. He'd unearthed the fact that Nick Kamanedes didn't believe in electronic sensors, or even barbed wire. He relied on regular patrols by security guards to ensure his privacy. "Worse than that, his sons hire some of the biggest blockheads in New Jersey as guards. On the cheap. Nick doesn't know Ricco and Nunzio are salting away the surplus," Bill had reported with a cynical chuckle.

Gabe boosted her up, and she once again found herself flat on her stomach atop a wide wall. After making sure no guards loomed on the other side, she inched over the edge feetfirst and dropped to the ground, landing in some sort of deep, springy ground cover. Juniper, she decided, as the fragrance of the bruised twigs reached her nostrils.

As instructed, she melted into the shadows to wait for Gabe.

Moments later, he dropped to the ground beside her. He coiled the slim nylon rope with a three-pronged hook on the end that he'd used to reach the top of the wall and tucked it behind a shrub at the base of the structure, pulling her close to point out its hiding place. When she looked at him questioningly, he shook his head. In the fading moonlight, she saw his hand motion to the left. She fell into step behind him. His need to point out his precautions to ensure her escape without him made Jenny nervous. What had made Gabe so jumpy?

The guest house was located in the far corner of the compound, fifty yards from where they stood. A broad patio, edged with decorative urns and low shrubs, surrounded the rear half. Heavy draperies concealed any lights from within. Gabe's hand pressed her shoulder. Puzzled, she nonetheless cooperated when he pushed her down behind a stone bench and threw himself beside her. With his hand at her nape, he turned her face toward the ground to avoid detection in the fading starlight.

Seconds later, plodding footsteps approached. Jenny heard the click of a lighter. The smell of tobacco smoke wafted toward them. After a pause, the footsteps continued along the path and faded in the distance. Gabe's lips moved against her temple. "Do just as I say. I'm going in first. If I don't signal you to follow within ten minutes, you're out of here." He dropped a kiss on her forehead, sprang to his feet, and was gone.

If she could have reached her gun in time, Jenny would have shot him. They were to have gone in together, in hopes the unexpectedness of their arrival would keep Kamanedes quiet until they could convince him they hadn't come to kill him. Damn the man for being overprotective! She noted with satisfaction that mental cursing had begun to come easily to her. Gabe Daniels was enough to drive her to much worse than that.

The thin blade of Gabe's knife easily released the latch of the French doors; he edged the left one inward a scant half-inch. The hairs on the back of his neck were standing on end. The setup was all wrong. He'd had a bad feeling about this from the start. Kamanedes wasn't alone. The musky odor of sex, overlaid by a heavy fragrance similar to the one Jenny had worn the night before, reached him.

A coaxing voice reached his ears. "You sure you don't want me to stay for another round, Nickie honey?" Apparently, classic slapstick wasn't the only thing that kept Nick entertained through the early hours of the morning.

"Today was a bitch. I'm going to hit the sack. You run along home, Susie. Make sure one of the guards walks you to your car."

Gabe smiled in the darkness. Nick Kamanedes's voice rasped like a rusty door hinge as it made the naive suggestion to the departing prostitute. He was willing to make book the compliant Susie picked up a second, if smaller, fee for action in the backseat of her car before she left for home.

Moments later a door closed, and the bickering voices of the Three Stooges broke the silence. Nick apparently really was indulging himself in his ostensible excuse for the seclusion of the guest house. Gabe hoped to hell he'd put clothes on. His stomach sure as hell wasn't up to the sight of the aging warlord in the nude. Drawing a deep, quiet breath, he edged the door inward and slipped inside, behind the lined, antique satin draperies. Leaving the door ajar a hair's width, he moved to his right. He was reaching behind his back for his gun when Nick's voice said, "Come on out, Daniels. I've been expecting you. My lookout signaled when you came over the wall."

Gabe counted to ten, then edged aside the heavy fabric, his hands hanging free at his sides. "You're an easy man to underestimate, Nick."

"It comes in handy." Nick beckoned to him from the

lush brocade sofa. A short, garish, electric-blue satin robe was belted around his considerable middle, not quite reaching his knobby knees; his bare feet were propped on a fat ottoman. Waving the remote in his left hand, Nick muted the sound emanating from the television. His right hand cuddled an Uzi in his lap.

"Nice equipment, Nick. Your supplier must have a pipeline to Russia," Gabe quipped.

Nick's small eyes retreated farther into his face as he growled, "You're a cool bastard, Daniels, I'll give you that. Now convince me why I shouldn't just blow you away. Word on the street is you're a real smooth talker."

Gabe kept his gaze on Kamanedes. He sensed, rather than saw, a faint movement behind the louvered door at the other side of the room, and knew he had to get out of range of the opening.

Keeping his eyes level and his hands in sight, he sauntered over to stand facing his captor. "Thanks for the compliment. The word on you is that you're a real reasonable man. That's why I'm here. I thought I could help clear up some misunderstandings for you."

"Yeah. Sure. And then maybe I'll set you straight on a few things," Nick said jovially. He pitched the remote to the cushion beside him and snapped the fingers of his left hand. "Roberto . . ." The louvered door swung open and a slim, dark-haired man in his thirties stepped through. "This damn gun is getting too heavy. Search him. Then get lost. We got business to discuss."

The bodyguard's hands were a little too personal, but Gabe decided not to make an issue of it. With regret, he watched his guns disappear into the other room. He prayed Jenny was already climbing the wall and heading for safety.

Nick shoved the Uzi carelessly between the cushions of

the overstuffed sofa. "So. Did you come to bring me the number of that little weasel's Swiss bank account?"

Gabe shook his head and waggled his fingers derisively. "Nick, Nick, Nick. Have you been reading fairy tales again? Sterling has first dibbies. His lawyers are already filing the paperwork to claim his share."

Kamanedes laughed mirthlessly, the movements of his substantial belly loosening the belt of his robe. The older man's dark, beady eyes turned crafty. "How about his lawyers sharpen their imaginations and claim the whole apple? Then your grandpa can hand over what's mine to get you back."

Gabe sank into a nearby chair and stretched his legs out in front of him. He crossed his ankles. "Not in this lifetime. Haven't you heard? I'm nothing but a thorn in his side. Anyway, why should Sterling do you any favors? Some of the dirt might rub off. Right now his shirttails are clean, but he has enough solid information on you to put you in a penitentiary for the rest of your life. Last I heard, he was itching to clean out his files."

"You're bluffing." Sweat appeared on Kamanedes's broad forehead.

"Then call it. Your fingerprints were all over DeWitt's murder. Sterling has a copy of the kill order from your E-mail." Gabe grinned broadly, hoping Nick wouldn't recognize a bluff. "Shit. Those damn computers are supposed to be secure."

"You know what they say. Some days you get the bear; some days the bear gets you. Tough luck, Nickie." He kept the louvered door in sight.

Kamanedes glared at him, then snarled, "You goddamn college boys are too damn smart. I want my money! That son of a bitch DeWitt skimmed over three million from my operation! Now everyone thinks I'm a patsy. You and that snake-in-the-grass Travino have screwed me around long enough."

Pretending innocence, Gabe said blandly, "Travino's screwing you, too? You do have your problems."

Jenny edged her way through the side door. After listening at the French door, she'd looked for the exit the call girl with the big hair had used and found it unlocked. She wanted to tell Nick Kamanedes he should be more security-minded, but now wasn't the time. Freeing Gabe had to come first.

Then she intended to use every bit of sincerity she could muster to convince the mob boss that Uncle G. hadn't broken their agreement.

She found herself in a dark, box-like service hall. To her relief, a line of dim light showed beneath a door at the left. Taking a deep breath, Jenny pressed her ear against the panel. When she heard no sound, she closed her hand around the knob and twisted slowly. The latch receded, and she pulled the door toward her until the opening was wide enough to peer through.

She'd found the kitchen. The only light in the room came from beneath the vent above the stove. Gabe's Beretta and his two-shot lay on the end of the counter, just above a dark figure crouched on the floor with his ear pressed against a louvered door. He held a small tape recorder against one of the slots.

Nerves jumping, all the while praying the door hinges were oiled, Jenny eased the door open bit by bit.

The man was so intent on eavesdropping he never heard her approach the counter and swoop up Gabe's Beretta. When she struck the side of his head with the butt of the gun, he crumpled. Jenny grabbed the tape recorder from his hand and tucked it in her back pocket. Then she sank down beside his limp body to listen.

"Don't play stupid, Daniels. I got it all figured out. Travino ordered DeWitt's house searched after my messengers killed him. He'd had that blonde broad in place there in that hick town to weasel her way into DeWitt's mind so he'd tell her about his business with me, but we offed him. She had enough sense to snatch the cat, but you caught her before she could give him the number. They blew the place up to let you know they meant business, but you didn't cave. Since then you've been carting her all over the country. Tell you what. If she knows the number, you can turn her over to me, and I'll let you go."

"What use is she to you? She's just another piece of tail." Gabe sounded bored.

Jenny bit back one of Gabe's favorite words.

Kamanedes's voice raised. "She knows the number. My shysters will deal for my money, and Uncle G. will deal for her. Christ, I'm surprised you hadn't figured all the angles yourself. You're almost as dumb as my sons!"

Beside her, the crumpled figure stirred. Feeling no compunction, Jenny struck the back of his head a second time. She wondered if she had become as callous as she had once accused Gabe of being.

His voice interrupted her thoughts. "You don't have all the angles on this yet. Travino didn't send her, Nick."

"Don't bullshit me, Daniels. Those two rockheads who took him out was supposed to get the cat when they delivered my message. Then Travino's locals blasted the house before I could send someone else in. By the time I discovered you'd snatched both the woman and the cat, all I could do was track you and hope." He leaned forward and smiled triumphantly at Gabe. "You saved me a lot of trouble by coming here tonight. Now I got Sterling by the short hairs."

His gravelly laugh grated on Jenny's ears. She was tired of being a pawn, and she wasn't going to allow Gabe to be one, either. No matter what he felt about her. Without further thought, she stood, kicked the door open and stepped into the room. Holding the Beretta steady with both hands, she aimed at the back of Nick's head. "I don't believe so, Mr. Kamanedes."

Gabe groaned. He should have known Jenny wouldn't do as she'd been told. Abandoning his lazy pose, he stood, crossed the room in two strides and jerked the Uzi from between the cushions. He waved the muzzle in an upward arc. "On your feet, Nick, just in case you've got more firepower stashed in the upholstery."

"Find him a straight chair, and take one yourself, Gabe . . . after you put that thing down on the floor over there by the door." Never had Jenny's speech been colder or crisper. "Since I'm who Mr. Kamanedes really wants, I intend to do the dealing. Even a 'piece of tail' likes to be in charge once in a while." She rounded the end of the sofa and gestured toward the small dining table and chairs near the louvered doors. "Those will do nicely."

Gabe wondered if Jenny realized the danger of their situation. "Why don't you let me hold that thing?" he coaxed.

"I'm quite comfortable with it, thank you," she answered coolly. "Just do as I suggested. Mr. Kamanedes wasn't responding well to your approach, but then perhaps you've given him the impression you're dealing from the bottom of the deck. I feel sure he'll see the light once I've explained the truth to him. He knows I've no reason to lie." Jenny gestured sharply toward Kamanedes, who had lurched to his feet and was looking back and forth between them. She released the safety on the Beretta and waggled the gun at her prisoner. "I'm quite capable of removing a toe, or an even more cherished part of your anatomy, if you don't do as I say immediately."

"She means business, Nick," Gabe interjected. Half-afraid to annoy her in her present mood, he pulled out two cushioned chairs. He turned to face Jenny and sat, unable to avoid noticing how ridiculous Nick looked as he attempted to scuttle toward the chair and snug the belt of his short robe at the same time. His veined bowlegs and bare feet reinforced his age and triggered a faint twinge of sympathy in Gabe's subconscious. It must be hell to get old and be surrounded by incompetents.

Nick fixed a belligerent gaze on Jenny. "I take it you're the broad Travino sent." He smiled and leaned forward. "Tell you what. You give me the account number and I'll forget you was ever involved. After I bypass Mr. Stinking Rich Thomas, I'll settle this other business with Uncle G. my own way."

Jenny rested her hip against the arm of the chair Gabe had vacated and looked at the aging crime lord with disgust. "You're being extremely foolish. Sterling Thomas has the power to put you and your idiot children out of business. Before breakfast. You'd be better off claiming the proceeds Mr. DeWitt skimmed off the top as a business loss when you file your taxes." Her tone dismissed the three million dollars as trivial. "I didn't come here to talk about money."

She stood and moved a foot closer. Keeping her face expressionless, she said, "I am only going to tell you this once. If you don't believe me, I swear I'll shoot you."

Gabe shifted on his chair, and she threw him a look that

nearly froze the tips of his ears. He considered saluting, but decided against it. Now wasn't the time for flippancy.

She turned back to Kamanedes. "You are operating on a false assumption when you claim Uncle G. sent me to trick DeWitt. I knew nothing of his past nor of his activities when I moved to Donhaven. Neither did Uncle G. From the day of Trent's funeral, I'd had no further connection with the Travinos."

"Then what were you doing all tarted up at The Stuffed Olive last night?" Kamanedes broke in. "According to my boys, you and the old man was pretty chummy."

Gabe interjected, "Your boys did a piss-poor job of pursuit, too. Let her finish."

Jenny's cheeks had acquired a pinched look, and Gabe wondered if she would be able to go on with this. He shifted his feet slightly, distributing his weight so he could move in a hurry.

"Sit still, Gabe. I can handle this without your help. You're underestimating me again."

Jenny turned back to Kamanedes. "I attended that party in disguise, for only one reason. To talk with Uncle G. without any members of his family knowing what was said, or even that I was there. You complain about your incompetent sons. Uncle has an even larger problem; someone within his own circle is making it look as if he's breaking the agreement he made with you ten years ago."

"We had a nice little trade going out there. The profits was good until DeWitt started taking his cut off the top. Then Travino muscled onto my turf!" Nick exclaimed.

"You're not listening. Someone else, a person he trusted, was behind that," Jenny countered. "He now knows who the ringleader is. When he discovers how many others are involved, he'll clean his own house." Her voice softened. "He told me to give you his apologies."

"Why should I believe you?" Nick said belligerently. "You just said he cut you loose."

For the first time, Jenny looked disconcerted. Guessing she had nearly reached the end of her ability to intimidate, Gabe interjected, "The maverick planned to kill two birds with one stone, Nick. First, she hired locals to make it look as if Uncle G. was muscling in. After they screwed up, they were eliminated so they couldn't tell anyone she was the one who hired them. She wanted you to make the connection between Jenny and Travino and to take Jenny out. You almost succeeded."

Jenny's face turned white and the Beretta slipped from her suddenly slack fingers. Gabe dived for the weapon and missed. On the second bounce, the gun fired.

SEVENTEEN

Gabe grabbed at his calf and tumbled from his chair, swearing viciously.

Horrified, Jenny knelt beside him. "Oh, God! Gabe, I'm sorry. I'm so sorry." She reached to pull his hand away.

He rolled to his other side to avoid her touch just as the French doors burst open. Three guards crowded around Gabe and Jenny, pointing guns, shouting threats and jostling each other. Roberto, one hand cherishing his head, erupted from behind the louvered doors. Jenny threw herself over Gabe and looked up at the henchmen fiercely. "All of you back off. Right now!" she ordered. Oddly, she had no fear for herself, only for Gabe.

"You heard the lady. Enough!" Nick's voice thundered over the babble, and Jenny glimpsed the authority that had kept him at the head of his organization for so many years. The guards lowered their guns and Roberto sidled back toward the kitchen. "Hugo. Get Doc Larabee over here." One of the guards pulled a cell phone from his belt and dialed.

"No doctors," Gabe gasped. "The bullet just creased me. We don't want a gunshot wound reported." He tried to sit up. "Get off me, Jenny. I don't think Nick wants me to die yet."

Nick smiled at him mirthlessly. "Doc Larabee don't report nothing. He can't practice no more. I want you patched up so we can talk. If you talk good, maybe you'll convince me the lady's right." Without turning his head, he asked, "What happened to your head, Roberto? You got blood running down your ear."

"I hit him. Twice." Jenny remembered the tape recorder. When Nick eyed her in disbelief, she continued, "It was the only way I could get through the kitchen. Did you tell him to record your conversation with Gabe?" She reached into her hip pocket, pulled out the miniature machine, and offered it to him.

Swearing comprehensively, Nick grasped Roberto's shirt and jerked him so close their noses nearly touched. "Who are you spying for?" When he received no answer, he nodded to the other two guards. "Take him into the kitchen and find out who's paying him." He spat, as if to clear a bad taste from his mouth.

Once again retying his belt, he extended his hand for the tape recorder, which he dropped on the table beside him. Then he crossed the room and sank onto the edge of the sofa near where Gabe sat clutching his leg. "The little scum is ratting to someone." He spread his hands helplessly. "We spy on each other to keep a step ahead. Nickel-and-dime stuff, like some damn book. Enough to eat your guts out. Used to be, Uncle G. and I played straight with one another. Things was fine."

He looked gravely at Jenny. "I like your style. You're an up-front lady. You didn't have no business married to Trent Travino. He was twisted."

Unwilling to discuss Trent, now or ever, Jenny pretended she hadn't heard. She seized a box of tissues from the table next to the sofa and folded several together. Pushing Gabe's hand away from his leg, she enlarged the tear in his black jeans and pressed the thick pad against the shallow furrow on the outside of his left calf. The bleeding had nearly stopped. "Stop pulling away," she ordered as he tugged against her hand.

"Dammit, quit fussing over me. It's just a scratch," Gabe said irritably.

"Don't try to play hero. Your wound has to be cleaned. You should thank Mr. Kamanedes for calling in a doctor." Jenny pressed harder against the wound.

"Dammit, you're crying. I didn't think you cared," he said arrogantly.

"She's crying because you ain't got the manners to thank me for what I done. The lady's got too much class to cry over you," Nick pointed out.

Gabe cupped her face with one hand, dabbing at her cheeks with his other. She realized tears were trickling down both sides of her nose. "Mr. Kamanedes is right. I'm not crying over you. Why should I care if you bleed to death?" She pushed his hand away. "He's right. You should thank him for calling the doctor."

"I hope to hell not. I've cut myself worse than this shaving." His gruff voice held embarrassment. "My manners aren't your problem."

Everything was too much for Jenny. "You could have d-died! Those p-poor stupid boys in Donhaven . . . and Faith . . . and Lord knows who else. Dead. Just because I married Trent. And now I don't even understand why I did it!" Jenny pressed the pad of tissues more firmly against Gabe's leg and let her tears fall.

"Jesus, woman, not so hard. I don't need a tourniquet," he said tenderly, prying her fingers loose and cradling her against him. "Stop crying, or Nick's going to think you were bluffing when you threatened to shoot him. If he decides you're a weak sister, he'll change his mind about negotiating. Who said you were so important that all of this has been your fault?" He pulled the black silk cap from her head and her hair fell loose.

His tenderness surrounded her like a magic quilt. Her tears slowed. She opened her eyes and saw Nick watching her intently. For the first time, she saw the intelligence in the dark eyes nearly buried in his fleshy face. "Mr. Kamanedes won't try to trick me. He knows I told him the truth."

A scuffling sound from the kitchen drew Nick's attention. "I gotta see what Roberto spilled. When I come back, we'll deal. You got yourself a classy broad there, Daniels." As he stood, a tall, distinguished-looking man stepped through the French doors. Nick pointed at Gabe. "There's your patient."

An hour and a half later, one of Nick's guards drove Gabe and Jenny back to their car. Gabe limped to the passenger side and held out his hand to Jenny for the key.

She retrieved it. "Your leg must hurt terribly. Do you want me to drive?" she asked in a subdued voice.

He made a disgusted sound, unlocking the door and swinging it open before gesturing her in with his other arm. "Don't hover. I'm treating you the way a classy broad should be treated. Nick said you should go home and rest. Who am I to disobey him?" After she settled herself on the seat, he rounded the car and slid behind the wheel. "Of course, I'm the one with the hole in my leg and the black market pain pills in my pocket. If you drive and Nick gets wind of it, he'll probably send his boys to work me over. What is it with you and these aging syndicate types?"

He twisted the key in the ignition and pulled away from the curb.

Jenny smiled sadly. "I treat them with respect. Haven't you figured out yet that that's the one thing they crave most?"

"Yeah. Sure. So I'm supposed to respect people who dole out murder on order, distribute drugs, steal, run prostitutes and protection scams?" Gabe grimaced at the throbbing in his leg. His wound hurt like hell. "And that's just for starters. I could get into the really good stuff if you want to hear."

"I mean on a personal level. Their underlings, even their families, are like employees. They say what their boss wants to hear, but deep down, most of them are hoping he'll die or step aside to give them more power." She rested her head on the back of the seat. "You've never lived with them. Since I wasn't really ever included in the conversation at weekly family gatherings, I observed a great deal. Believe me, I'm right."

Gabe accelerated around a slow-moving car. Jenny's insight amazed him. His mind recoiled at the thought of her six-year immersion in the murky world of the Travinos. That she had emerged with her values and her honor intact was a miracle.

Jenny continued. "Nick's a perfect example. I think he's better friends with that poor unlicensed doctor than he is with his own sons."

"They sure showed up fast. Probably hoped he was dead." The younger Kamanedes had arrived while the doctor was cleaning his wound; for one nervous moment, he'd braced himself for gunfire.

"Dr. Larabee was quite drunk, Gabe. Was he competent?"

Gabe glanced in the rearview mirror, relieved to see nothing suspicious. "Bastards like that do their best work when they're buzzed, and most are buzzed twenty-four seven." Jenny's concern while Larabee bandaged his leg had touched him. His poor tired mother had been so immersed in her own misery that she'd had little sympathy left over for his minor hurts. "I don't think he appreciated your suggestions about cleanliness."

Her only answer was a disgusted sniff.

"I hope your magic works on Sterling when you tell him you promised he'd file a claim on DeWitt's account for twice as much money as the bastard stole from him . . . and then give Nick his share." He savored the thought of how her promise would outrage Sterling's ironclad ethics. Should he break that bit of news before or after reminding Sterling of his orders to Gabe to neutralize or remove any threat to Jenny's existence?

Listening to Jenny assure Sterling she was sure he'd want to do the right thing would be better than a Broadway show. The woman certainly had a way with men of a certain age. He grinned, admitting to himself that her power worked pretty well with him, too.

Gabe snatched a quick sideways look at her. Jenny's head rested against the headrest; her eyes were closed. In the eerie glow of halogen lights, the purity of her profile made something inside him clench. A subtle tension flattened the skin around her lips, and he knew she was brooding on the events of the past week. Gabe felt an urge to commandeer Sterling's jet and fly her to a remote island in the South Pacific, far away from danger and jealousy and greed and filth. He would pamper her and cherish her and make love to her until they both fell over from exhaustion. And then he'd begin all over again.

For the first time in his life, he envisioned a future that included a woman. Not just any woman, but Jenny. He imagined what it would be like to hear her soft, cultivated boarding-school tones at the breakfast table each morning, close to his ear in the dark hours of the night. He groaned softly at the realization that he had never before wanted a woman so desperately.

Her voice broke into his fantasy. "Your leg is more painful than you'll admit, isn't it. You needn't play macho man for me." The words, uttered in such prim tones, and the touch of her hand on his thigh, affected him so strongly he nearly rammed into the back end of the old Dodge lumbering along ahead of them. Lost in his fantasy world, he'd forgotten his wound. "Sure it hurts. The pain'll go away in a few days. Nothing to it," he lied.

"Gabe." She said his name as if she enjoyed the feel of it on her lips. "What are we going to do about Tania?"

He sighed. Leave it to Jenny. Gabe wondered if he could convince her to forget about Tania and run away. Let Uncle G. handle the murdering bitch. Asking wouldn't hurt. "Why don't we let things play out? Uncle G. will take care of that one. You and I have to lay our deal with Nick on Sterling's table, remember?"

After a long silence, she replied, "She's as much Trent's victim as I was. She didn't kill Trent, and I'm terribly afraid Uncle G. will have her eliminated if he thinks she did." She turned her head to look out at the passing cars. "As much as she's damaged me, she doesn't deserve that. I want to warn her. Not just about Uncle G., but about something else. Is there any way I can meet with her? She should have the chance to run while there's still time."

Gabe wondered if he should just deliver her to Bellevue. "She'd slit your throat with a dull nail file if she got a chance. Jesus, woman!" He pounded his fist on the steering wheel. "Someone who'd start a gang war to cover up your 'accidental' death has no conscience. She doesn't deserve a warning. She wants you dead." He jammed on the brakes as a truck trundled out from a side street in front of them. "Dammit, she's frustrated as hell that I'm protecting you."

"Then she may try to kill you first. To get to me." Jenny's voice tightened. "I wish you'd go away, to someplace safe. I . . . I don't want anything to happen to you."

A balloon of hope expanded in Gabe's chest. "Don't worry. I watch my backside very carefully. If she gets to me, she'll wish Uncle G. had caught her. Sterling will send in an army." As he turned into the warehouse district, he scanned the sidewalk outside his building from force of habit. The headlights surprised movement in a doorway across the street, then reflected off metal at the opening to the alley at the corner of his building. Keeping his speed steady, he drove past his garage and on to the next intersection.

"Gabe, wasn't that your place back there?"

He turned left and accelerated. At the next intersection, he took another left, circling the block to drive past the opposite side of the building, all the while monitoring the rearview mirror. As they passed Bill's garage, he caught a flicker of movement in a nearby doorway. "Yeah, it was. And I don't like the look of things on Bill's side any better than I did on mine." Pulling his cell phone from beneath the seat, he dialed Bill's number, eternally grateful for his friend's gadget that doubled the security of the digital line. Bill answered on the first ring.

"Have you noticed the increased activity outside?" he demanded.

"Where the hell have you been? I tried to call you nearly an hour ago! There must be ten guys out there lying in wait for you, and I didn't know if you were dead or alive." The annoyance in Bill's voice didn't disguise his relief.

"I'm just down the street." Gabe's mind worked rapidly, sorting his options. "There was too much pedestrian traffic around both garages when I approached, so I drove on. Your boys can send them home without starting a war, can't they?"

Bill laughed. "You're insulting my people. I'll call you when the street's clear."

"No good. They'll just come back. Jenny and I squared

things with Kamanedes tonight, so these must be Tania's." Gabe paused, glanced at his passenger, and made a snap decision. "We're going underground. I'll call tomorrow to let you know where we are."

"Watch your back."

He disconnected and tucked the phone back beneath the seat. Jenny's appearance had made his decision for him. Her face looked shrunken, the skin tight over her cheekbones. She sat very straight, her head high. He should have realized that her bravado earlier would sap what little reserves she had left. She needed rest and a chance to regroup. Since that was all he could offer right now, he announced, "We're going on a vacation, Tess."

His use of her false name jolted Jenny from her haze of fear. Minutes earlier, everything had fallen into place. She'd realized who had murdered Trent. Gabe's cryptic conversation with Bill had come to her as if from a distance, and for what seemed like the thousandth time in the past week she felt cut adrift. Knowing he expected her to protest, she challenged, "Where?"

"In view of the crowd at the loft, I thought we'd take a trip into the mountains. My fake ID's in a compartment under the backseat. You're carrying your Tess ID in your tote, aren't you?"

"The mountains? Why?"

"Because they're there," he answered lightly, reaching over to clasp her hands, which were clenched in her lap.

The feel of his warm hand wrapping around her cold fingers revived Jenny's brain. "Tania will find us."

"Not until I want her to." He executed yet another left turn and accelerated. "As soon as we're far enough out of town, we'll pull into a motel for some rest. Then we'll head southwest. I know a place in Virginia that rents tourist cabins so remote I'm not sure the proprietor knows where all of them are." He squeezed her fingers. "We can pick up gear along the way."

As they sped through an intersection, Jenny watched his face in the light of the traffic signal. He looked so competent, so solid, so resolute, yet there was no reason for him to . . . "Gabe, why are you doing this?"

Without turning, he countered, "Why do you think?"

Memories of the passion she'd found in his arms the night before, and again that afternoon, flooded her senses. He had been exquisitely tender, as if his only concern was her pleasure, not his own. In her limited experience, that could only mean one thing. He hadn't really been involved. She may have lost control, but he'd remained detached, no matter what he claimed. Humiliated heat flooded her face. "I forgot. I'm Sterling's charity case. You've just been following orders."

He sighed. Honking at a slow-moving van, he swerved into the next lane before saying in a deceptively soft voice, "Jenny, that's a crock of the finest. It's four in the morning, traffic is becoming a bitch, and I've got a damn bullet wound in my leg. Can we save this conversation until I have both hands free so I can knock some sense into that thick, beautiful head of yours?"

He stole a quick glance at her as he spoke, and the expression in his eyes confused her. Was that resignation she saw? How inconvenient it must be for him to have her thrust into his care like . . . like poor little Choc. She had been a mercy f———. Jenny couldn't form the word. Not even in her mind. Instead she said primly, "Of course. Rest assured I'll not bother you again." She closed her eyes and began thinking furiously.

"Jenny . . ." His voice trailed off, as if he were at a loss for words.

By the time they exited the Holland Tunnel, Jenny knew she had to escape Gabe. Somehow, she had to reach Tania and urge her to run—if it wasn't already too late. And she would tell her who really murdered Trent, thus exorcizing her own guilt at not being able to mourn him.

If she were gone, Gabe would be safe; he wouldn't be in danger of being killed in a turf war fueled by Tania's belief that she, Jenny, was responsible for Trent's death. Confronting Trent's vindictive cousin terrified her, but she had no choice.

Her decision made, she focused her gaze to the right of the car's hood. During the years with Trent, she had perfected the ability to mentally remove herself from any situation that made her uncomfortable. Within her mind she was already in the mountains, surrounded by plants and trees unfurling their best springtime green. The sky was a blue she knew she could never duplicate on a canvas, and somewhere nearby a stream rushed, its clear, bubbling water nearly bursting its banks.

Gabe's voice brought her back. "You can come back to the present. I'm going to check us in at the Ritz over there."

Jenny looked in the direction he indicated. Thin morning light revealed the uninspired architecture of a Motel 6 registration office with a neon "Vacancies" sign glowing in the window. To the west, a wing of sheltered doors faced the parking lot. She felt numb and disoriented.

"Are you going to be okay?" Gabe asked. Furrows of concern creased his forehead.

"Yes. Yes, of course." Jenny blinked rapidly, trying to clear her mind. "I must have dozed off. I'll be wide-awake in a minute." She watched him enter the office. He had sounded solicitous, as if he truly cared. Jenny wished things were different, because in her idyllic dream, he had been with her. The worst had happened. She had fallen in love with him.

She allowed herself a brief bout of self-pity, then sat up straight and smoothed her hair. How ridiculous to waste time feeling sorry for herself when she had so much to do during the next few hours. As soon as she could get away from Gabe.

Gabe propped himself against the counter while the clerk imprinted the platinum card that identified him as David G. O'Shaughnessy, grateful that the tall, molded-plastic work space shielded his torn black jeans. He leaned against its sturdy contours, taking some of the weight off his injured leg. The pain in his wound had subsided to a manageable ache, just enough to make him aware it was still there. He'd suffered much worse.

Through the office window, he saw Jenny smooth her hair and square her shoulders. He wondered what decision she had just made. Her body language invariably announced her state of mind.

"Room 126. One night," the sallow-faced clerk said, waving his arm toward the rank of doors. "Parking's right outside your door, and there's a McDonald's and a Kmart just down that access road." He pointed in the opposite direction.

His stomach growled. Kmart wouldn't be open yet, but he could at least get them some breakfast. Gabe signed his new name with a flourish and ran his tongue between his teeth and his cheek. "You wouldn't have any courtesy toothbrushes in the desk, would you? My wife and I started out sort of on an impulse."

The clerk gave him a "Yeah, right, buddy" look and

produced two plastic packets. The toothbrushes were small, with even smaller tubes of toothpaste, but they were better than nothing.

Scooping up his plastic key card and the packets, Gabe winked and smiled back. "Thanks a lot. These'll be great."

He returned to the car quickly, tossing the toothbrushes on Jenny's lap before sliding behind the wheel. "They were free." He started the engine and turned in the direction of their room. "You go on in and take a shower. By the time you're done, I'll be back with breakfast. You want lots of cream in your coffee?" He watched her fingers curl around the little plastic packets.

Jenny nodded without speaking.

"Stop looking at me as if you think I'm going to abandon you," he ordered as he braked the car angrily in front of their room.

"You'd never do that, Gabe. Your conscience wouldn't let you walk away once you accepted a duty." She held out her hand for the key. "I'll open the door and bring this back to you."

Gabe wanted to back her up against a wall and hold her there until he'd kissed some sense into her. She returned and reached through the car window to put the card in his outstretched hand. "You're a real knothead, you know that? If you weren't nearly asleep on your feet, I'd show you just how screwed up your mind is." Exasperated, he watched until she disappeared into their room, then drove off to find breakfast.

When he returned, the door to the bathroom was closed and the shower was running. One of the toothbrush kits lay precisely in the center of the bed closest to the door. The other bed was turned back. Gabe put the paper bags containing their breakfast on the desk and emptied his pockets, dropping his new identity cards beside them. Then he removed both of his guns, which he placed on the bottom shelf of the Formica phone stand.

The bathroom door opened, and Jenny walked out surrounded by a cloud of steam. She'd put the black slacks and turtleneck back on, and her hair was wet. Walking over to the desk, Gabe selected a comb from his little stack of belongings. "Here. Comb your hair before you eat." Her grateful smile as she took the comb and made a show of sniffing the fragrance of the fast food brought him little comfort. For some reason, his own appetite had vanished. "I'm going to take a shower before I eat," he said brusquely and headed for the bathroom.

Jenny watched him limp through the door. Would he remember not to get his bandage wet? A reminder poised on the tip of her tongue, but she never gave it life. Then she was alone. She listened for the sound of the shower before scooping one of the sausage McMuffins from the sack. She grabbed a cup of coffee and set it down again. Snatching Gabe's wallet, she extracted a twenty-dollar bill and tucked it into her pocket.

Easing the door closed behind her, Jenny fled toward the truck stop across the highway. She refused to think about Gabe. The greatest gift she could give him was to stop the killing and the danger.

EIGHTEEN

Gabe limped around the end of the bed, realizing that in his panic he had used the motel phone instead of his cell phone. He interrupted Bill's greeting to ask, "Is your scrambler in place? I'm not calling from my digital."

"Shaken are you, old man?" Bill's voice held a wealth of amusement. "I scramble everything. Go on."

"The damn broad has some half-assed notion of warning Tania," Gabe roared. "Sure as hell that's where she's headed." He cursed himself for losing Jenny. He should have listened to his instincts and indulged his hormones as soon as they checked in.

"What do you mean, calm down!" He strode toward the door, and the phone base crashed to the floor. Cursing, he turned to pick it up, demanding to know if Bill was still there. In the same breath, he continued, "If she makes it to New York without getting robbed, raped or murdered, Tania and her hoods will hop on Jenny like flies at a county fair the minute she shows up." Still carrying the base, Gabe paced the length of the bed.

When he'd emerged from the bathroom and discovered her gone, he'd rushed to the window. When he saw the Honda was still there, his attention had swung immediately to the truck stop across the way, where an eighteen-wheeler was pulling out. Another idled up to the exit. His imagination hadn't required much stretch to picture Jenny sitting primly next to the burly driver of either one.

He forced his attention back to Bill. "Okay. But do your

damnedest to get a tap on Tania's line, even if you have to send someone to scrub the street. I want to know what they say to each other if Jenny calls her. Is the coast clear at your place now?" When Bill answered in the affirmative, he continued, "I'm heading straight back. She has fake ID. I entered the particulars in your file, so you know who to look for. Put a tag on her new credit card in case she uses it. If I think of anything else on the way in, I'll call you." He slapped the receiver in place and pitched the telephone in the direction of the bed.

Retrieving his guns from the shelf, he jammed them into their respective holsters. The ritual reminded him that Jenny still had the two-shot Gigi had given her. The thought depressed him as much as it reassured him. In her hands, the gun was no more use than a peashooter. Jenny didn't have the experience or killer instinct to defend herself against Tania and her goons.

With that pessimistic thought, he pulled on his jacket and seized the bag containing a Styrofoam container of cold coffee and a sausage biscuit, then dropped the plastic room key on the desk. As he stepped out the door, the sun cleared the horizon in the east. "I hope to God that's a good sign, because if not, this is going to be the longest day of my life."

Four hours later, Jenny stood beside a bank of telephones in Bloomingdale's, waiting for an open phone. The gruff truck driver who had given her a ride into the city had dropped her at the stop closest to Manhattan and insisted she accept a fifty-dollar bill to go with the twenty. "You gotta take a cab the rest of the way into town, ma'am. Can't do that with peanuts."

Realizing the truth of his words, she had insisted on

writing down his address so she could repay him. Once she reached the center of New York, her first stop had been a bank, where she paced the sidewalk until it opened, boldly using her new credit card to take a cash advance.

Then she had headed for Bloomingdale's to lose herself in the crowd drawn by the discreet sales signs in the windows. The batteries on her cell phone were dead, so she needed somewhere anonymous from which to call Tania. In another lifetime, she would have felt out of place in her rumpled black turtleneck and jeans. Looking around, she realized her unkempt appearance helped her fade into the crowd.

A harassed-looking brunette slammed the receiver back in place and manhandled a stroller holding a screaming two-year-old through the crowd. Before any of the others around her could move, Jenny leaped forward and seized the available telephone. Depositing the coins she'd been clutching, she dialed. The distant ring scarcely registered; her thoughts were consumed with Gabe. What had he done when he discovered she was gone? He'd never find her in New York City. She could lose herself in the fast-moving masses of people more easily than anyplace she could think of.

"What do you want?"

Tania's voice was raspy with sleep, and Jenny's gaze dropped to her watch. She'd called too early. Bloomie's doors had opened ten minutes ago, and Trent's cousin seldom surfaced until noon.

"Dammit, who the hell is this?" Irritation laced Tania's demand.

"Tania, it's Jenny."

Silence pulsed back at her. Then, "Jenny! My God, where have you been? I was afraid you were injured in that terrible explosion after I left, but I couldn't find anyone who knew anything, and the TV news skimmed over it . . ."

Tired of being treated like a gullible fool, she cut in, allowing her impatience to surface in her voice. "You needn't keep up that fiction any longer, Tania. I know who caused the explosion . . . and I know about you and Trent." She clutched the receiver so tightly her hand began to lose feeling, waiting breathlessly for an answer from the woman she had once thought her friend. Any kind of response would serve.

There was none, and Jenny realized she had momentarily gained the upper hand. She continued, "All this killing can't continue. We need to talk. As soon as possible."

"We have nothing to say to each other," Tania said sullenly. "Trent married you, and now he's dead. And you're alive."

Jenny glanced over her shoulder at the man at the next telephone before whispering, "I can't bring Trent back, Tania, but I can tell you who killed him."

"I know who killed him," Tania said harshly. "His goody-two-shoes worthless wife! And Uncle G. helped you!"

"You have everything all wrong! You're in danger."

Jenny heard Tania's quick indrawn breath before she said defiantly, "You're the one in danger."

"I want to help you. Meet with me, Tania. Then I'll disappear. I promise."

Jenny despised herself for the pleading note in her voice, but now that she knew the truth, she was determined to share it. Surely once Tania also knew, she would leave her alone. "Believe me when I tell you, you'll never have to see me again." She would walk away from that chapter in her life. Warning Tania and giving her a new target for her hatred should wipe the slate clean.

The silence stretched interminably. The phone slipped within her grasp. Her fingers were wet with perspiration. Or was that moisture tears? She realized she was crying.

"Midnight. Central Park," Tania offered. "At the softball diamonds."

Jenny's nerves jolted. Central Park at night was the last place in the world she'd meet anyone, much less a woman who hated her and was attempting to have her killed. "Too late. My . . . my flight leaves at nine," she lied. "I'll meet you at five. At the public library."

The silence on the line stretched her nerves taut. Jenny would have sworn she heard Tania's thoughts processing. "No, someplace less public. I told you I'm living with Rose now, didn't I? Come here. If you don't want to come inside, we can talk in the garden."

"Why should I think I'll be safe?" Jenny countered. The homes of other Travino family members surrounded Rose's house.

Tania's sigh crackled over the receiver. "You'll be safe. But if you insist on bringing your stud along, the meeting's off. I don't think he likes me much anymore."

Her callous dismissal of the explosion that had taken one life and endangered four others horrified Jenny. "You killed his friend, Tania. What do you expect?" No need to tell her that she'd run away from Gabe to keep him safe.

"Yeah. Well, she shouldn't have gotten in the way. Be here by one-thirty. Uncle G. has called a meeting for after lunch, so there shouldn't be anyone around." Bitterness crept into her voice. "Naturally I wasn't invited. We'll have time for our talk before anyone returns."

Tania's mention of Uncle G. startled her. In her excitement over her discovery, Jenny had almost forgotten his quest for the ringleader of the group undermining his status. Was he about to move on Tania and her group of rebels? Logic told her it would be safer to call off her visit with Trent's cousin and allow mob justice to kick in. She shook off the moment of cowardice. Her pride insisted she convince Tania of her innocence. "Will Rose be home?" she asked cautiously.

"Don't you remember? She plays mah-jongg after lunch. We'll be alone."

Jenny quaked inside at the idea of going to the heart of the Travino enclave, but she knew this was her only chance. "I'll be there," she said.

"She drew two thousand in cash on her credit card from Empire State Bank an hour ago," Bill informed Gabe as he entered the office on the second floor of the building they shared. Gabe gave a massive sigh of relief. Jenny had surfaced.

Bill turned on the speaker and removed his headset. "She's talking to Tania right now. Don't worry about what you missed. I'm taping."

Gabe spun a wheeled chair across the tile floor and sat beside Bill at the console. His high-speed trip from the motel had been filled with nightmare visions of the dangers she faced, and his heart contracted with fear as he heard her voice, tight and high, as if she were at the end of her emotional resources.

When the connection ended, Gabe asked sarcastically, "Whatever would you suppose Uncle G.'s meeting's about?"

Bill shoved his tongue into his cheek and rolled his eyes, assuming the naive look that served him so well in the security field. "Shucks, Gomer, I wouldn't have the faintest idea." He glanced at his notes and became deadly serious. "Tania's probably under tight surveillance."

"And Jenny's walking right into the line of fire." Gabe pushed to his feet and paced the room. "Where did she call from?"

"Pay phone. Bloomie's. The little broad's not as dumb as you want her to be, although I don't think she's admitted to herself how very evil Tania is."

"Dammit, I want her to be smart enough to stay alive. You'd think she'd have figured out that woman long before Trent was killed. I read her in ten seconds."

"Yeah, but you grew up with a tough crowd."

Gabe acknowledged the comment with a nod. "Maybe if she survives this she'll have learned a little something. I hope so. I won't always be around to pick up the pieces." Unless I'm lucky.

Evading direct eye contact, Bill flicked off the speaker and lined up the pencil and pad in front of him. "Of course not. How do you want to handle this afternoon? We'll be invading their turf, you know."

Exiting the rank of telephones, Jenny slipped through the bargain-happy crowd to a first-floor exit. Her stomach reminded her that it had been hours since she'd forced herself to eat the cold sausage biscuit. Bile rose in her throat at the thought of food; more than anything, she needed to conquer her fear.

She fought her way through the pedestrians outside the store and flagged a cab. Throwing open the back door, she said, "St. Patrick's Cathedral." Her subconscious had furnished the destination automatically.

After what seemed like hours, she mounted the steps of the church and hurried toward the tranquility of the chapel.

An hour later, emotionally refreshed and resolute, she descended the same stairs in search of a restaurant. If she was going to be killed, she would do so on a full stomach.

Jenny noticed the taxi driver's growing discomfort. Before they left the city, she had extracted his promise to wait for her while she conducted her business. Now, after one look at the neighborhood, he appeared to have changed his mind.

"Lady, I know where I am. The people who live here don't like cars hangin' around. Why don't you just call for another cab when you're ready to go?" he said, casting an anxious glance in the rearview mirror.

Perspiration darkened the collar of his plaid sport shirt. Jenny suspected it wasn't caused by the heat. A driver picked at random knew that Travinos occupied nearly every house on the street, while she had spent the first month of her marriage naively delighted that so many members of Trent's family lived close by. "Because I don't want to do that," she replied calmly.

Tania wasn't going to like what she had to say. Intuition told her that once they finished talking, her only chance of escape would be to leave immediately, before Tania's volatile disposition prompted her to kill the messenger. She reached around the half-open glass divider and rested her hand, a hundred-dollar bill clasped in her fingers, on his shoulder. "I truly need you to wait. It would mean a great deal to me."

Without turning, he palmed the bill. "Crap, lady. If it means that much to you, I'll be here. But I'd be lyin' if I told you I'm happy about it. See, it's not just the money."

"I understand completely, Mr. . . ." —she looked at the mounted photo and license— "Saweki. I appreciate your help. Believe me, I have no intention of returning here myself." She opened the door and stepped out onto the grass at the curb.

Her nerves twanging, she took a deep breath and headed up the curving drive to the venerable stone house Tania now shared with Trent's mother, Rose. Octagonal paving stones marked a path leading around the house to the formal garden that was Rose's hobby, and Jenny followed them with no little trepidation.

Her footsteps dragged as she reached the corner of the house. What if Trent's mother had stayed home today? She'd never made a secret of the fact that she hated Jenny. Not from the moment they'd met. Her presence would make what Jenny had to tell Tania impossible. She stopped walking, torn between going ahead and running for the sanctuary of the taxi as fast as she could.

"I was sure you'd chicken out." Tania's voice came from the direction of a wrought-iron bench on the other side of a shallow pool where several gigantic goldfish circled lazily. She was dressed in impeccably tailored cream slacks, with a matching cardigan draped casually across the shoulders of her sapphire blue shirt. Jenny felt like a refugee in her wrinkled black slacks and turtleneck. Caught, she had no choice but to do what her conscience demanded. She walked toward Tania.

"You were always such a prissy mouse," Tania continued as Jenny rounded the pool toward her. "At the beginning, I almost felt sorry for you because you didn't know the score. Later, I hated you because you were so dumb you never caught on."

The venom in her voice startled Jenny. "I never guessed." She swallowed the lump in her throat and continued, "You were the only one who was kind to me, and I was grateful."

"Like I said, you never knew the score." Tania stood and waved imperiously toward the garden beyond the fish pool.

"Let's go back there. Rose decided not to play mah-jongg today, so she's home. I don't want her to know you're here. It will upset her."

Tania led the way to a sheltered area behind the yew hedge surrounding the rose garden. Absurdly, Jenny found herself focusing on the dark red shoots on the bare rose canes and how beautiful the garden would be in the months ahead. From nowhere, she remembered poor Mr. Dolan. The dead embezzler would never see his roses bloom. Her hands began to tremble so violently that she jammed them into her pockets.

They passed through a small opening in the hedge, into an area Rose must have ordered the landscapers to redesign. Strings were tied to dowels marking off sections that had been rototilled, and equipment lay where the workers had left it, apparently to take a break.

"Well, what do you have to tell me that's so damned earthshaking?"

Jenny's heart sank. Tania's arms were tightly folded across her chest, and her ex-friend's expression was as closed as her body language. Gabe was right. Nothing was going to change the dark-haired woman's thinking. But she had to warn her. "Uncle G. knows you're the one trying to take over the family, Tania. He's only waiting until he knows the names of everyone who's gone over to you."

"What are you talking about, you stupid slut! What take-over attempt!" All color had drained from Tania's cheeks.

"He knows, Tania," she said sadly. "Consider my warning a payback. You can still get away. Even though your friendship was a game to you, it once meant a great deal to me."

Tania's hard voice was like a slap in the face. "I'm not going anywhere until you've been punished for Trent's death!"

Jenny was tired, tired of taking the blame for something she hadn't done and tired of beating her head against a brick wall, but she pushed on. "Once I learned you and Trent had been lovers, even after he married me, I understood why Rose would invite you to live here with her after Trent and I married. You were as close as she could come to having him back."

A cloud obscured the sun, triggering a chill of apprehension about what she was about to say. "I never minded that Rose hated me. I understood. Trent was all she had, and he'd chosen someone from the outside. Maybe if I'd had a baby, she might have at least come to tolerate me. But that didn't happen."

She wrapped her arms around herself, gaining little warmth from the gesture. "It just never occurred to me that she would want to kill me." Tania's look of surprise gave her the strength to go on. "I was the one who was supposed to die that day. The disappointments in her life must have made her a little crazy."

"That's ridiculous!" Tania stalked closer. "Do you know what I believe? You put out the hit on Trent yourself. Being his wife wasn't as glamorous as you thought it would be, and the only way you could be free was for him to die."

The hatred on Tania's face and the venom in her voice as she stalked toward her brought home to Jenny how foolish she had been to come here. Her deep inner loneliness that had cherished Tania's early friendship made her the perfect victim. The debt she felt she owed was a cruel joke, an unforgivable weakness in Tania's eyes. Oh, God! Gabe was right. I am too dumb to live.

"I didn't!" Jenny protested. She put out her hands to fend off Tania's approach, all the while looking frantically for a way to escape. "I wouldn't even have known who to ask. Don't you understand? I was supposed to die. It was Rose, not Nick Kamanedes or someone from another family. She arranged for the bomb, thinking I would answer the door. She forgot I wasn't the good, obedient wife she kept telling Trent I should be. I was in the kitchen making salads, and Trent . . ."

Jenny's words faltered when a dark-suited figure stepped from behind a budding lilac bush. The cloud went on its way, leaving the sun to burnish the golden hair of Dave Lassiter, the man who had taken Trent's position. The silencer on the muzzle of his gun looked larger with each step he took.

Tania motioned him to her side. "You can't shift the blame, Jenny. Uncle G. not only covered up for you . . . I think he helped you plan. He was always foolish over you." She advanced menacingly. "He'll pay, too," she promised. "We'll bring him down. Then I'll be in charge."

Tania was as crazed as Rose. With a flash of insight, Jenny demanded, "Is that why you seduced Trent in the first place? All those years ago, were you planning to use him to destroy his own uncle?" She looked past her to Lassiter's expressionless face. "Aren't you afraid she'll discard you once you help her succeed?"

Hips swinging, Tania sauntered forward, her dark eyes malevolent. "David knows what his reward will be after you're dead! I'm going to marry him." She stopped directly in front of Jenny, raised her hand and swung toward Jenny's face.

Jenny leaped backward. Then every nerve in her body jumped at the sound of a harsh voice entirely too close by. "My Trent should still be alive. You were supposed to die!" A sharp pain between her shoulder blades sent her to her knees. A flat shovel struck the ground beside her with a thud, a shovel wielded by a tall, full-bodied woman with streaks of white in her dark, well-cut hair, and eyes burning with manic fever.

Jenny hadn't seen Rose Travino since Trent's funeral, where the woman had glared venomously at her across the church. She had hoped never to encounter her mother-in-law again. Was it possible the woman would beat Tania to the privilege of killing her?

Only if she didn't continue to stay sprawled on the ground as if paralyzed. Jenny threw herself to one side and rolled.

"Let me do it, Rose!"

Tania rushed to the older woman and tried to wrest the gardening tool from her hands.

"No!" Rose shouted. "I was his mother! It's my right!" She wrapped her arms around the handle, clutching it as if it were a holy relic.

Jenny pushed up onto her hands and knees. As the two struggled, she inched farther away from them. When her foot encountered an obstacle, she glanced over her shoulder. A pronged garden tool, its claws curling outward, was propped against a wrought-iron bench. Jenny reached back and snatched the handle. Its solid heft sent a surge of hope through her.

The turf shredded inches from her hand. Jenny had forgotten Dave Lassiter's gun. Another divot flew into the air close to her face. She leaped up and looked around frantically. Tania was heading toward her, but a thicket of yew toward the bottom of the yard offered possible sanctuary—if she could reach it. She turned right, stumbling over a low pyramid of half-moon tiles which had been stacked in readiness. The pyramid collapsed, sending broken pieces of tile flying as she fell headlong on the grass.

"Don't let her get away!" Rose shrieked, joining Tania in pursuit. She clutched the shovel with both hands.

Jenny's fear of Tania and Rose wasn't nearly so great as her conviction that David Lassiter's next shot would kill her. Sobbing, she scrambled to her feet and ran deeper into the garden, too terrified even to retrieve the gun holstered at her ankle. Looking over her shoulder, she saw him aim. Hypnotized, she watched his hand contract.

A shot rang out in front of her. An unsilenced shot.

Grass tickled her nose. Jenny realized she had thrown herself to the ground and buried her face in the luxuriant spring growth. Cautiously lifting her head, she saw Lassiter crumple. She pushed to her feet and ran faster than she had ever run in her life.

Her heart beat loudly in her ears. Her breath hitched in her chest. Pain stabbed at her side as she dodged her way through the landscaper's maze of string and dowels. A second gunshot, still from in front of her, made her want to throw herself to the ground. Fear made her keep running.

She didn't dare look back a second time. Somewhere ahead, at the back of the garden, she remembered a gate opening on the lane shared by the other estates. Sweat poured down her forehead into her eyes, blinding her. Another series of shots shattered the silence of the afternoon.

Gabe stepped from behind a clump of evergreens and lowered his rifle. He watched, as in the distance, five dark-suited men surrounded Rose and Tania. Another stood over Lassiter's writhing body. He recognized Uncle G.'s commanding figure approaching the group. Waving Bill back, he set down the gun and stepped into Jenny's path. Her momentum was so great that the impact threw him backward.

He collapsed. His first instinct was to wrap his arms

around Jenny to protect her, but she transformed into a twisting, biting, wild thing. He felt as if he'd captured a whirlwind. Wincing when the toe of her shoe struck his wound, he tried to calm her. "Jenny, it's Gabe." Her elbow jammed into his chest and he flinched. "Ouch, dammit!" From the corner of one eye, he saw the prongs of the weeder descending. Snagging her wrist just before the tool made contact, he shouted, "You're safe, dammit!"

"No, no," she cried wildly, struggling against his hold. Her tears rained on his face. Stark terror contracted her colorless features. "I'll never be safe, she'll find me no matter where I . . ." Her struggles ceased abruptly. He loosened his hold.

"Gabe?"

Even as the tension drained from her body, Gabe sensed her distancing herself. Still within his grasp, she drew away, as if anticipating a blow. A curious blankness filled her eyes.

"You're safe, Jenny. Look behind you." He spoke as gently as he could.

When she didn't respond, he grasped her chin firmly. She resisted. Gathering his legs beneath him, he sat up, still holding her arms to her sides with his other arm. He forced her to turn around. "I said look."

Three guns were leveled at Rose and Tania, who stood at the intersection of two paths. Uncle G., his shoulders sagging and sorrow creasing his already lined face, faced the two women. His lips were moving, but he spoke too softly for them to hear.

"I think your ex-in-laws just met mob justice. Uncle G.'s meeting must have been called to discuss Tania's extracurricular activities," Gabe said gently.

Jenny stiffened against him. "How did you know about . . ." Her eyes widened. "You listened when I called Tania!"

Relief made him respond violently. "Jesus H. Christ, woman! How the hell do you think I got here in time to keep you from getting yourself killed? I was terrified that socio- path would murder you. Uncle G. listened to the call, too, or he and his boys wouldn't have arrived so conveniently."

"I could have escaped, you interfering idiot. I didn't need your help."

Gabe's temper escalated. "Yeah? And what if the old bat had had better aim with that shovel? What if your old buddy Uncle G. hadn't come through? What then?"

"None of those things happened. I'd have escaped. Somehow." She wrenched free of his hold. In a voice thick with tears, she said, "Tell Sterling your mission's accom- plished. I'm not in danger anymore. You don't have to watch over the charity case." With that, she turned and ran toward the open gate.

Before Gabe could set off in pursuit, Bill seized his arm. "Don't make any more of an ass of yourself than you already have, old buddy."

"What the hell's that supposed to mean?" Gabe demanded. He watched Jenny's slight figure until it disappeared from view. He tugged to free his arm, but Bill's grip was unbreakable.

"You've been acting like a seventeen-year-old with tes- tosterone overload ever since you showed up with her."

"Dammit, she was one step from dead meat even before I took over." Gabe had never felt so vulnerable. In a few short days, Jenny had become the most important thing in his life.

His body tightened as he remembered the heart-stopping moment she had come to him in the night. Her passionate response to his lovemaking couldn't have been simple relief at surviving her gutsy performance at The Stuffed Olive.

He'd hoped desperately that it meant much more.

Bill shot a wary glance at the grim little gathering in the rose garden. "Let's get out of here before we're forced to mingle. As a good citizen, I should call in the police, but since the neighbors are all family, and they haven't complained, why should I?" He grinned nervously. "I learned long ago never to intrude on family matters."

Gabe let his friend haul him toward the wrought-iron gate, which hung open after Jenny's hurried departure. He glanced back once over his shoulder. Apparently his shot hadn't damaged Lassiter too seriously. One of Uncle G.'s men had forced the lawyer to his feet and was hustling him away. Rose had thrown herself on the ground, where she continued to scream, but Tania stood rigid, aloof from Rose's hysterics and the circle of thugs. Gabe couldn't dredge up any sympathy for her. Not after her relentless pursuit of Jenny.

He shook off Bill's hold and strode ahead. Dammit, he had more important things to worry about than the fate of two unstable women and a mob that still operated on the principles laid down by Al Capone. He had to find Jenny. He had to make her understand how he felt. If she couldn't love him, life wouldn't be worth living.

Just as he reached the gate, his cell phone rang. Swearing raggedly, he answered. "Sterling? . . . What the hell do you mean you want a report?"

NINETEEN

Jenny folded her portable easel and rinsed her brushes, then poured the contents of the glass jar into the sand and held it up to the sun now slanting over the Gulf of Mexico. Light poured into the streaky colors clinging to the inner sides. Ever since she'd torn herself from Gabe's arms and run away to lick her wounds, her life had been just as empty, its colors homogenized into a blur.

She wrapped the jar in the faded dish towel she'd used to dry her brushes and dropped it into the large canvas tote, then collapsed the easel and stuffed it in the bag legs first before hefting the strap onto her shoulder. Ignoring the frame nudging the back of her head, she picked up her plastic watercolor case and the canvas portfolio.

Coarse sand shifted beneath her bare feet as she set off along the beach to the remote cottage Uncle G. had loaned her two months earlier. Behind her, the Gulf glistened in the sun, its constantly moving surface a mosaic ranging from deep emerald to angry sapphire.

During the time she had been here, she had seen the waters in a variety of moods, including the towering gray-brown waves that had battered the shore during the hurricane which had passed less than a hundred miles from her the week before. The focus it had taken to accept the Gulf's volatile nature had soothed her heart and mind by keeping her attention on the here and now. Today she felt bruised, but at peace.

Setting down the watercolors and portfolio, she took off

her floppy-brimmed canvas hat and shook her head. A quickening breeze nuzzled through her sweat-soaked hair, giving her a moment's relief from the heat. She dropped the hat back in place over her hair, tilting it forward until her vision was limited to the small area ahead of her feet. The notion that her life had narrowed to this small, controllable space pleased her.

She relished the luxury of not looking any farther ahead than the instant of time she occupied. That way she didn't think of Gabe. She no longer writhed with embarrassment when she recalled the way she had crawled into his bed like a . . .

Now she merely shuddered when she recalled how close she had come to telling him she was in love with him—just like a besotted adolescent. Or a naive idiot.

After examining their relationship in the clear light of the Florida sun, she'd realized their love could never have endured. They were too different.

A hand appeared in the framework of her limited vision to slow her progress. "My dear, you must be careful to watch where you're going. You could trip and fall."

Jenny stopped so suddenly she nearly fell. Her tote slid from her shoulder and landed in the sand with a clatter of the easel's legs. She pushed her hat back from her forehead and stared up at Sterling Thomas.

How typically Sterling. His stance, even with her rustic little house not a hundred feet away, managed to convey the impression that he was a king surveying his kingdom. He was clad in immaculate tan linen slacks and jacket. In an apparent concession to the heat, he wore no necktie with his white linen shirt.

Mild annoyance was the strongest emotion she could muster. "How on earth did you find me?"

She couldn't read the expression in the eyes behind the mirrored sunglasses, but she heard gentleness in his voice when he said, "I approached your benefactor. I wanted to see for myself that you had survived all the unpleasantness intact. Gabe merely reported that the loose ends were tied up and that you had disappeared. I preferred to confirm your safety for myself."

Although mention of Gabe's name made her pulse leap, Sterling's revelation startled her even more. "You met with Uncle G.?" she gulped.

"An interesting gentleman." Sterling retrieved her tote bag, adjusted the awkward burden on his own shoulder, then took her arm. "Our business interests lie in somewhat different areas, but we share one thing. Heartfelt concern for your well-being." He led her toward the little screened porch. "I took the liberty of bringing a picnic lunch as an apology for disturbing your peace. Perhaps we can talk while we eat."

Jenny tensed. In the past, when someone had offered her food as an excuse to talk, she inevitably ended up agreeing to something she had never intended to do. She replied warily, "We've very little to discuss. You were kind enough to provide me protection when I needed it, for which I'm very grateful." She forced herself to smile naturally as she swung open the screen door. "Did the painting arrive?"

"Indeed. My dear, you were in Palm Springs but one day, yet you captured the view from my study perfectly." He chuckled as he propped the tote against the screen and followed her over the threshold carrying the cooler he had left waiting outside the door. "Now I can never change that particular fountain. By the way, several of my friends who have seen your gift have inquired about your work. Are you accepting commissions?"

Jenny nearly laughed at the notion that any of Sterling's wealthy acquaintances were desperate enough to collect the work of an obscure unknown, an artist whose only reputation so far lay in quirky illustrations for children's books. The novelty of the idea softened her feelings toward the older man, however, and she gestured toward the glass-topped table before answering, "Now I know the truth about why you've searched me out. May I get you some iced tea before we talk business?"

"Thank you, my dear. I believe everything else we'll need is in here." He gestured to the cooler at his feet.

By the time she returned with tall, sweating glasses, Sterling had set out two plastic-covered china plates of exotic fruit, a flat platter of nut bread spread with soft cheese, and linen-wrapped flatware. "This is the best I could procure on such short notice," he apologized.

Jenny put the tea in place and seated herself across the table from him. "Most days I eat very simple lunches, so to me, this looks like a banquet," she said as she removed the plastic wrap from her plate. The fruit was fresh and luscious, the plate was Wedgwood, and the fork she retrieved from the Irish linen napkin was heavy, embossed sterling. If this was his idea of roughing it, she wondered what he would think of the peanut butter sandwich on a paper plate she was accustomed to.

Sterling Thomas had not become a multimillionaire without considerable experience in manipulating people. The man wanted something. He was fussing with his plate, and although he had removed his sunglasses, he avoided making eye contact. Anticipating pressure of one kind or another, she resolved to send him away empty-handed. The irony was that she recalled condemning Gabe for defying his grandfather's wishes; suddenly she empathized with how cornered he must have felt as a teenager—and how much he enjoyed the power he possessed as he'd matured.

She pierced a luscious strawberry with her fork and asked, "How is Choc coming along?"

"He is a delight," Sterling answered eagerly, as if grateful for a neutral subject. "He has endeared himself to my staff, so he doesn't suffer unduly when I am forced to leave him." He sighed and his erect shoulders sagged. "Although as I become older, I find I don't enjoy the travel as much."

Jenny suppressed a smile. Sterling wasn't yet seventy, and he had the appearance of a man fifteen years younger. The industrialist undoubtedly had another thirty vigorous years ahead of him. Why this ploy for her sympathy? Deciding to give him the compassion he apparently wanted, she soothed, "You have so many responsibilities. Can you delegate the travel and decisions to some of your younger people?"

Sterling chewed a section of pineapple wistfully, as if he were gratified that she thought he had one foot in the grave. He swallowed, then said, "At one time, I had hoped Gabe would assume a leadership role. Now, unfortunately, that is impossible."

At last we're coming to the point, Jenny thought. Although she hungered for news of Gabe, she couldn't ask. Instead, she sipped her iced tea and sympathized. "Perhaps he still resents the methods you employed when you rescued him from the juvenile system. Or perhaps you reached him too late for the two of you to bond properly."

"Bond? Oh, er, of course . . ." Sterling put down his fork. "Whatever the problem, I fear I have lost him." The corners of his lips drooped. "After reporting the outcome of your adventure, he moved into his loft on a permanent basis. Apparently he plans to take more of a role in the security business he and that friend of his started." A brave smile creased his cheeks.

"What an ungrateful wretch!" Jenny blurted, "I mean, you're his grandfather. After all you've done for him, I can't believe he'd desert you now that you're entering your golden years." Her last jab made him wince. Maybe the "golden years" description was laying it on a little thick. Whatever, she hoped he'd soon get to the point. Jenny nibbled on a slice of nut bread and waited.

Sterling gave up all pretense of eating and leaned his linen-clad arms on the table. His sincere expression would have looked more at home on a television evangelist. "My dear, that's why I'm here. Poor Gabe isn't himself. I can think of only one reason for him to break all the promises he has made me. The boy is heartbroken. When he set out on his own after the debacle in Baltimore he demonstrated a degree of fear for your safety that I found quite touching. I must admit, I allowed myself to hope something might come of the two of you."

Jenny spotted the calculating gleam behind the supplication in his eyes. She busied herself with cutting a chunk of melon, refusing to make this any easier for him.

He eyed her closely. "I realize this is a terrible intrusion on your privacy, but do you by any chance return my grandson's, ah . . . affection?"

Tears crowded behind her eyes. She should tell him the truth. That she had made a fool of herself. Jenny was grateful she'd gripped the edge of the table, or she might have hit Sterling Thomas with one of the pots of azaleas that edged the little screened porch.

She sat up very straight, desperately hoping lightning wouldn't strike her dead, and said, "Mr. Thomas, you've come on a fool's errand. I assure you, Gabe has no love for me, nor I for him. Otherwise, he would be sitting across from me at this table, not you. Although I appreciate his efforts to insure my safety, your grandson was simply following your orders. Any attraction either of us felt was purely physical, due undoubtedly to the days we were forced to spend in close company with each other. Other than that, we're quite incompatible."

"You're remarkably forthright, my dear. I had so hoped . . ." Sterling stood and patted his mouth with his napkin. "I fear disappointment has made me lose my appetite."

"I am sorry, Mr. Thomas." Jenny stood, praying he'd leave before she burst into tears. The old sonovabitch had broken her peace into millions of slivers.

She had to restrain herself from clamping her hand over her mouth. Throughout her days with Gabe, she'd condemned him for cursing. Now she'd mentally called his grandfather Gabe's favorite word. And it had felt good.

"Allow me to leave you the tableware and cooler as an apology for my presumption," Sterling said as he clasped her hands in farewell. He managed a shaky smile. "I wish things had transpired differently. You're a lovely young woman."

Jenny pulled her hands free, surprised at the press of tears against her eyelids. As angry as she was with Sterling's meddling, if his compliment affected her this strongly, perhaps she wasn't as much in control of her emotions as she thought. "Thank you," she managed over the lump in her throat.

"My friends are quite serious about wanting to commission your work, Jenny. How shall they contact you?" He swung the screen door outward and paused for her answer.

Grateful for the opportunity to look away, she reached

into her watercolor case and pulled out a card. "This is my agent. She'll be glad to talk with them."

The next day, Jenny left the beach, heading for the Massachusetts coast and the home her parents used as a base when they were in the country. She no longer had any reason to hide, and she loved the old converted lighthouse.

After a night spent soul-searching, she didn't believe for a minute that Gabe had left Sterling's employ. He loved his grandfather, whether or not he would admit it, and it was obvious the affection was returned.

Sterling Thomas had come to Florida on a fishing expedition—but he'd been the wrong messenger.

She was reconciled to the difficult months ahead. Months during which she would work at the task of cutting Gabe from her heart and building herself a new life.

Gabe propped his feet on the coffee table in Sterling's Palm Springs sitting room and read with masochistic interest an article in the *New York Times* concerning the disappearance of Rose and Tania. "Somehow I don't think they're wearing concrete booties," he commented cynically. "Rose is Uncle G.'s sister, and it's my guess she's nearly certifiable. Tania's his niece. He's probably stashed the two of them someplace under guard and left them to hate each other to death."

"Have you noticed how careful the newspapers are about avoiding mention of Trent's death as a possible link in the chain of tragedies affecting the alleged crime family? Some enterprising reporter even asked about Jenny, and quoted Uncle G. as saying Trent's widow has severed her ties with the family. He says she's been unavailable for comment," Sterling replied.

"Dammit, she was never anything but an innocent

bystander in this whole mess!" Gabe glared at his grandfather, who lay on the couch across from him with Choc sprawled across his chest.

"Calm down, my boy. I agree completely. Otherwise I wouldn't have gone to so much trouble to assist Uncle G. with her disappearance. I believe the man has a true affection for her."

Gabe shoveled his fingers through his hair as he continued to scowl. "Involvement in this latest mess would be the final straw for Jenny. As furious as I was at the time, your idea of letting her regroup, stashed where no one could find her, was a good one. She shouldn't be within miles of this witch hunt."

Stroking the cat's sleek fur, Sterling smiled and shook his head. "You underestimate her. Jenny has extremely deep resources. She is even somewhat devious at times. Of course, I realize your obsession with protecting her makes you blind to such strengths." He gazed across the room at the painting she had sent him.

"What the hell's that supposed to mean!" Gabe demanded.

"You have a delightfully chivalrous and somewhat antiquated view of womanhood. I confess I find it as charming as I do surprising. Jenny is like an oak tree. The winds and storms of life may batter her, but she is a survivor. Admirable. She is everything I hoped you would find in a woman. If, however, fate should declare otherwise, she will fare much better than you."

For one brief moment, Gabe pondered the best way to kill his grandfather. Then he began to laugh. "You sly old bastard. You've seen her, haven't you. All this time you've been preaching patience to me, you wouldn't tell me where she was." Suddenly intent, he demanded, "You asked me to hold off tracking her down, and I did. But I'm tired of waiting."

285

Sterling pulled a card from the pocket of his shirt. "I thought you would never ask. When I visited her, I received the impression she felt you considered your time with her a duty. Perhaps even a charity. I'd no idea you were so ineloquent. You'll have to dispel that impression. Tactfully. If you attempt to correct her misapprehension with shouting, you will lose her."

Gabe stared at the address printed on the card, cursing beneath his breath. Then he grinned at Sterling, and for the first time in his life, addressed him properly. "Thanks, Grandpa. For everything."

"You're welcome, Gabe." Tears glistened in Sterling's eyes. "I love you."

"Yeah, I know," he managed to force out around the lump in his throat before tucking the card into the pocket of his shirt and heading for the door. "We'll talk about that some other time. Right now I'm in a hurry."

Gabe peered through the rain blowing against the windshield. Between gusts, he saw the whitewashed column of the lighthouse perched on a promontory above the angry Atlantic. Light flowed from the lamp room, creating the illusion that the lantern still functioned. He pictured Jenny using the room as a studio, standing before her easel in a prim button-down shirt, her blonde hair brushing her slender neck, stroking deliberately with a brush. Damn, no matter what Sterling claimed, to his way of thinking, she was fragile. Why did she have to be so stubborn!

Swearing, he parked his rental car as close as he could before killing the engine and lights. He'd felt fear this intense only once before in his life—the day he'd met his grandfather. Now, as then, his future hung in the balance. He took a deep breath and, aware the pearly gates might fall off from the shock of hearing a petition from him, murmured humbly, "Please, God. Don't let me screw up."

Rain sluiced across his face and soaked his shirt before he reached the deeply inset door. Huddling in the shelter of the alcove, he tugged the old-fashioned bellpull. He pictured Jenny abandoning the splashy, flower-strewn painting on her easel. He even imagined her graceful descent of the circular stairs, the movement of her slender feet and ankles blurred in her haste. Maybe she wouldn't hurry. The sudden summons in the middle of an afternoon storm might make her hunker down in the safety of the tower.

He was dithering. He stepped back into the rain so the sight of him crammed into her doorway wouldn't startle her. He waited.

Months earlier, the jangle of the doorbell echoing up the tower would have sent waves of apprehension skittering along her nerves. At this juncture, Jenny felt only annoyance. Until the storm had hit an hour earlier, the lamp room, stripped of every vestige of its original purpose, had made a perfect light-filled studio. Fortunately, she was past needing the light. She'd nearly finished the portrait she was determined would exorcize the heartache she had been unable to heal.

"Dammit, I'm coming," she muttered as she put aside her brush. She had reached a point where her casual use of the word scarcely deserved notice. The word was a link to Gabe. Once she returned to sanity, she would deal with that disturbing lapse, but for now, she could slay only one dragon at a time.

As she scurried down the circular stairwell, she absently wiped her paint-stained hands on the tails of her denim work shirt, adding a final swipe down the sides of her knit shorts for good measure. At the bottom of the stairs she collected the

Lady Smith from its nook. Revolver in hand, she blew at the strand of hair that had drifted over her eyes, threw open the door, and said, "Whoever you are, I don't want any."

"You look like Ma Barker on a bad day."

Jenny had released the door and wrapped her left hand around her other wrist to steady the gun. At the sound of Gabe's voice she nearly dropped it. When he stepped closer, she leveled the muzzle toward his flat stomach, instinctively seeking protection from the yearning that filled her. His dark hair lay in tousled damp tendrils over his forehead. Even his curling lashes were wet and spiky. The dim light made it impossible to read his eyes, but she didn't want to. She was afraid she hadn't been as successful as she thought at ousting him from her heart.

"I just want to talk, Jenny, to be sure you're . . . squared away," he said softly. He stood very still.

Unsure of what she heard in his voice, Jenny countered, "We can talk right here. Don't come any closer." Her heart thunked against her breastbone.

He stepped into the scanty shelter afforded by the doorway. "What happened to your fancy manners? Do you pin everyone who rings the bell at gunpoint? What if the minister comes to call?"

Jenny's wrists trembled beneath the weight of the gun. She looked down at the weapon, a puny defense against the humor she heard in the familiar sexy purr that made her nervous system go into meltdown. Ignoring the flutter of her heart, she let the gun fall to her side. "You told me never to lower my guard."

Gabe moved closer and looked at her intently. She resisted the urge to back away, but refused to meet his gaze. "That was when the wolves were after you. Jenny, I swear I . . . dammit, Jenny, I love you. Will you marry me?"

Her body reacted as if she'd just stuck her finger into a light socket. The gun slipped from her suddenly lifeless fingers.

Gabe dived forward, catching the weapon before it hit the floor. "Dammit, the safety's off! You're going to kill me yet!" He flicked the safety and set the gun carefully on the narrow table beside the door before he turned to scowl at her.

Jenny was almost relieved to see the familiar expression, the one he'd worn the first time they'd met. Its appearance gave her a chance to regroup.

His leap for the gun had brought him inside. Now she backed away, all her senses focused on the words thrumming in her head. "I don't believe you."

"Well, you already shot me once," he said.

She shook her head at him for deliberately misunderstanding her. Then he flashed her a grin that made her toes tingle. "That's what I get for falling for an amateur."

Jenny retreated toward the little sitting room tucked beneath the curve of the stairway and fumbled behind her back for the doorknob. She'd be a fool to believe him. If she could just escape with her pride intact . . . "I mean, what you said before. I know I threw myself at you once, but you needn't feel compelled to bolster my self-esteem any longer." Her hands didn't seem to work right. She couldn't find the knob.

"What kind of crap is that?" he demanded. His brows lowered. Moving rapidly, he backed her against the door.

Jenny struggled against her body's response to his familiar scent and fixed her gaze on the vein that pulsed in his throat, punctuating each of his next words. "Do you think I make a habit of running around giving mercy f——?"

Her hand miraculously obeyed her, covering his mouth. "Don't you dare say that word," she commanded, ignoring the fact that the same phrase had formed itself in her brain on a regular basis each time she allowed herself to remember that night.

He wrapped his fingers around her hand and drew it down to his side, then stepped even closer, lowering his head until they were nose to nose. "Then don't be an idiot. Of all the fuzzy-headed damn women in the world, you take the prize. Did you really think . . ." His voice dwindled as he cradled her cheek with his other hand.

Closing her eyes, she twisted her face away, helplessly relishing the feel of his callused fingers.

"Christ, what an idiot you are," he said, wrapping his arms around her and gathering her close. "We were so damn good together I couldn't believe it. The next morning, I was so shaken I could scarcely look you in the eye because I was afraid you'd think I was an idiot if I told you I loved you."

Jenny glared at him. "How was I to know that! You could have told me something." She wanted to kill him. After she'd had her way with him.

"I came as close as I could without confessing the truth. If I had, you'd have looked at me like something that just climbed out of the swamp. What would have been wrong with you telling me how terrific it was, or how you felt about me?"

Warmth blossomed inside her. Gabe had been just as vulnerable as she. Wrapping her arms around his back, she buried her face against his damp chest and drew a deep breath of his scent. All the ache and misery of the past two months vanished as if it had never been. She wanted to purr.

Leaning back in his arms she met the indigo heat of his gaze, unleashing all the yearning she felt. "You ought to get out of this wet shirt, Gabe. Why don't we go upstairs and find you something dry . . . like a sheet."

Minutes later, after peeling each other's clothing off in record time, Gabe followed her down onto the sleigh bed in the quaintly shaped bedroom just below the lamp room. He nuzzled the soft skin of her neck with his chin. "Damned if I don't think I'm an optimist. I shaved before I drove here." When she walked her fingers up his shoulder to fondle his cheek, he captured them with his lips. "Jenny? Have you noticed anything missing here?"

He received a contented sigh in reply.

Gabe tried again. "I love you, Jenny." He waited a beat. "Do you have anything to say to that?"

She hooked her leg over his thigh and pulled him close, plastering her breasts against his chest.

He anchored her shoulders to the mattress and glared into her half-closed eyes. "I've created a monster. I should never have told you how happy you make me." He made a halfhearted effort to discourage her questing hands, which were burrowing between them and forging a path over his abdomen. They arrived at their destination, causing his groin to contract painfully. "I'm not that easy. You don't get what you want until you say the words."

When Jenny's clever artist's fingers drew him into her heat, Gabe forgot his ultimatum until her body clenched around him, until she placed her lips against his ear and moaned, "Oh, dammit, Gabe! I love you."

Hours later, Gabe stood behind Jenny, holding her close to his chest with one hand flat against her stomach and the other possessively cupping her breast, watching the storm blow out over the Atlantic. The setting sun lit a partial rainbow in the saturated air to the left of the lighthouse. He kissed the vein pulsing faintly at her temple. "That's a good sign. Sterling must have ordered it."

Her laughter vibrated against him, and Gabe wished he could capture this moment forever.

"You really love him, don't you," she said.

He should have known she'd guessed. "He's an interfering old bastard, but he's the only grandfather I've got."

"Then you haven't really left him to spend more time on your business with Bill?"

Gabe turned her in his arms and kissed her as hungrily as if they hadn't just spent an entire afternoon in bed. "He lies when it suits him." She giggled, and the vibration of her chest felt so good he looked around for a flat surface in the converted lamp room. "Damn, this place has no walls." When he noticed the easel half-turned away from him, he released her. Without a word, he crossed to the painting and shifted the canvas so the watery sunlight struck the surface. After several minutes, he said, "Oh, God, Jenny. You make me feel so humble."

His own unsmiling face looked out at him. In the deep-set eyes was an expression he recognized, for the depth of emotion buried within them had looked at him from the bathroom mirror minutes before he'd set out on this mission to claim Jenny. The mixture of love and hope she'd portrayed matched what he felt each time he thought of her, and each time he had been filled with fear, frightened she would be out of his reach.

Gabe felt her arms slip around him. Her breath was warm against his shoulder blades as she spoke. "I started that, hoping I could exorcize you from my heart. No matter how many times I redid the eyes, you looked out at me like that. You were making me crazy."

"You saw what I tried to hide from myself." He turned and pulled her against him. "This is a hell of a lot more complimentary than that mural on my wall. Sterling is wild about the thing, by the way. He wants you to finish it. He thinks your portrayal of him as a spider shows creativity." Her closeness rekindled his desire, and he buried his face in her hair.

Jenny burrowed into him as if attempting to crawl beneath his skin. "My mood's different now. I may change the mural. What if I put you in silver armor on a white horse? Sterling can be King Arthur."

A reluctant laugh burst from Gabe's throat and he eased his hips onto the table he'd backed into. "That's a cliche. The flowers are a lot more fun." He drew a deep breath and looked closely at the top of her head. "Jenny darling, did you know you have paint in your hair?"

Laughter filled her face as she looked up at him. "Gabe darling, did you know you have paint on your slacks? You just sat on my palette."

The shadows which had haunted her eyes were gone. If Gabe had his way, the bubbling joy that replaced them would remain there forever. Laughter wasn't a bad way to start their life together. Not bad at all.

ABOUT THE AUTHOR

JUSTINE WITTICH is a former journalist and jack-of-all-trades who abandoned the glamour of her past jobs—teaching, editing, publicizing and "secretarying"—to write the stories that grabbed hold of her imagination and wouldn't let go.

She lives in rural southeast Ohio with her husband, Pete. They are owned by a party cat and a princess cat.